BRIDE OF A WICKED SCOTSMAN

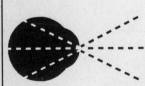

This Large Print Book carries the
Seal of Approval of N.A.V.H.

BRIDE OF A WICKED SCOTSMAN

SAMANTHA JAMES

THORNDIKE PRESS
A part of Gale, Cengage Learning

GALE
CENGAGE Learning·

Detroit • New York • San Francisco • New Haven, Conn • Waterville, Maine • London

GALE
CENGAGE Learning™

LIBRARY OF CONGRESS CATALOGING-IN-PUBLICATION DATA

James, Samantha.
    Bride of a wicked scotsman / by Samantha James. — Large print ed.
      p. cm. — (Thorndike Press large print romance)
    ISBN-13: 978-1-4104-4313-7 (hardcover)
    ISBN-10: 1-4104-4313-2 (hardcover)
    1. Husband and wife—Fiction. 2. Scotland—Fiction. 3. Large type books. I. Title.
PS3560.A395B75 2011
813'.54—dc22   2011032081

Published in 2011 by arrangement with Avon, an imprint of HarperCollins Publishers.

Printed in the United States of America
1 2 3 4 5 6 7 15 14 13 12 11

BRIDE OF A WICKED SCOTSMAN

PROLOGUE

AN ANCIENT IRISH MYTH

From out of the mists and magic steeped in time came a myth — a myth that was born on the lands of the people who came to be called the Clan McDonough. It was here, on the very tip of the peninsula, in this place where the wind meets sea and sky, and the sky the earth, where Druids reigned and pagans came to worship their Celtic gods in a temple ringed with standing stones. It is here, said the tale, that the Circle of Light first came to be, conjured by the Druid priests. Conjured up from sea and sky, water and earth, a symbol of the eternal cycle of life. Of purest silver it was made, a simple pattern, weaved together, a circle that had no end and no beginning.

The Circle of Light resided high upon an altar of stone — floating, suspended with a power of its own, slowly rotating, ever turning, shimmering with myriad color and warmth. The Druids proclaimed that all people of the Clan McDonough who worshiped — all who believed in its powers of endurance — would be blessed.

So wondrous was the Circle of Light that St. Patrick himself came to see it. He, too, blessed the Circle, and all of the McDonough and their lands. He decreed that it should remain forever in this place of ancient worship; the clan was charged with its guardianship. In thanks for this blessing, the Clan McDonough built their church in honor of St. Patrick, bringing fortune and favor to their lands and people.

As time and tide went by, the McDonough came to believe that to lose the Circle of Light — this enduring cycle of life — would be to lose their good fortune. Such was their belief. Such was their faith. Night after night throughout the centuries, in the church of St. Patrick, the Circle of Light was seen through the window to the north, casting out its glow. Shifting and shimmering through mist and moonlight and the darkest night, bringing forth luck and prosperity to the lands of the McDonough as promised. Like a crown of warmth and hope, its light could not be dimmed.

Until the night the Black Scotsman came plundering across the seas, to the land of

the McDonough, where he seized the Circle
for his own . . .

And the truth of the legend came to be.

CHAPTER ONE

The day began as any other.

Yet for some vague reason, Lady Maura O'Donnell reflected, something seemed different that day.

While the curtain of night retreated, dawn began its awakening. Snug in the warm nest of her bed at Castle McDonough, Maura watched as pale pink light hovered as far as the eye could see; it banished the shadows and deepened to amber and rose, at last spilling across the earth until it poured through the open curtains.

Ha! Whoever said that it rained in Ireland more than anywhere in the world had never lived here, on the northernmost tip of the isle!

Wide-awake now, Lady Maura rose from her bed. It was mid-June, but the mornings carried a chill yet. There was no rug on the floor, so she yanked back her toes at the feel of the cold wood. Jen the housekeeper had seen the once grand carpet beneath the four-poster whisked away while Maura was gone one day. A hazard and a relic, Jen declared with a glint in her eye, daring Maura to refute it when she yelped at its absence. Maura admitted that Jen was right when the threadbare carpet joined the burn pile and burst into flames thrice her height — why, thrice the height of Jen's husband Murdoch, truth be told.

Papa had promised her another the next time they made the trip to Dublin.

Maura hadn't reminded him. It was she who kept the books. There were no funds for such extravagances as beautiful, hand-woven carpets. The household staff had grown smaller through the years, as more rooms of the drafty castle were closed off. Now it was only the earl, herself, Murdoch, and Jen who resided in the main section of the castle. Maura's mother had died before she was six; she could scarcely remember her.

Shivering, she finally braved the cold floor and scampered toward the washstand. A floorboard creaked. She paused and glanced down, only to stub a toe on the edge of the next. Stopping, she ran the other toe along the loose edge of the long, pitted plank. As she washed her face, then combed her hair and tied it back with a length of ribbon, she decided she would have to call Patrick the Woolly in to fix it before she fell flat on her face. Her father had always claimed that Patrick the Woolly — not a soul in the valley called him otherwise — was the best carpenter in County Donegal. And he was, provided one used his services early in the day, before he'd had a pint too many. And if she did not have it fixed posthaste, her father would be wondering if she herself had imbibed with Patrick the Woolly.

A wistful sigh escaped. How dearly she wished there were funds to see the castle restored to its former glory. Oh, how Papa would beam . . . But she knew it would never be so. Little by little it had become necessary to begin selling off items of value. They were not destitute, not yet, but she feared that someday it might come to —

No. No. She must not think like that. She had to believe that better days were ahead.

Elsewhere in the castle, the morning ritual had begun as well. Maura heard her father's boots cross the floor in his room at the end of the hall. Slipping into her petticoats and gown, she heard Murdoch's heavy footfalls on the stairs. More creaks there than she could count, she decided.

A heavy door opened, then closed. Another creak. Maura stifled a sigh and turned. As always, Jen's timing was impeccable.

The shorter woman gave a curtsy, as much as her portly form would allow. "Good morning to you, milady."

"Milady? What?" Maura teased. "What misdeed have I done that I have lost your good graces?"

The older woman shook her head. It was a long moment before she lifted her head. Maura stared. Her eyes seemed overly bright. Was she . . .

"Jen. Jen, what is this? Why these tears?" Maura grabbed her hands and pulled her into her room. "Jen, tell me! What's wrong?"

"Nothing is wrong." Jen spoke strongly, then her tone wavered. "It's just that — well, you are a lady, Maura, a most beautiful one at that."

Maura was still stunned, taken aback at the tears Jen couldn't quite hide, the unsteadiness of her tone that she couldn't control. She scoured her mind but couldn't recall ever seeing Jen cry before. Not even when both her sons had left for America, and she and Murdoch knew they'd likely never see them again.

"Jen," she whispered, and all at once there was a huge lump in her throat.

"You've grown up before I even knew it.

And I — I thought you should know. I oft tend to see you as a child. But you're a lady," Jen said again. "So much a lady and so beautiful you bring tears to my eyes. Soon, Maura, some dashingly handsome young man will appear and take you away as his bride. I'll miss you, Maura. I'll miss you so." Trying desperately to smile, she smoothed one velvety black curl that lay on Maura's shoulder.

Touched beyond words, Maura reached out, wrapped her arms around Jen's sturdy form and hugged her tight. After the death of her mother, her father had never remarried, and Jen, the woman who raised her, was the only motherly figure she'd ever known. She had comforted her, tended her scrapes — and oh, there were many! — and scolded her soundly when she was into mischief. Why, both Jen and Murdoch had done so. They were more than servants. Much more.

They were her family, as much as her father.

For a long time they stood that way, clinging to each other. In the back of Maura's mind was that same sensation as when she woke . . . that something was different. Yet still it eluded her.

Finally, Maura drew back, searching Jen's

15

face. There were new wrinkles there — and it was something she had never noticed until now. With her thumbs she traced them, tiny grooves etched into the housekeeper's cheeks. To Maura they were not wrinkles of age, but those of beauty — a beauty that came with life and loving and giving — beauty that bespoke her character and goodness and spirit.

"I shall not be going anywhere, Jen." Maura sniffed, striving for a smile and succeeding. "Why, the only young men I know are most certainly not dashingly handsome. Those I know of the male gender are still throwing stones at their sisters! So I'm hardly ready to acquire a husband or become a bride." She stuck out her tongue, making Jen laugh even as the housekeeper wiped away her tears with the corner of her apron.

Castle McDonough was her home, Maura thought. In truth, she could not imagine ever leaving the land of her ancestors.

They hugged again, then parted ways as Maura continued down the hall. She'd heard her father call for his newspaper — the footsteps on the stairs had been Murdoch delivering it. The newspaper from Derry was usually a day or so late, but it was the earl's habit to read the news and sip a leisurely cup of tea before venturing downstairs for breakfast. Maura rapped lightly on the door to wish her father good morning.

There was no response.

She rapped once more. When he didn't answer, she opened the door and poked her head inside. "Papa," she said laughingly, "I do believe you and Jen have contrived to play games with me —"

She broke off.

"Papa?" she whispered, and then it was a cry. "Papa!"

Her father stared at her, an expression such as she had never seen before on his face. Shock, surely. And . . . something else. Something she couldn't define. He was white as snow. The newspaper he had been reading fluttered to the floor, while the earl struggled to push himself to his feet.

Maura rushed forward, screaming for Murdoch. She managed to wedge a shoulder beneath her father's just as he would have pitched forward. Wrapping her arms around him, sheer force of will helped to keep him upright — her father was not a small man — until Murdoch arrived to help him to his bed.

Her father fell back. His skin was ashen. He tried to rise, then fell back again. He

17

sought to speak, yet could not.

Maura laid a hand on his chest. "Shhh," she soothed. "Stay where you are, Papa. Let it pass."

But whatever had overtaken him, he fought it. She sensed it; saw it in the anger and frustration and myriad expressions that chased across his face. His lips parted. Once again he sought to speak.

Maura took a deep breath, steadying herself even as panic loomed. She had never seen him like this.

She glanced back at Murdoch, who stood beside the bed. "Summon a physician," she said, keeping her voice low. She was aware that fear lay vivid in her eyes as she looked at Murdoch, but she revealed no sign of it in her tone. Nor would she allow her father to see it.

All at once she could feel the heat emanating from his body. She laid her fingers on his forehead. He burned with fever. His eyes squeezed shut, then opened. He gazed at her, through eyes as green as the fields in the valleys far beyond — eyes the color of hers. All at once they clouded over.

"You know what this is, Maura. You know."

"You've taken a chill, Papa. That is all —"

"It is always thus for the lords of McDon-

18

ough. You cannot fight it, child. You cannot stop it. It happened just this way to my father, and my father's father before him. Death, without warning. Death, so unexpected, to the lords of McDonough. Since the time of Randall O'Donnell, grandfather to my grandfather!"

Anguish twisted across his face.

"Ah, Maura!" His cry of regret was almost pitiful. "The McDonough were once among the most powerful clans in Ireland, lass — our home, Castle McDonough, a powerful stronghold, safeguarded by our blessed Circle of Light. But no longer. Why, not for . . . what? A hundred years or more — no, nearly two! Two hundred years since the night the Circle was stolen from our church by that blackguard, the Black Scotsman!"

Behind her, where Jen hovered, Maura heard the other woman suck in a breath. From the corner of her eye she saw Jen cross herself. It had been thus throughout her life. Even now, those who still remained on the land of the McDonough crossed themselves at the very mention of the Black Scotsman's name.

Inside, Maura trembled. To hear him speak so . . . A sickening rush of certainty swept over her. Always, he was hearty and robust. Always. Now, to see her father like

19

this . . . to hear him speak with such anguish . . . it was like a knife in the heart. Despair encircled her. She tried to stave it off. She would not be weak. She must be strong for both of them.

She shook her head. "No," she said. "Papa, it is only —"

"Nay, child. It is not myth. Not legend. You know it as well as I! From the night the Circle was stolen, a shadow stole across our lands, the lands that belonged to our family — to the earls of McDonough! My grandfather spoke of it — how the rolling fields of our valleys, so fertile and thick with crops, grew ever more barren, year after year. Sorrow and misfortune have been our legacy."

She knew of what he spoke. The Circle. The Circle of Light. God, she almost hated it.

It spun through her mind how the church had been laid waste by fire nearly a hundred years ago. It was rebuilt by the people, for this was the church of the ancients, the church of St. Patrick. But then a fierce windstorm such as the isle had never known blew it to the ground. Again it was rebuilt, but even then those who had been loyal to the clan for centuries began to depart, family by family. And when the Famine spread across the land, there were some who believed the curse had spread across the whole of Ireland.

If only she could refute it. But she could not. She had only to climb high to the hills to see it, to know it for the truth.

Maura could not remember a time when she hadn't known of the havoc wrought when the Circle was stolen. One of her forebears was known to cover his ears and run for the earthen cellar when storms battered the headland. Their castle towered on the tip of the peninsula, the once fertile valleys below. It was said he believed the castle would fall into the seas, as the kitchens of Dunluce Castle had in the year 1639.

Castle McDonough remained. Outside McDonough land, the rolling hills beyond still flourished, while the lands of the McDonough began to wither and die. Little by little, year by year.

An awful foreboding seized hold of her, flooded her entire body like a shroud from which there was no escape. It was as if she knew the outcome of this night . . . even before it happened.

No, she told herself. No!

With shaking hands she removed his boots, then pulled up the coverlet. He moaned and thrust it aside.

"It calls to me. The Circle calls to me. It cries out to come home. It cries out that I have failed to bring it home — failed as our ancestors have failed." Something strange passed over her father's eyes. "I can hear it," he whispered, his tone almost haunted. "This is my punishment, Maura. This is my judgment for failing to seek the Circle, to claim it and guard it as we were charged. Randall O'Donnell spent the remainder of his days seeking the Black Scotsman, to reclaim the Circle and return it to the church where it belongs, that our family and lands would once again be blessed!"

Maura went very still inside.

"To no avail," she reminded him quietly. Randall never succeeded, nor did any of his sons. One by one the Clan McDonough abandoned their quest. It was rumored the Black Scotsman was a nobleman. Whoever he was, his identity was destined to forever remain secret, the Circle forever lost.

Her father railed, "I should have tried. Why did I not? I should have taken to the sea. To Scotland!"

Maura smoothed his brow. "Too many years have passed, Papa. Too many to —"

She broke off as he tried to rise and failed. A spasm racked his body. "You see, Maura?

Death will take me. Death will take me this day."

Her heart wrenched. "Do not say such things," she pleaded, choking back her fear — her tears. "You will not die, Papa."

By the time the door was flung open and Murdoch arrived with the physician, Dr. Mulligan, her father alternately burned with fever, then shivered as if he'd been plunged into the icy waters of the sea.

Maura leaped to her feet. "Help him," she pleaded. "Help him please!"

Dr. Mulligan peered at her over his spectacles. "Let us see what can be done," he said gently. He motioned her outside, along with Murdoch and Jen.

Tensely, they waited. When Dr. Mulligan finally emerged, Maura stepped forward.

"What is wrong with him?" she asked. "What ails him? Tell me you can save him!"

The good doctor's manner was one of resignation. It was unmistakable. He removed his spectacles, blew on them and rubbed them with his handkerchief, as if searching his mind for the right words. He settled them on his nose again before he cleared his throat.

"My lady," he said, "I have examined the earl to the best of my ability. I wish I could

23

help him. I truly do. But I fear there is nothing I can do, for I do not know what illness plagues him. All I know is that he is sick." There was a long drawn-out pause before he gently added, "Deathly sick, I fear."

Jen let out a wail.

Maura braced herself inwardly. "How long?" she asked evenly.

He hesitated.

She pressed on. "How long, if you please?"

"I cannot say."

No, Maura thought. He would not say. But there was pity in his eyes. Even he knew.

Superstition, some might have called it. Nonsense. But deep in her soul she knew it was the curse. The curse that had plagued the McDonough since the night the Black Scotsman — the scoundrel pirate who hid his real identity from both Scots and Irish — had sailed away into the night with the Circle of Light in his possession. They all knew.

Before the day was out, the earl of McDonough would be dead.

She inclined her head. "Thank you," she said quietly. "Murdoch, will you please escort the doctor to the door and see to his payment?"

Maura let herself back into the bedroom. Her insides twisted in sick dread. A sharp, tearing pain split her heart in two. Her father lay weakly against the pillows. She was stung by the change in him, in but the short time she had been outside in the hall. His cheeks were sunken, the bones of his face taut, his skin almost papery thin. With a finger he beckoned her near.

"He comes, Maura. He comes again."

She drew up the chair beside the bed, then leaned close. "Who, Papa?"

"The Black Scotsman."

Fire raged inside her. "That bloody pirate!" she cried. "He is dead and I pray that he has burned in Hell these many years! I curse him as we have been cursed!"

A fit of coughing seized the earl. Maura held a glass of water to his lips and made him drink.

"It will do no good to curse him," he rasped when he was able. "He is already cursed. By the old earl of McDonough, Randall O'Donnell himself, who saw his ship disappear into the night." He began to wheeze again. "But you can save us, Maura. You are the one."

A wave of despair broke over her. If only it were true. If only there were some way she could save them! But with every year that passed, a few more tenants moved

25

away. Those who remained eked out a living.

Throughout the rest of the day and into the evening he railed. "Maura," he whispered again and again. "You are the one. The only one who can save us. The only one who can save our people and our lands."

For a time her father was quiet. Maura was dimly aware of Murdoch and Jen hovering behind her. She thought he was sleeping — a restful sleep, a healing sleep, she prayed. Just when hope unfurled in her breast, he coughed anew — it sounded like the scratching of winds across a field of straw bleached dry and brittle by the sun.

It was almost as if she could see him shrinking away before her very eyes. She tried to soothe his wild ramblings, but all at once he heaved himself up with a strength that astounded her. His eyes opened and fixed straight upon her.

"The Black Scotsman," he whispered again. "Did you not hear me, child? He has returned. He is in Ireland. In Ireland, girl!"

He was hallucinating, surely, for nothing he said made any sense now.

"Papa —" She tried to press him back, but he reached out and seized the paper he'd been reading when he fell ill; Maura had tossed it aside, onto the bedside table.

He thrust it into her hands, then collapsed back upon the pillows. "Read," he commanded in as stout a voice as ever. "Read!"

As if guided by some force from above, her gaze homed in directly on the line that read:

Alec McBride, Duke of Gleneden, has arrived in Ireland for several weeks of angling. Prior to his return home to Scotland, Lord Preston, Baron of Killane, will play host to the duke for the last week of his visit. On Thursday, 10 June, Lord Preston will honor the duke with a masquerade ball to conclude his grace's visit. One cannot help but wonder if the dashing Black Scotsman will capture the hearts of our Irish lasses as surely as he has captured many a heart in his homeland . . .

Stunned, Maura went very still. The paper slid from her hands onto the floor. A strange sensation seized hold of her.

"You see, Maura? You understand now, don't you? The Black Scotsman has returned. He has returned!"

Maura shook her head. "Papa, this man . . . this duke . . ."

"I see it, Maura. I know it. Promise me you will find him."

His breath grew heavy and labored. She almost hated herself for thinking it, but he had not long to live. She could almost see him slipping away.

Tears filled her eyes. "Stay, Papa. Stay." It was a cry of outrage, a desperate plea, as if she could stop the inevitable.

There was a suffocating tightness in her chest, as if her heart was being chipped away, piece by piece. She battled to hold back tears. It was useless. A tear slid down her cheek, followed by another. She didn't want to promise. She didn't want to let go of him. She didn't want to lose him.

She gripped his hands. He held tight — so tight it was as if lightning flashed inside her brain, her very blood — as if a current of some strange unknown energy passed from his body into hers.

It was believed by many that her father had the sight. It was true things often happened as he said they would. He often dismissed this belief in his usual, jovial way. Yet now Maura realized for the first time — and with an unswerving certainty — that it was the truth.

Some might have argued there was no reason to believe that this man whom the newspaper called the Black Scotsman could possibly be related to the pirate of yesteryear, the Black Scotsman who stole the Circle of Light. Yet, with an uncanny certainty, Maura felt the truth to the core of her being. This man, Alec McBride, Duke of Gleneden . . . carried the blood of his pirate ancestor, the Black Scotsman.

Her father cried out, "I see in your eyes that you feel it, too. That you understand. That you know it as I do. Oh, aye, girl, it was his ancestor who stole from us, stole everything. Go to him, Maura. Seek him out. Go to Lord Preston's and find this Black Scotsman and follow him to his home — to his lands, for it is there you will find the Circle. Find it and bring it home, child. Take back what is ours. End this curse, that our lands and people will again be blessed with good fortune. Promise me, Maura. Promise me you will find this man. Promise me you will find the Black Scotsman."

Her throat was so raw she could barely speak. "Papa, I do not know —"

"You will find a way, my child. You are the one. The only one who can save us. I feel it here." He thumped his heart. Tears filled his eyes.

Just as tears filled hers.

"Promise me, daughter. Promise me you will bring the Circle home, home where it belongs."

Her voice was but a shred of sound. "I promise, Papa."

Relief flooded his eyes. Then all at once he tipped his head to the side. "Listen," he whispered.

A sound echoed eerily through the night.

The howl of a wolf.

And there were no wolves left in Ireland.

An odd shiver filled her heart. It was a sign, she realized. A sign that transcended belief and reason and explanation. A sign of all that had been . . .

And everything to come.

He squeezed her fingers. "All will be well, my darling Maura. All will be as it should be." A faint smile graced his lips. Her promise had given him peace, she decided vaguely.

The thought came the instant his grip slackened. The very instant she was aware of life draining from his body.

Downstairs the clock tolled midnight.

Now she knew what was different about this day, for it came to her then. Her father, the earl of McDonough, chief of the Clan McDonough, had died on the very day the Black Scotsman had stolen the Circle.

Two hundred years earlier.

Wiping the tears from her cheeks, Maura kissed his brow. "I will not forsake my promise, Papa," she whispered. "I will not."

She rose to her feet, a determined resolve beating in her blood, her very heart.

She would honor her promise to him. She would bring the Circle home to their lands.

She would not fail him.

CHAPTER TWO

Go to him, Maura. Seek him out.

And she had. She could scarcely believe it. She was here. In the home of Lord Ellis Preston, Baron of Killane. In a lovely, damask-papered room, with a round-cheeked maid named Eileen assisting her as she readied herself to attend the masquerade given in honor of the Black Scots— Good heavens. She must stop thinking of him that way. He had a name, a title . . . She fought to remember it, for already she'd grown accustomed to thinking of him as the Black Scotsman.

Alec. Yes, there it was. Alec McBride, Duke of Gleneden.

Besides, as she and Murdoch had discovered, the Black Scotsman was a name given him by the debutantes in England, who apparently considered him quite the catch.

A faint bitterness filled her. Less than a fortnight had passed since her father's death. Less than a fortnight before the Black Scotsman departed Ireland. Her father was scarcely in the ground after the wake before a straggling line of tenants gathered before the stone steps of the castle. There had been no time to waste, to grieve or to mourn.

She had bid good-bye to each of them. She cautioned Daniel the Swift that he must keep his hands from the neighbor's sheep and gave a tug to Patrick the Woolly's beard. He grinned in return.

When it came to Jen, Maura had hugged the housekeeper very hard. Releasing her, feeling as if her heart would break at any instant, she'd glanced toward the church-yard, high on the hill. She thought of her father then — his stanch pride — his love of his home and land.

Before she even thought about it, she'd reached for the small velvet pouch inside her purse and dumped the coins it held into the bottom of the bag. Her emotions ran rampant as she bent low and scooped a handful of dust and stones into the now empty pouch. The move was sudden, unex-pected, and appeared to startle Murdoch, who stepped forward.

"Lady M—"

He stopped short. Rising to her full stat-ure, Maura's chin came up and she defiantly yanked the strings of the pouch closed. Her best pair of white gloves was now ruined. She gave not a whit. If she must leave her home and lands, by heaven, a piece of Mc-Donough land would always be with her. Murdoch's expression changed from puzzlement to something else as he helped her into the carriage. Maura deliberately glanced away. When she turned back, she could have cried.

She saw Murdoch kiss his wife, and Jen cling to him a moment longer, as long as she could. She had looked on with a sensation so painfully acute she could have cried out. Then Murdoch stepped into the carriage and sat down across from her, his hands settled on his knees. Maura had almost hated herself for what she was doing — in all the days of her life, Murdoch and Jen had never spent a night apart.

She'd almost been relieved when the driver gave a crack of the whip. She waved to the assemblage. Patrick swept off his hat and offered a swaggering bow. Toothless Nan gave her a wink. Her pulse speeding up, she in turn gave Nan a tiny little nod.

And then they'd set off, en route to the Baron of Killane's estate.

Almost from the night her father died, Maura's mind had been working furiously.

34

Somehow she had to get to Scotland — to the Duke of Gleneden's estate. She weighed several possibilities. What if she were to pass herself off as a distant relation? Too risky, she decided, for several reasons. He might not believe her. Plus she had no way of making certain she could manage an invitation. Even if she did, it would likely be for only several days, at best, and she had no idea how long it might take to find the Circle.

What if she landed a position in his household staff? Ah, but what if there were no positions available? Provided she did manage to secure one, what if she ended up as a scullery maid? But such a post would doubtless offer no chance for her to search for the Circle. Even a position as a house-maid might not give her the opportunity she needed.

And what she needed was the ability to roam about freely, wherever she wished. Whenever she wished.

Maura recalled what the newspaper had stated: *One cannot help but wonder if the dashing Black Scotsman will capture the hearts of our Irish lasses as surely as he has captured many a heart in his homeland.*

It simply would not leave her mind. And with that in mind, she had conceived her plan . . .

Her first obstacle was getting herself into the Baron of Killane's masquerade. The second — and this the hardest! — would require boldness and daring. It involved a very great risk.

A very great deal of luck, for everything had to fall perfectly into place!

A very great deal of boldness and daring.

She was prepared to take that chance. Within her breast beat an unwavering resolve.

She would do whatever she must to find and bring home the Circle of Light.

With a stash of funds from her father's room, she and Murdoch had taken modest lodgings at a hotel not far from the baron's estate. During the journey, she had purchased several new gowns, and saw to it that Murdoch was fitted with several new suits of clothing as well. For her plan to succeed, Murdoch had to appear a proper gentleman. Luckily, he needed little training in manners and the like. Though Maura's father did not insist on formality, both Jen and Murdoch were familiar with the proper deportment when needed. Their first position before being hired by Maura's parents had been with the Earl of Rawlins in County Cavan.

"Murdoch!" she'd chuckled after commanding him to show her one of the new suits. "Oh, if Jen could see you now! I vow you'd take her breath away as you did those many years ago!"

"It is indeed my breath that causes me worry," he'd grumbled, running a finger between his stock and his throat. "It reminds me most heartily that if your father had insisted I dress like this day in and day out, my time in his employ might never have landed beyond a week!"

"Oh, cease!" Maura had given him a mock frown. Both Murdoch and Jen were more family than servants. "I," she said rather airily, "maintain that you look quite handsome" — she pretended to flick off a wad of wool from his sleeve — "my dearest uncle."

It was crucial that they arrive early so they might ferret out what information they could about the Baron of Killane. It was Murdoch who discovered at a pub in the next village that the baron was elderly; his wife, Lorraine, had been dead for nearly a decade.

Perhaps it was rash. Perhaps it was foolish to think that she could gain entrance to the ball. But by Jove, she would sneak in if she had to.

They had taken lodgings not far from the baron's home. Several days after their arrival, Maura sat down at the wooden desk in her room, her heart thumping madly, her mind running wildly. Yet slowly, ever so slowly, she reached for quill, paper, and ink, and began to write.

Lord Preston,
Please allow me to convey my condolences on the death of your wife. It comes years late, I know. For that, I apologize. My own dear father, you see, has just passed on as well. In going through his belongings, I discovered a packet of letters written to my dearest father from my mother while they were courting. In her letters, my dear mama spoke of your beloved wife quite fondly — they were, it would seem, great friends when they were young.

As I am staying in the area with my Uncle Murdoch for several days' rest, I cannot help but think of my dear mama and your wife. I pray you will forgive my forwardness in sending you this letter, but again, please accept my condolences.
Yours truly,
Lady Maura O'Donnell

A coin was pressed into the hand of the innkeeper's house boy and the letter dispatched. The baron might call her bluff. He might call the authorities, Murdoch warned, were he to know her claim was untrue.

Instead the baron called on her . . . at tea, the very next afternoon in the inn's tiny dining room.

"Your mother," he observed, casting her a look beneath the bushiest pair of white brows she'd ever seen in her life. "Gone, too, I gather?"

"Aye," Maura said earnestly. "I was but a girl when she died." She had lowered her eyes, as if it were painful for her to think about. "But, oh, how she loved the rolling hills and masses of flowers in County Clare!"

Another fact that Murdoch had unearthed.

"Oh, aye, that she did, my Lorraine!" the baron had replied. He scratched his great droopy moustache. "I must say, I've always found the weather in Clare a wee bit wet for m'taste."

Maura laid her spoon upon the saucer. "Well, perhaps Uncle and I should journey to the south and east," she said brightly. "My father was not one to travel far from home. But Uncle Murdoch and I have not yet decided precisely where our journey will lead us. Perhaps as the wind takes us, as they say."

"When do you leave?" the baron had asked.

"We thought to leave tomorrow." Murdoch spoke before Maura had a chance to.

"Tomorrow! Oh, but you cannot leave so soon! Your journey — you travel at your leisure, do you not?"

Maura cleared her throat. "Yes, but —"

"Then stay! I have a masquerade planned tomorrow night," declared the baron. "It would please me to no end if the two of ye would attend. It would please me even more if you would come stay at the manor with me now! I have a house full of guests already — and room for more."

This was exactly what Maura had wanted. Exactly as she hoped. But the baron was clearly a man of great, hearty, and welcoming demeanor, and she winced inside at her deceit. She liked him, she truly did, and lying to him was like the scraping of tooth upon stone.

But then she thought of the Black Scotsman.

She bit her lip. "I've never been to a masquerade before, Uncle."

Murdoch was frowning. Pretending to consider, as she well knew. "Well —"

"Come now," said the baron. "Never been

to a masquerade! Why, almost a sin, it is, for our lovely Lady Maura to miss such an event! I implore you, stay, the both of ye now! I've a room full and more of costumes that you may choose from."

Murdoch arched a wiry brow and heaved an exaggerated sigh. "Ye know I cannot refuse ye, girl."

The baron had let out a laugh. "Then do not, man!" He clapped Murdoch on the shoulder. "I shall send a man over for yer things as soon as I arrive home —"

"Oh, but we are quite comfortable here for the night, are we not, Uncle?"

Murdoch nodded. They both knew better than to appear too eager.

It was perfect. So very perfect.

"At least for the night of the masquerade, then," the baron had insisted. "Please, you will offend me deeply if you refuse."

Murdoch extended a hand. "Then we have no choice but to accept your gracious offer. But we will be off, bright and early, the morning after."

So it happened that she was here, in the baron's home.

Beneath the same roof as the Black Scotsman.

The sound of Eileen's cheery voice

brought her back to preparations for the masquerade. "Shall I tighten the back laces of your vest, my lady?"

Maura clasped her hands around the bedpost.

"Goodness, my lady, never before have I tended a lady with so tiny a waist!" the girl marveled as she began her task. Maura scarcely heard.

Knowing the Black Scotsman — she might as well leave off trying to think of him otherwise — was here, somewhere, sent a skitter of anxiety all through her.

Eileen guided her to the dressing table, chiding her. "Do not frown so, my lady. A woman's brow must be smooth as a baby's bottom. Can ye imagine that? I never believed it until I tended a lady from England. Beautiful she was, with nary a wrinkle. It was achieved, she informed me, by neither frowning nor laughing. And if a smile must be displayed, it must be done only with the most demure sense possible." In the mirror behind her, the girl demonstrated. "Her face was wooden. She even walked about as if she had wooden sticks for legs!" She started to laugh, then clapped a hand over her mouth. Her eyes widened. "Oh, forgive me, milady —"

But Maura was laughing along with her.

She realized it was the first genuine laugh she'd had since Papa's death nearly ten days ago. Perhaps, she decided cautiously, the luck of the McDonough had already begun to change . . . for the better.

"The baron," said Maura. "Does he entertain often?"

"Oh, two or three times a year." Eileen picked up a hair brush. "A house party later in the summer. It's lovely then, milady, ye should see it! All green and bright with flowers. He keeps the garden exactly the same as when his dear wife was alive, ye know. And usually another house party during hunting season."

Eileen ran the brush through Maura's hair. "Such lovely hair ye have, milady," said the girl. "So thick and dark and shiny. Will ye be leaving it loose beneath yer scarf?"

Maura nodded. Eileen had already proved to be a font of information. Her father was the head groomsman for the baron. She was the eldest of eight children and had been in the employ of the baron for three years.

"And this party? The masquerade?" Maura edged her back to tonight's event. "Will there be many guests?"

"A fair amount. The baron's friends from Dublin and neighbors mostly," Eileen supplied. "And the masquerade is in honor of the duke. His father and the baron were great friends, ye know. The duke's father often came to fish, and the duke has continued the tradition every few years, I'm told."

The girl already knew how she and her "uncle" had met the baron, because of Maura's letter regarding the baron's late wife. Maura feigned innocence. "The duke?" she queried. "I wasn't aware there would be a duke in attendance."

"Oh, aye." Eileen's eyes began to sparkle. "The Duke of Gleneden. Scots, he is. I heard Mrs. O'Hara say at luncheon today that when she was in England last, she heard that every young miss in England and Scotland longed to become his duchess — and not only for his money and title. I should imagine it's surely the same for any woman in our fair isle! The Black Scotsman, he's called."

"Really." Maura feigned indifference. "And what other reason would these women have for wanting to marry the man other than his wealth and title?"

Eileen fairly giggled. "Ye will know when you see 'im, milady."

Maura raised her brows. "How can you be sure?"

Eileen chuckled. "Oh, I doubt ye will miss 'im, masquerade or no. His hair is as black as yer own. He towers over every man 'ere, why, a giant he is. A fair handsome one, which is why the ladies take to 'im so!

"He and the baron have been out at the streams fishing most days, as the baron and his father used to do," explained the girl. "According to Mrs. O'Hara, he takes to the ladies as much as they take to 'im!"

That was precisely what Maura had been counting on. By now her strategy was well conceived; it involved both daring and dread. Daring because of her deceit to the baron, as well as the fact that she must play a part she had never played before; dread that if her plan failed, she might never have another chance such as this.

A short time later Eileen applauded Maura's costume with clasped hands and a delighted laugh. Maura turned to the mirror almost reluctantly.

She had fashioned her costume with an almost defiant determination. Her skirt was of crimson satin, its ragged hem barely covering the top of her riding boots. She wore no petticoats. Maura noticed dimly that she felt remarkably unencumbered. A crimson and white striped scarf covered her head. Her hair flowed in loose waves over her shoulders and down her back, nearly to her waist. She'd tucked a loose, gauzy, peasant cut blouse into the skirt, cinched tight by a wide leather belt, and borrowed a cutlass from among those in the baron's costume room.

But it was the blouse that gave Maura pause. Not wanting to be trussed up twice over, she had discarded her corset for the night. She wore a sleeveless, black leather vest over it. Eileen had tightened the laces of the front of the vest quite tight.

One fleeting glance at her reflection and her jaw dropped. Her eyes widened in consternation. Her breasts swelled high and round and full, straining against the nearly sheer white cloth. "Oh, my," she breathed. "Oh, my." She longed to snatch up the coverlet and sling it over her shoulders.

But that would have been so very counterproductive.

Eileen left with a smile. Maura jumped when a knock on the door sounded a few minutes later.

"Maura?"

She slipped a small silken pouch — different than her other — held by a black ribbon, over her head and between her breasts. She opened the door to Murdoch, dressed as — very apropos — a butler. She stepped into the corridor. He blinked when he saw her costume but made no comment. "We are late," Maura said hurriedly. "We should go."

Murdoch closed the door. "You have the pouch from Toothless Nan? The —"

"Yes, yes, I have it."

"You realize, Lady Maura," Murdoch said worriedly, "if we cannot discover who he is, one of us will have to query the baron."

Maura said nothing. Somehow she sensed that she would know exactly who he was, no matter his costume. But she didn't say so. Instead she said, "Remember the plan. When I do not appear downstairs promptly at seven to —"

"Yes, yes. I know where to find you." Murdoch's tone was unmistakably grim. "And now I must warn you, Lady Maura, that if all does not go as planned, do not hesitate to do what you must to prevent him from —"

"Yes, yes, Murdoch, I shall!" Maura was impatient.

Just before they ascended the stairs that led to the ballroom, Murdoch laid a hand on her arm. His gaze searched hers questioningly. "Are you certain," he said quietly, "this is what you want?"

Maura's eyes darkened. "Pray do not ask that, Murdoch. It is what I must do. You know that I promised Papa."

47

He sighed. "I know, child. But there is an old Irish proverb: 'If you dig a grave for others, you might fall into it yourself.' That is what worries me."

"I shall be fine, Murdoch. Truly."

In the ballroom, the baron, dressed as King Henry VIII, greeted them heartily. There was food, but Maura could scarcely eat. Her gaze roamed the room.

She spied a jester. A small-statured man dressed as Napoleon. No, that was definitely not the duke. Eileen had said he was tall.

Maura's palms were damp. She would never have called herself vengeful. And it wasn't revenge that filled her chest. Fear, excitement, all the chaos in the world. She spied a priest garbed all in black. Eileen's words echoed in her mind. *Takes to the ladies, he does.* Now that would have been irony indeed, if he chose to dress as a priest!

Growing restless, she began to walk the perimeter of the ballroom. Her gaze seemed to scour every inch. They'd missed the introduction of the duke. Why did this have to be a masquerade? She or Murdoch would have to ask his whereabouts after all.

Maura felt her mouth pinch tight. She sought to soften it. She'd conjured up a far different vision of the duke than Eileen had described. Oh, aye, she could well imagine

48

his appearance. She pictured him as his pirate ancestor. A scurvy, slimy runt of a man. With yellow, rotted teeth — what teeth there were left! No doubt Alec McBride, Duke of Gleneden, was surely the ugliest man to walk the earth. On that thought, she stopped short.

And then . . . no sound in the world, no image, no words could have prepared her for what she saw next. Lingering near the hall entrance stood a man. An exceedingly tall man. One eye patched, a tartan thrown over one just as exceedingly broad shoulder.

Maura froze.

Her heart thundered.

Her pulse lurched.

Their eyes met . . . and held. Held endlessly, she thought vaguely.

Yet in that mind-shattering instant their eyes caught, that same sizzling sense of certainty slid over Maura, the way it had the night her father died. She had felt it in her father's blood — she felt it in hers.

By heaven, it was him. Alec McBride, Duke of Gleneden. The man known as the Black Scotsman.

It spun through her mind that perhaps it was fitting that she had chosen her garb as she had . . . She stood as if anchored to the earth, unable to move, to even blink, as she watched him slowly make his way toward her . . .

Together they stood.

Face-to-face.

Toe-to-toe.

Pirate-to-pirate.

CHAPTER THREE

Alec McBride, Duke of Gleneden, stood at the edge of the ballroom and scanned the crowd once more. It was quite a crush. A faint smile rimmed his lips. He'd never been particularly fond of masquerades. But as he was the guest of honor, he was obliged to work his way around the room, shaking the hands of those he'd met during his time here — despite the costumes.

He spied Lady Alicia McDormand, dressed as a vampiress. Another dressed as Marie Antoinette with her great white wig. A man sauntered by, enrobed in black, with a deep cowl that completely shadowed his face. The man paused, and when a hand with great claws emerged to bring the fingers of a gaily laughing witch to his lips, Alec chuckled. He was acquainted with the inspiration for the man's costume. Tonight he was the Demon of Dartmoor, penned by his brother Aidan's wife, known to the world as F.J. Sparrow.

They would laugh when they learned the frenzy had extended to Ireland. Of course now they were halfway around the world on their honeymoon.

Ah, yes, while he'd enjoyed his time in Ireland, he was chafing to be home. He'd remained in London in the spring for Aidan's wedding. He'd visited Annie and Simon in Yorkshire and his mother in Bath prior to making his trip to Ireland. He wouldn't forego the baron's invitation, not when his father and the baron had been such great friends. But the thought of returning to Gleneden, sitting in the great hall in his favorite chair, his feet propped up and sipping a whiskey at his leisure, was appealing beyond belief. And —

The thought stopped mid-stream.

He was obliged to revise it.

Ah, yes, he decided. Appealing beyond belief . . .

His return to Scotland was forgotten. He stood some twenty paces distant near a tall fluted column when he spied her . . . a woman who gazed into the throng as if searching for someone.

The set of her shoulders was proud. She was tall for a woman, but small-boned. Brave of her to appear with her hair loose

— and bold of her, he thought with a vent of admiration, to wear a skirt that clung to her hips, revealing the shape of her buttocks as she turned ever so slightly. Aware of a low simmer alight in his belly, he surveyed her, an admiring assessment.

She was exquisite. Indeed, there was much to appreciate about the lady.

And most fortuitous for him that her costume of choice was the same as his, for it provided him an avenue of introduction.

Almost before he knew it, Alec found himself standing before her. He had no memory of crossing the black and white tiled floor.

He executed a slight bow. As he straightened, he secured two glasses of wine from a passing footman and handed one to her.

"Good evening, my fellow pirate," he said smoothly. "Are you expecting someone? Your escort, perhaps?"

He gazed straight into her eyes, eyes that were a startling, vivid shade of green. At his question, the lovely said nothing, but shook her head. The tip of her tongue came out to run over her lips, leaving them dewy and damp, the color of blooming heather after a misting of rain. Desire, sharp and swift, clamped hold of him. He was a little startled at its strength.

Alec's gaze had already roved her from head to toe. Her skin was almost iridescent, and no doubt as smooth as a pearl, he was certain. And there was a goodly expanse of it revealed, he noted in satisfaction, battling the impulse to reach out and touch, to confirm his assessment.

As if he needed such an excuse. He was well aware he was right.

Those delectable breasts quivered with a deep, indrawn breath. He quite enjoyed the view. She gazed up at him. Her feet were braced slightly apart, one slim hand on her cutlass, as if, indeed, she balanced herself on the rolling deck of her ship.

And certainly there was nothing tentative in her appraisal of him. It was no less thorough than his. Alec took a swallow of wine, aware of her forthright study. Was it bedding she wanted? If so, he would accommodate. Oh, indeed, quite obligingly.

But he discovered himself rather impatient. Dammit, he wanted to hear her voice. Sweet and musical? Low and sensuous? The latter, he decided.

"I applaud your costume." He allowed a faint smile to curl his lips. "I believe it is the first time I've seen a lady play the part of pirate."

"Indeed." He was right. Her voice was

low. Vibrant. "Have ye never heard of Ireland's most famous lady pirate, Grace O'Malley?"

"I have not. Pray tell me of this pirate."

She smiled, running her tongue over her lips again. A stab of sheer, raw desire bolted through Alec. Vaguely he wondered how she would taste . . . He had to drag his gaze away from her lips to concentrate on what she was saying.

"Many called Grace O'Malley the Sea Queen of Connaught. Her father was involved in shipping and trading. Irish legend tells it that as a young girl, Grace wished to accompany her father on a trading expedition. When she was told she could not because her hair would catch in the ship's ropes, she cut it off." She gave a low, husky laugh, flipping her own hair back over her shoulder.

Alec took a sip of wine. His gaze had sharpened. Beneath her pirate's scarf, her hair was beautiful. Thick, tumbling waves flowed down her back, the glossy black of a raven. Of course, if they had met under other circumstances, her hair would have been hidden, neatly tucked beneath a bonnet or pulled back into a tight, restrained bun, no doubt. Instead it was wild and unrestrained . . . as wild and unrestrained as she was, he suspected.

"I should imagine every man here is glad you did not do as the young Grace O'Malley," he murmured. "I should consider it almost sacrilege."

She made no comment on his remark, but continued with her explanation. "Even once she was wed, Grace sailed the seas. A fierce sailor, our Grace O'Malley, who would not be beaten down by the English as they tried to take over Irish lands."

"She sounds quite fierce. Why, I almost hate to reveal to you that I am half English."

Her head tipped to the side. Black, piquant brows arched high. Wordlessly, she eyed his plaid.

Alec gave a mock sigh. "And aye, half Scots."

"In truth?"

"Oh, aye, in truth. Does that mean I shall be unable to curry favor with you?"

A slow-growing smile edged her lips. "Are you familiar with the Giant's Causeway in Antrim?"

"I am. I visited there a scant three days ago." Alec was reminded of the huge basalt columns descending from the cliffs to the sea like giant steps.

"Then perhaps you've heard of the legend of Finn McCool, who lived there with his

56

wife Oonagh. From across the channel there, the Scottish giant Benandonner began taunting him, telling Finn that he was but a wee giant compared to him. Benandonner declared that he was the stronger and he could prove it, if only the channel did not stand in the way."

She ran a finger around the rim of her wineglass, all the while maintaining that alluring smile. "Now, Finn could not stand for such insult from his Scottish rival. So Finn built a causeway out of the stones to cross the water and demanded that Benandonner come prove himself. Alas, Finn was so exhausted from building the causeway that when Benandonner came, he needed a wee rest before battling him. Thus, his wife Oonagh disguised Finn as a baby and put him in a cradle, should Benandonner come before Finn was ready."

His lady pirate spread her hands wide. In some far distant part of his mind, he noted her tendency to speak with her hands as well.

"And Benandonner did indeed come chasing after Finn, thinking to best him. Yet when Benandonner arrived and spied Finn sleeping quietly in his cradle, he feared the mighty giant Finn even more after seeing Finn's 'baby.' So frightened was he that he had not the courage to face Finn. He fled back to Scotland, terrified, tearing up the causeway so Finn could not follow."

Alec tipped his head to the side. "I have heard this story. But I was told the Scottish giant was much larger than the Irish."

His lovely lady pirate waggled her finger back and forth. "Oh, no, no." She spread her fingers, turning her hand palm up. "However, even if that were true, Finn's wife Oonagh proved herself the smarter of either of them."

Alec laughed softly. "At first I was convinced I must prepare to defend my Scottish heritage. And now I find I must defend my gender as well." He gazed down at her. "Perhaps we should resume our role as pirates. Are we acquainted with each other?"

"I think not."

"Never on the high seas? Fighting over the booty of a ship gone down? In port where we shared . . . perhaps . . . a pint or two of ale or a bottle of rum?"

"I daresay," she said lightly, "that we are evenly matched on the high seas, sir. And —" she drank from her wine, smiling as she did so. That seductive smile was still in place as she lowered the glass. "— perhaps elsewhere as well," she finished with a faint laugh.

"I see." Alec leaned against the pillar, as if considering. "A pity. I could hardly call myself a pirate were I not the sort to kidnap ladies and do . . ." He let the sentence trail away, his meaning clear.

She met and matched him full-on. "Perhaps you should fear what I might do were I to kidnap you, Scotsman. Why, I might take you to some warm, distant island across the ocean. You'd be forced to spend long nights alone in my cabin. And when we arrived, why, I might bind you. Tie you to a tree so I might indulge my preferences. You see, at such times I have this urgent . . . need, shall we say."

"Need?" He arched a brow. "What need?" Her lips were damp and red from the wine. He wanted them wet with the wash of his tongue.

"It is the land, you see. After those many days and nights at sea, I revel in the feel of land beneath my feet. And it's then . . ."

"Yes?"

". . . that I prefer to dance naked round the fire. I fear it is the pirate in me."

Alec threw back his head and laughed. A coquette? Without question. No timid miss here. The brazen display of her breasts, her suggestive, outrageous banter, all proclaimed otherwise.

A tiny smile lingered at the corner of her lips. He watched as she swallowed the remainder of her wine. "Why have I not seen you before today? Are you a guest of the baron's?" Lord above, he'd have remembered those emerald eyes. He'd never seen such lush, brilliant green . . . as green as the landscape of this rocky isle.

"Only for tonight," she said.

"Then perhaps introductions are in order." He wanted to know who she was. "I am —"

"Wait!" She held up a hand. "No, no! Do not tell me. This is a masquerade, is it not? A night to disguise our true selves. What say we dispense with names?" That tiny smile evolved into seduction itself.

Alec laughed. She was sheer delight. And quite the flirt. "As you wish, Irish."

"That is my wish, Scotsman."

Alec settled down to enjoy the thrust and parry. "May I get you something? A plate perhaps? The desserts are quite exquisite." God help him, the dessert he had in mind was her.

"I am quite satisfied just as I am."

He was not, he thought with unabashed fervor. "Well, then, Irish, perhaps you would care to dance?" Manners dictated he ask. He allowed a smile to curve his lips. "Much to my regret, however, I fear you'll not be able to dance naked round the fire."

Oh, but that was a sight he would dearly love to see! Beneath her eye mask, her cheekbones were high, the line of her jaw daintily formed. He longed to tear away the mask, to see the whole of her face, to appreciate every last feature.

She gave a mock sigh. "Alas, you are right, Scotsman. And truth be told, I should only be so inclined if you were to dance naked 'round the fire with me."

By heaven, he was right. She was not just a flirt, she was quite an accomplished flirt!

Their eyes met. Meshed. Alec moved so their sleeves touched. Her smell drifted to his nostrils. Warm, sweet flesh, and the merest hint of perfume.

He wanted her. He was not a rogue. Not a man for whom lust struck quickly and blindly. He was not a man to trespass where he should not. He was discreet in his relationships. He was not a man to take a tumble simply for the sake of slaking passion.

Never had he experienced a rush of such passion. Moreover, so quickly. He'd wanted women before, but not like this. Never like this. Never had he desired a woman the way he desired this one. What he felt was immediate. Intoxicating. A little overwhelming, even. Of course he desired her. She was, after all, a woman who would turn any man's eye. It was simply that the strength of his desire caught him by surprise.

Perhaps it was this masquerade. Her suggestion that they remain anonymous.

He cupped his palm beneath her elbow. "There are so many people. The air grows stale. Shall we walk?"

Laughing green eyes turned up to his. "I thought you should never ask."

A stone terrace ran the length of the house. They passed a few other couples, strolling arm in arm. All at once she stumbled. Quite deliberately, Alec knew. Not that he was disinclined to play the rescuer.

He caught her by the waist and brought her around to face him. "Careful, Irish."

"Thank you, Scotsman. I am in your debt." She gazed up at him, her fingertips poised on his chest, moist lips raised to his.

Alec's gut tightened. She was so tempting. Too tempting to resist. Too tempting to even try.

A smile played about his lips. Behind her mask, invitation glimmered in her eyes. "Is it a kiss you're wanting, Irish?" He knew very well that she did.

"Are you asking permission, Scotsman?"

The smoldering inside him deepened. "No. But I have a confession to make." He lowered his head so their lips almost touched. "I've never kissed an Irish lass before."

"And I've never kissed a Scotsman before."

"So once again it seems we are evenly matched, are we not?"

"Mmmm, so it would seem —"

Alec could stand no more. That was as far as she got. His mouth trapped hers. A jolt shot through him the instant their lips touched. He felt a tremor of reaction in her, and he knew then just how much she returned his passion. His mouth opened over hers. He'd wanted women before. But not like he wanted this one. It was as if she'd cast a spell over him.

And he kissed her the way he'd wanted to since they met — with a heady thoroughness, delving into the far corners of her mouth with the heat of his tongue. Tasting the promise inside her. Harder, until he was almost mindless with need.

She tore her mouth away. She was panting softly. "Scotsman!" she whispered.

Alec opened his eyes. His breathing was labored. It took a moment for him to focus,

for her words to penetrate his consciousness.

"What if we should be seen?" she said.
"Perhaps . . . we should go elsewhere."

There was no mistaking her meaning. His
Irish lady pirate was willing — and he was
quite wanting. Oh yes, definitely wanting.

"I agree, Irish. I quite agree." He tugged
at her hand and started to lead her toward
the next set of double doors.

"Where are you taking me?"

He stopped short. "What! I thought you
knew, Irish."

"Tell me."

He slid his hand beneath her hair and
turned her face up to his. "Why, I'm about
to kidnap you, Irish." He smiled against her
lips. "I fear it is the pirate in me."

CHAPTER FOUR

I prefer to dance naked around the fire. I fear it is the pirate in me.

Inside, Maura cringed, in utter mortification as her words played through her mind again and again. Lord, had she really said that? What had she been thinking? Something within her administered a stern admonishment, reminding her that pirates were adventurous. Pirates had no scruples.

She and the Black Scotsman had parted inside the ballroom, so as not to arouse suspicion. They met again at the landing of the stairs. He laughed softly when he saw her wave down a servant bearing a tray. An instant later a full bottle of wine and two goblets were in her hands.

He didn't realize it was the means by which she would tame him.

And the fortification of courage for her.

From the moment he presented himself before her, panic threatened. A part of her longed to flee. To hide. It was as if all time had stopped. The pulse of her own heartbeat resounded in her ears.

Despite Eileen's prattling on about how the ladies flocked to him, he was nothing like she expected — yet exactly as she should have expected.

His breeches were of skintight leather, tucked into high, cuffed boots. Like her, he wore a loose white shirt. The strings were untied, revealing a hair-roughened chest. Over the shirt was a vest, much like hers.

There the similarity of costume ended. He wore neither hat nor scarf, as she did, but rather a narrow bandanna tied around his head. Eileen had not exaggerated, Maura decided with a flutter of her pulse. He was handsome, disturbingly so. Disarmingly so. Almost wickedly so!

Jet-black hair tumbled over his forehead. It deeply emphasized the contrast between the pale blue of his eyes and the pitch-blackness of his hair. A patch covered one eye, and only served to heighten the aura of danger he exuded.

It spun through Maura's mind that this was exactly how his ancestor must have looked. Raw. Dangerous. Deadly.

Added to it was a sense of tightly leashed control. A coolly disguised arrogance. She

66

was certain she didn't imagine it. Most disconcerting of all was his regard. Bold and almost possessive, it trickled slowly down her body.

And it was scarcely that of bored indifference.

When their eyes finally met, it was as if a bolt of lightning shot through her. In that fraction of a heartbeat, she knew . . .

Alec McBride, Duke of Gleneden, was a man who got what he wanted, she was certain of it. He was a man of unrelenting purpose — and she, she realized shakily, was what he wanted! Whatever had she been thinking, to presume she could control a man like this!

But everything had been set in motion, the players — herself and the Black Scotsman — ready and in place. It was too late to turn back. Whatever trepidation she felt must be stifled. Whatever uncertainty she felt must be smothered. She had a part to play, that of coy seductress. Play it she must — and play it she would!

With that, Maura mustered her purpose. It was steady and firm. She would not stray from it. After all, she had just proved she could assume the role of flirtatious lady. The ease of it had shocked her a little.

But in truth, thus far all had gone according to plan. She must remember that. And, appalled as she was at the discovery, kissing the Black Scotsman had proved . . . well, exciting. Exciting in a thrilling, dangerous sort of way, she scrambled to assure herself . . . and that, too, would serve her purpose.

He took the wine, along with her hand, and led her up the stairs. When they reached his bedroom, he relieved her of the glasses and gave a nod toward the door. Maura opened it, quelling a fleeting sensation of dread. She closed it with both hands. For the space of a heartbeat she stood as if transfixed, one hand splayed wide on the wood, the other curled around the handle. It occurred to her that there was still time to yank it wide and —

"Lock it, will you, Irish?"

His tone was casually offhand. All at once Maura was not feeling casually offhand. But resolve prevailed. She was strong. Resolute. She'd made it this far, hadn't she?

The lock clicked shut. Slowly, she turned. The duke deposited the wine and glasses on a long, low bureau angled across one corner of the room. Turning, he slanted her a wicked half smile and extended a hand, one pale blue eye smoldering.

Their fingertips touched. Fire. Heat. It

raged all through her.

"Shall we begin where we left off?"

He sat on the bed and tugged her between his knees. His gaze was level with her breasts. When she realized where it dwelled, she longed to smack that approving smile from his face. It struck her then that she was breathing hard, as if she had just run a very great distance — which only obliged him more!

He trailed a fingertip down the deep hollow between her breasts. Maura sucked in a breath, reining in her instinctive impulse to pull back. A blunted male fingertip lifted the ribbon with the pouch from her neck. "What is this?" he murmured.

Her fingers closed over his. She wouldn't allow him to open it. "What else could it be?" She tossed her head with a breathless laugh. "Pirate's booty."

His chuckle was low. "Yes. Of course. I'd forgotten."

Deft male fingertips dispensed with the front leather fastenings of her vest. The vest parted. He tugged it from her shoulders and tossed it toward the chair beneath the window. Her breasts spilled forth, as if to protest their confinement — and bolster his enjoyment, the cad!

She bemoaned her modesty as well as his

avid scrutiny. Beneath her blouse her nipples formed tight little buds, while her breasts swelled heavy and full. A lamp burned on the bedside table. She was well aware her nipples were clearly visible. One corner of his mouth tipped up, conveying his approval. It took every ounce of willpower she possessed not to clamp her arms over herself. Instead she flicked a finger at the front of his vest.

"Your turn, Scotsman."

He gave a soft laugh. "You give no quarter, do you, Irish?"

"No quarter asked, none given. A heartless pirate, am I not?"

He laughed again. His vest joined hers on the chair. He dragged off his bandanna, and then his shirt, which landed on the floor behind her.

Maura smothered a gasp. She hadn't expected that. It wasn't as if she'd never seen a man's naked torso. The farmers and tenants in the fields often worked shirtless. But she'd never been so close to a man's naked chest. She tried not to gape. He still wore his breeches, but for all the clamor inside her, he might as well have been naked!

Curling dark hair covered his chest, the flat of his belly narrowing before disappearing into the waist of his breeches. It scarcely registered before a hard arm slid around her back, bringing her down on the muscled stretch of a powerful thigh.

"Come here, Irish."

Self-conscious did not even begin to describe how she felt. Warm hands settled on her waist, nearly burning her with heat. Confronted with the brazen masculinity of the man before her, she had no idea what to do with her hands. Where to put them without touching bare, naked flesh. Or bare, naked, hair-roughened flesh. She battled an almost hysterical desire to laugh. She was supposed to be a sultry seductress, well able to negotiate her way around a man's naked body, not a maidenly virgin.

Which, of course, she was.

Almost desperately she framed his face with her palms. The skin of his cheeks and jaw was faintly rough. Absurdly, she liked the slightly abrasive feel of it. "Your patch," she said. "Remove it."

"What if I have but one eye? What if it has been gouged out in battle and I am so horridly disfigured you will scream in horror at the sight of me?"

She arched a brow. "Will I?"

His smile seemed even more devilish than before. "I would much rather that you scream in pleasure than in fright."

Maura's smile slipped a notch. To hear him say it aloud made her want to run screaming from the room.

"Well, Irish? Do you still wish to see me without my pirate's patch?"

Her tone was as level as she could make it. "I do."

A faint light flickered in the one eye visible to her. "Then remove it."

Despite her banter, her heart was already pounding hard, almost painfully. She started to reach for the tie fastened at the back of his head.

He shook his head. "Not that way," he said.

Bemused, she frowned.

He bared his teeth, a gleam in his eye. A most challenging gleam.

For a heartbeat she didn't understand . . . Her heart began to thunder. She couldn't back down. She wouldn't, no matter how much she wanted to.

Her heart was pounding madly. "Ah," she murmured playfully, "you may regret this, Scotsman. I might nip you."

"Please do," he invited with a rakish grin.

With a kittenish growl, Maura half raised herself and caught the end of the string in her teeth. Her breast brushed his jaw and her pulse leaped. But then his scent seemed to envelop her — soap and the fresh woodsy fragrance of his cologne. She gave a little tug on the string. Rats, she'd pulled the tie into a knot! Now she was forced to catch it fully between her teeth and tug it clumsily up over his head.

A tremor shot through her. His hair was soft. Silky. Somehow she hadn't expected that. And it appeared her effort was futile, for now that cursed patch was half on, half off. It took three tries before she succeeded, and by then she was laughing.

The patch fell to the floor. Maura plopped down on his knee again.

Her laughter faded.

For now she beheld a face that was starkly masculine, yet utterly striking. So striking that for one heart-pounding moment it stole every last breath from her lungs.

He gazed at her steadily, with nary a blink, as if nothing in the world were amiss. Perhaps nothing was amiss in his world, she thought with an aching twist of her heart. Had his people gone hungry? Watched as their world — their livelihood — withered and died with every year that passed?

Every emotion roiling in her breast was fraught with conflict. Her hands had fisted, falling awkwardly on the broad width of his

73

shoulders. Slowly, she uncurled her fingers. She didn't want to touch him. She didn't want to look at him. She wished that he was disfigured — that he was one-eyed, the ugliest of men, the most vile creature ever to walk the earth.

Yet never in her life had she seen eyes so beautiful, the color of blue crystal. He looked different without the patch. Not quite so . . . dangerous. Ah, but she had to remind herself this was a dangerous game she played.

No, she thought vaguely, that wasn't right.

It wasn't a game at all.

The risk to herself was as nothing compared to her goal. Everything depended on her. On recovering the Circle of Light and bringing it home. The thought brought with it a bounding resurgence to attain her goal. Her promise to her father.

And a reminder of the cost.

One mistake and all might be lost. There might never be a chance like this again. But she couldn't deny what she felt.

She found him daunting.

But she must remain undaunted.

She longed to snatch her hands away from their perch on his shoulders. His skin seemed burning hot. She felt seared clear through to the very marrow of her bones.

Yet her hands held steady.

It wasn't that she was afraid. Oddly, she was not. Not in the sense that he might hurt her. He was a gentleman, albeit a very amorous one at the moment.

A tremor shot through her. She fought the irrational flutter of her pulse. Oh, who did she fool? She liked the feel of his hands, so large and strong, circling her waist. Outside, on the terrace, she'd liked it when he kissed her, the heat of his lips, warm and smooth against hers. She wasn't supposed to like it. Any of it.

"It's your turn now, Irish. Off with your mask."

Maura pulled her hands into her lap, folding them as if in submission. "I pray you, good sir, do not bite hard. I've tender flesh, you see."

"Do you, now. Well, then, I vow I shall be gentle."

Maura arched a brow. "I daresay a pirate's oath is hardly one to be believed!"

She felt the laughter that rumbled in his chest. "Then I'll grant the leniency you think I lack. Your mask, Irish."

There was a moment of stillness, of utter quiet before she raised her hands and untied the mask. Pulling it free, she laid it on the nightstand.

Her vision focused on her hands, once again clasped together in her lap. She couldn't look at him. She didn't dare.

Oddly, he was no longer laughing either. "Your scarf," he said softly. "Remove it, please."

Please.

Slowly, Maura raised her hands. However reluctant she was, she knew she mustn't display it. She tugged the scarf free, then combed through the strands with her fingers. Her gaze was downcast, focused on a point somewhere distant on the floor.

"Look at me, Irish."

She did not want to. She truly didn't. In that moment, she had not the words to explain how she felt. Why she felt the way she did. It was as if, by revealing her face, her hair, that she yielded something he had no right to see. As though she would give away some part of herself that didn't belong to him. It belonged to her. To her.

"Irish." The word was little more than a breath.

Calmly, she raised her chin. She even managed a glimmer of a smile. Those incredibly blue eyes roved her face, in much the same way that hers had roamed over his. The fixed intensity of his gaze was unnerving, the silence excruciating. It stretched out until she was certain she would scream. Her stomach knotted.

Then, without a word, he reached beneath her hair. Warm fingers brushed her nape, shaped themselves there. Slowly. Oh so slowly. He slowly lowered his gaze to her lips. She made a sound. Or was it he? Maura had one glimpse of his face before his mouth met hers. His eyes were ablaze, like blue fire. She screwed hers shut, as if to close him out.

Scant hope of that. This was nothing like his first kiss. It was as if that kiss had been playful. But this kiss was anything but playful. She tasted headiness. She tasted hunger. She tasted longing. She tasted a passion that was all-consuming, worlds beyond what she had ever imagined. A passion that so far eclipsed what she was prepared for, it was almost frightening.

Gasping, she dragged her mouth free, literally coming up for air. She aimed for a seductive, inviting laugh, and feared that she'd succeeded only in revealing her anxious panic. She needed to get hold of herself.

"Faith, but I find myself suddenly thirsty," she said. "Where is the wine?"

She tried to slide away. He caught at her

elbow. "Ah, Irish, not yet. Just one more kiss."

She tried to pull away, but he held firm. She couldn't yank herself free without arousing suspicion.

"I shall make it up to you, Scotsman. I am parched, sir. Truly I am!" She touched her throat, shocked at how hot her skin was. Why, as hot as his! And her voice was indeed hoarse, drier than bone. "Besides, why waste what I'm sure is an excellent bottle of wine?"

There was the faintest amusement in his tone. "The flavor of you is all I desire, Irish. However, I surrender to your wish. But I will hold you to that promise." His head bowed low. He brushed his lips against the bare flesh of her upper arm.

"And I will make certain that you are not disappointed." The touch of his lips made her insides tighten. It was difficult to think clearly, let alone speak. "As pirates," she heard herself say in what she prayed was a provocative tone, "we seek treasure, do we not?"

"And the pursuit of pleasure when and where we chance to find it, eh, Irish?"

"I do believe we shall find both, Scotsman. Now, allow me to pour a glass for you."

78

Maura slid from his lap, hoping she didn't appear eager to be away from him. Slowly she walked to the bureau where he'd placed the bottle of wine and the two goblets.

It was then she spied a letter opener. Shaped like a dagger, it looked lethal and sharp; much sharper than the tiny little knife sewn into the pocket of her skirt. She could have trilled her luck. Could she have asked for anything more? Throughout the evening, fortune had been her foremost ally.

Thankfully, the bottle was already open. The servant had been on his way to the ballroom, and Maura made certain it was uncorked when she took it from the tray.

The wide neckline of her blouse slid down over one bare shoulder. She resisted the urge to drag it up. Such modesty would surely give her away. Casually, hoping he would think nothing of it, she slid the pouch that hung from her neck up and over her head, laying it atop the surface.

There was a rustle of movement behind her. "Do you need assistance, Irish? I'm happy to —"

"No, no." Every nerve inside her clamored. Hurriedly, she poured wine into one of the goblets. In her nervousness, she nearly overfilled it. She glanced back over her shoulder, slanting him what she hoped was a seductive smile. "But I do believe it might be wise to close the curtains. We wouldn't want to shock any of the baron's guests, would we?"

She heard him rise. While his back was to her — and hers to his — she grabbed the pouch and opened it, emptying a tiny stream of silvery-white powder into the wine. She hastily stirred it with a fingertip and sucked the liquid from her skin, then filled the other goblet.

When she turned, the duke had just swiveled away from the window. Maura retraced her steps and handed him a glass. "Pirates we may be, but the fact that we have no rum will not stop us from enjoying a bit of beverage." She raised her glass high.

He quirked a brow. "To you, Irish."

"To a night you shall never forget, Scotsman." Ha! She was already assured of that!

Their glasses clinked. "Bottoms up," he declared.

Bottoms up? Maura sipped, her eyes on his goblet. She watched him, momentarily fascinated by the strong tendons in his throat as he swallowed.

His glass was nearly drained. Yes, she thought, scarcely daring to breathe. Toothless Nan was right. He would never taste her concoction, Nan had assured her. And it appeared he didn't. Bottoms up it was!

He was smiling, a half smile that flirted at the corners of his lips, when she finally drained her goblet. It was a smile she had already begun to grow familiar with, one that both challenged and invited.

Her own tantalized. At least she hoped it did. This time when he kissed her, she vowed, she mustn't react like a ninny. She must be bold, she told herself, as bold as he. As brazen and daring as he. To that end, she placed a hand on the center of his chest and pushed him toward the bed. He tumbled back with a husky laugh, reaching out to catch her as he fell.

She had no choice but to follow him down. Sweet heaven, she was lying atop him. On *top* of him.

The realization had scarcely registered than he moved, a subtle but deliberate movement. Strong fingers caught behind her knee, hiking it up to one side so her hips pressed hard against his. Her heart lurched, for what she felt was hard. Well, she decided, half amused, half frenzied, it seemed she'd managed to succeed in her quest. There was no question she had aroused him. The proof of it jutted against her. Why, the cad had managed to lock her into a shockingly intimate position — part-

81

ing her legs so she was astride him, the valley between her thighs riding against the ridge of his —

His hips thrust up.

Maura gasped.

The Scotsman laughed, a low throaty sound. "That pleases you, eh, Irish?"

The boastful boor! So he thought she was pleased, did he? Shocked, was how she would have described it. Shocked speechless, in fact. Shaking, every nerve inside quivering. Did he feel it? Yet what did it matter if he did? No doubt he'd mistake it for pleasure again!

A low rumble of laughter rushed past her ear. An arm about her back, he tugged her fully onto the bed so they lay face-to-face. His fingers encroached beneath the loose neckline of her blouse, catching it and dragging the cloth down, fully baring one breast.

That same, shameless hand now shaped itself around one buttock. Maura squirmed. Oh, but she knew it! He mistook her movements for reciprocation of his ardor. He kissed the arch of her shoulder, brushing his lips across her collarbone clear to the hollow where it met her neck. His fingertips grazed a blazing trail to the crown of her breast. Once. Then again. A touch that stunned her beyond measure. Her eyes widened in shock as his dark head bent low.

His tongue touched her nipple. Maura watched in shock as the pale peak disappeared into the wet cave of his mouth. He sucked hard, alternately swirling his tongue around the peak. Fiery sensation exploded all through her.

Her throat arched. A low moan escaped.

He raised his head. A husky, indolent whisper slid past her ear. "Patience, Irish. We have all night."

No, Maura countered silently. Desperately. They did not have all night. Toothless Nan, whose knowledge of herbs and the like had been passed down for generations, told her it wouldn't take long before her concoction took hold. Silently, Maura railed. She'd waited too long. She should have poured the wine earlier —

The thought was obliterated.

She hadn't noticed the Scotsman unlace his breeches. His hand engulfed hers. As if from a distance, she saw him tuck her fingers within his and bring them down. Down below his waist. Down until her knuckles brushed dark, wiry hair. Down until he guided her palm — finger by finger — around a column of thick, rigid flesh.

Maura felt the pleasure that vibrated in his chest. She was stunned to the core. It should never have progressed this far. A few kisses. A brief, forbidden caress at most. She had prepared herself to endure his touch, no matter how much she might dread it. Little had she realized there was pleasure to be found in it!

But the one thing she hadn't prepared herself for was a touch of such blatant explicitness.

Her heart raced. Had Nan been wrong? she wondered frantically.

She found herself praying. Oh, lord, oh, lord, oh, lord.

She sensed something was different, even before she felt it. The Scotsman eased to his back, throwing an elbow over his eyes.

Maura froze. The clock on the night table ticked away the seconds. Still afraid to move — to hope! — she swallowed.

"Scotsman?" she whispered.

He didn't answer. His eyes were closed.

"Scotsman?" she whispered again.

Still no reply.

Relief seeped in. Awareness crept in. Something else, Maura realized, was different as well.

Her gaze skidded down his body. Only now did she realize her hand was still in his —

With a cry she wrenched it free.

Triumph vied with disbelief. She had at-
tained the night's goal. But she felt as if the
world had gone a little mad.

Climbing over the Scotsman's limp form,
she set to work removing his boots. Mercy,
but he was heavy! It took at least three deep
breaths before she gathered the courage to
peel away his pirate's breeches. His legs
were iron-hard with muscle. Coated with
the same black hair that covered his chest.
As for that other part of him . . .

She tried. Truly she did. But she couldn't
make herself not look.

Even soft, that oh so male part of him was
impressive enough to make her eyes widen.

When she was done disrobing him, she
staggered back, falling into the chair. It was
as if she were looking through a haze. She
blinked. It took a moment for her to focus.
She realized then it was the wine — so
much, in so little time. She wasn't used to
it.

She divested herself of her skirt, drawers,
and boots, tossing them aside. It didn't matter where they landed. Indeed, she decided
vaguely, it would be all the more convincing.

But she wasn't yet finished. There was one
more thing to be done.

She stumbled to the bureau and picked

up the letter opener. Returning to the bedside, she leaned over the Scotsman and pricked her finger soundly. A thick drop of blood appeared, and she quickly smeared her bloody fingertip across the sheets.

Maura returned the letter opener to the bureau, then staggered back to the bed. Crawling over the Scotsman, she dragged the coverlet over them both, insinuated herself beneath a heavy arm, then fell back upon the pillow.

Her eyelids had closed but she couldn't let go of the thought. She was halfway to victory. She had accomplished what she sought. She was here. With the Black Scotsman. In his arms. In his chamber.

And in his bed.

CHAPTER FIVE

Alec woke the next morning with a hammer pounding dully in his head. Strange, he thought vaguely. Wine — no matter how much — rarely had that effect on him.

And then, good God, he felt soft, immensely pleasurable warmth nestled against his side.

His head still spinning, he opened his eyes.

Soft, silky skeins of black hair tumbled across his bare chest. Shocked, he took a strand between his fingers, following its length up, over the curve of her back. What the devil? Who the devil . . .

Remembrance swelled over him.

It was her. His lady pirate, who had bewitched him so the night before.

She was rousing. Stirring, snuggling deeper into the warm depths of the bed. She turned on her side, fitting herself against him.

And opened her eyes.

Slender, beautifully arched black brows drew together over her nose. In sheer, utter bewilderment, she beheld him. She stared at him as if . . . as if . . .

"You!" she gasped. She scrambled back against the wall, as far away from him as she could get.

Alec sat up and stretched out a hand. It was odd. His throat was cotton dry, his mind a fog. He remembered his midnight guest — how could he not? The previous night returned in jagged pieces that floated in and out of his brain. His mind groped. It was almost as if he didn't know what was real and what was not.

He sought to make sense of it. He remembered bringing her to his room, their teasing play. The last thing he recalled was a kiss, a hot, hazy, mesmerizing kiss that promised everything.

Yet now the chit regarded him as if he were an asp.

Something weaved in and out of his consciousness, a warning. A sense that something was wrong. He'd been drinking, yes, but he wouldn't have considered himself drunk. For pity's sake, what the bloody hell —

Someone was knocking at the door. He ignored it.

"Come now." He slanted a smile toward the girl, to soothe her. "There's no reason to —" He stopped cold. Blast! He didn't even know her name!

It didn't help that she remained wide-eyed and full of shocked wariness. She clutched fistfuls of sheet and coverlet and wrenched them all the way to her chin so that only her nose and eyes were revealed.

The knocking continued, sharply insistent.

Alec lost his temper. "Stop knocking and bloody well come back later!"

He turned back to the girl. Before he could say a word, he heard a key inserted into the lock. The door was flung wide. Alec was still considering why someone dared violate his privacy when a distinguished-looking, bearded man surged inside.

Alec leaped from the bed. "Who the hell are you?"

The stranger ignored him. "Maura?" The man's gaze circled the chamber, at last settling on the chit cowering in his bed. "Maura!"

The girl's beautiful eyes filled with tears. She scooted even farther back against the wall. "Uncle!" she cried.

The baron was suddenly there as well. He pushed a key into his breast pocket. "Your grace, forgive the intrusion. But please, let us not share this unpleasantness with the other guests."

Alec shoved his legs into his breeches. He swung around to face the baron, his rank no less impressive for the fact that he was bare-footed and bare-chested. "What the blazes goes on here? Who is this man?"

The baron had rather wisely insinuated himself between Alec and the bearded man. "His Grace, Alec McBride, Duke of Gleneden," the baron began, but the other man gave Lord Preston no chance to continue.

"I am Murdoch Maxwell," he said coldly. "You will forgive me if I do not shake your hand. I'm far more interested in knowing why the bloody hell you took my niece to your bedroom last night. I've searched for her all morning, until a servant told me she saw you leading her up the stairs last night."

Alec's head was spinning. Images flashed in his brain. Of his lady pirate's touch. Running her fingers through her hair. The certainty that she had lain atop him as they kissed. It was as if he could almost feel her slight weight once more, the precise angle of her knee between his.

He'd felt so strange. As if his blood were afire.

Aye, chided a voice in his mind, *the fire of desire.*

After that . . . God, but it was as if his mind had been wiped clean.

He raised his head. His jaw clamped together. His gaze slid from the she-pirate in his bed to Murdoch Maxwell. "This woman —"

"Lady Maura," Murdoch snapped. "Lady Maura O'Donnell, daughter of the late earl of McDonough. Please have the courtesy to use her name."

"I bloody well didn't know her name!" Alec ran a hand through his hair. Lord, but he sounded like a fool! This was unlike any other situation he'd found himself in. He wasn't a silly young pup who settled himself between any pair of willing white thighs that parted for him. He stayed away from trouble — he didn't make trouble for himself.

"Is this your usual manner of taking women to your bed, your grace?" The bearded man called Murdoch had turned toward the bed. "Did he hurt you, lass? Force you to come with him?"

Alec couldn't believe what he was hearing. Nor could he believe what he was seeing, for the chit — Lady Maura — had lowered her head, a pose of innocence. Her mouth opened, then closed. "I . . ." she stammered. "Uncle, truly, I cannot say how I came to be here —"

"The devil you can't!" Alec exploded. "I assure you, Lady Maura came to my room knowing full well what she was about!"

"Did she now?" Murdoch stepped forward. "I know my niece, your grace." His voice vibrated with feeling. "I know very well what she is, and what she is not. I also know full well the intent and desires of men who see a beautiful young woman like my niece — men who take what they want and care nothing about those beneath them. And I daresay the proof is in the pudding, is it not?" With one arm he swept aside the coverlet.

Blood smeared the sheet.

Maura yanked her eyes from it.

Alec was too stunned to speak.

Murdoch balled his hands into fists. He turned furiously on the duke. "I knew it. I knew it! You ravished her. By heaven, you've ruined her. I —"

The baron spread his hands wide. "Gentlemen, gentlemen! I beg of you, allow me to bid the remainder of my guests farewell. Let us meet in my study at noon. Then I'm certain this matter can all be sorted out."

Murdoch looked at Maura. "Maura, gather your things and go to your room."

She appeared stricken. "Uncle —"

"Maura!" he roared.

Her eyes downcast, the chit scooted from his bed, the sheet trailing behind her like a train. She looked around, searching for her clothes. He snatched her costume up from the chair and shoved it into her hand.

Alec opened the door wide. He spoke not a word while the others filed out.

Once they were gone, his jaw clenched.

He was not a man to cast aside his sense of honor. He was not cavalier when it came to the female sex. He set limits for himself and he adhered to them. Married women were off-limits. Virgins were off-limits. A woman's virginity was a gift to her husband — to be taken only by her husband.

So what the hell happened? Had he been so drunk he'd broken his own rule?

His gaze slid back to the stain on the sheets and remained there for a long, long time. The proof of the pudding indeed, he thought with a taste of bitter humor. He would never have made love to a virgin. Indeed, he couldn't remember making love to the enchanting Lady Maura at all.

But by God, it seemed he had.

He gave a black laugh. Oh, the irony — to have taken a maid — initiated her into the world of lovemaking . . .

So why the devil couldn't he remember it?

■ ■ ■ ■

Downstairs, Maura paused as she stood outside the baron's study. Murdoch had given her a long glance as they walked back to her room. She'd had no choice but to don her pirate's costume in an empty room across the hall from the duke's. The duke had hiked a brow, an unnerving half smile on his lips as she passed. He couldn't know that he had been drugged. Or could he?

Nothing had gone wrong thus far. Nothing.

Was it too good to be true?

He was a shrewd man. She sensed it keenly, as did Murdoch when they discussed the next step in their plan. Maura shivered a little. No doubt very little escaped the duke's notice. She could not stop her mind from running riot. She prayed he thought last night a tryst and not a trap. Or perhaps he knew it was a trap and not a tryst.

She must stop this, she told herself. Now. She pressed her fingers against her cheeks. Her fingers were cold, her skin burning hot.

As hot as his body had been.

She didn't know whether to laugh or cry. Murdoch was playing his part to the hilt. When she was a child and had done something naughty, a wordless glower from him had sent her scampering away. And when he scolded her soundly — for, oh, but she'd been a very mischievous child — she ran to her room as fast as she could.

Not that the Duke of Gleneden was intimidated.

She suspected there wasn't much that would rattle him.

Damn the man. She couldn't stay out here forever. They were all inside. Waiting.

Raising her chin, striving for regal demeanor, she walked into the library. Her gown was of crimson taffeta, to lend her courage.

She blinked hard, staving off tears, as she thought of all that happened last night. The wanton way she had acted. The way she had encouraged the duke. All that had brought her to this point.

All three men rose when she entered. Behind his desk, the baron executed a small bow. Murdoch extended a hand to Maura, indicating the chair beside him.

As for the duke, well, she'd never seen a man who stood so straight. Everything about him was impeccable. He wore a black coat over a shirt so white even Jen might have laughed and said it blinded her. Gold cuff links glimmered as he straightened his jacket.

This, she realized with a twist of her stomach, was her first true glimpse of Alec McBride, Duke of Gleneden. Haughty and tight-lipped, his manner one of cool disdain.

She stole a look at him. She couldn't help it — and oh, but she shouldn't have! For that glimpse of his expression sent a shiver all through her. His regard was scarcely that of delight, as it had been last night.

A part of her trembled inside. Another part of her was fighting mad. Still another warned her to be on guard. His eyes were like chips of pale blue. She felt them like the prick of ice.

And all at once she wished she dared to punch him in the jaw — to see it climb higher yet!

The Baron of Killane waved a hand that they should sit. He coughed, cleared his throat and coughed again. It was apparent he wasn't sure how to broach the events of last night.

"Well, then," he said finally, "while I dislike involving myself in the affairs of others, something happened in my home that must be addressed and set to rights. I do not wish for my home to be known as a place for raucous indulgence. I hope that this is an isolated incident."

Alec leaned an elbow on the armrest of his chair, completely at ease. "My lord," he said with a faint smile, "I can assure you, no one will assume that you host orgies in your home."

Murdoch glared at him. "Let us establish the events of last evening, then. Maura, I doubt that you wandered into His Grace's room on your own. Therefore, your grace, I am obliged to ask. Did you take my niece — Lady Maura — to your room last night?"

"I did," the duke said evenly.

"With the intention of —"

"Most certainly." Alec shifted his head to glance at the baron, then Maura. "Let us be frank. We are all aware there are times when a man and woman become . . . amorous. Such was the case between myself and Lady Maura last night. She is not a child" — he mocked her, and he knew it — "and I cannot imagine that she did not know the consequences of accompanying a man to his room. Alone, as it were."

Maura's gaze skidded to the duke's, then quickly away. She clasped her fingers together in her lap. Her deceit sat on her shoulder, a weight she could not discard. But she could not let it sway her.

She bit back a half sob. "I . . . Uncle . . ."

She faltered. "It was the wine, I think. Too much . . . Otherwise, I would never have . . . I should not have —"

"Do not offer excuses, Maura. What you have done has gone far beyond the pale!"

Tears welled in her eyes at her uncle's rebuke.

Alec eyed Maura coolly. Tears? he scoffed to himself. A quivering lip? She floundered so convincingly. And now she was wringing her hands. Oh, she played the shrinking violet so well! She knew just when to rail, just when to sob, just how to play the game. Why, she should have been on the stage!

He rose to his feet. "Blind yourself to the truth, sir, but your niece made herself an easy mark. She was quite amenable to my advances. I did not force her. Ask her yourself."

Maura gasped. How dare he sound so lofty! She was inclined to believe he was goading her. The beast! She knew full well he did when he continued, addressing himself to Murdoch.

"Perhaps," said the duke, "you simply do not know your niece as well as you think."

Murdoch pushed his chair back. "Your grace, I warn you —"

"Were you unwilling, Lady Maura?" Alec interrupted. He turned to Maura. His tone was as icy as his gaze. "Did I force you to do anything you did not want? I recall no protests. Or perhaps you wish to provide your account? In the heat of the moment, I find my mind a bit fuzzy as to all of the details. Perhaps you are better equipped to supply them."

Again he heard her give a half sob, and watched her shake her head. Tears of supposed shame welled in her eyes. Oh, she portrayed the picture of artless innocence so well! Too much bloody wine, hell! Where was the brazen pirate from last night? He was being played like a pawn, he decided furiously.

"Do not look at her like that," growled her uncle. "Do not dare to blame her! The fact remains, you have disgraced her! You took advantage of an innocent woman. And I defy you to tell me she was not pure."

Alec's eyes flickered. "Nonetheless, it occurs to me that your niece was —"

"Hold!" Murdoch roared, on his feet now and squared away toward the duke. "Be very careful what you say, your grace! Your rank will not countenance the ruination of my niece, and that is exactly what you have done!"

But for Maura, nothing could disguise the truth. It did not disguise her part in what

99

had taken place.

She was disgraced.

She felt ashamed.

But she could bear it. It was worth any-thing — everything! — if she found the Circle and brought it home.

Shakily, she got to her feet. Murdoch stretched out a hand. "Please let me be!" she cried.

The baron was up as well. He rounded his desk. "Lady Maura! Perhaps you'd like to compose yourself in the rose garden — my late wife's pride and joy. Mr. Maxwell, perhaps you'd like to accompany her."

A footman ushered Maura and her uncle through a set of double doors into the gar-den.

Alec gazed after them. The baron resumed his seat behind his desk and regarded him.

"I believe, your grace," Preston stated coolly, "that you are arrogant."

"Am I?"

"You are. And at the moment — rather reckless."

Alec shrugged.

"Headstrong."

"I fully admit, I am used to having my way."

"Too used to having your way, I suspect. By heaven, if your father had not been my friend, you would never be invited back," Lord Preston said sternly.

Alec gave a faint smile. "Am I being invited back?"

"That depends on you."

Alec arched a brow.

The baron's tone was gruff. "Lady Maura's mother and my wife were distant cousins. Even if her uncle were not here with her, you know that, as such, I would be obliged to stand up for her."

Alec's eyes narrowed.

"You know Murdoch will demand that you wed her. It is only right. Regardless of what you claim about her conduct, it does not excuse yours. All of us saw the proof, the fact that Lady Maura's reputation has now been irreparably damaged. She lost her virginity to you, your grace. You can hardly deny your part in it."

Alec's teeth were clenched so hard his jaw hurt. "And if we were to query her further, I would lay odds she planted herself in my bed for a purpose. If we were to query her further, perhaps she might admit she set out to catch herself a duke and his fortune!"

"What! And you had no part in it?" Preston scoffed. "Perhaps you should have thought of that before you took her to your room. To your bed." His tone carried a stern admonishment. "As the daughter of an earl," he continued curtly, "no man of good family will marry her now. She has no prospects —"

"None but a rich Scottish duke! And I didn't know who she was. But I'll wager she knew exactly who I was."

Preston glared at him. "Even if she did, that does not alter or excuse your behavior."

Alec made a sound of disgust.

The baron ignored it and went on. "It's entirely possible Lady Maura may well deliver your child. Have you considered that?"

How could he, Alec thought blackly, when he had no memory of ever bedding her!

"A Catholic girl who is no longer a virgin has no future. She and her family will face nothing but shame. It may easily follow them forever. If you do not do the honorable thing, Alec, she might as well go straightaway to the convent. Her life there would not be an easy one with such a taint. Would you subject her to that? Only one thing will restore her honor. Circumstances do not permit your refusal."

Alec felt like grinding his teeth. It gnawed at him, the notion that something was not right.

"Alec! Would you tolerate any less if a

member of your family was compromised in such a way?"

He would not, he admitted to himself grudgingly. He had not. A voice inside reminded him that he had demanded marriage to his sister from his present brother-in-law, Simon Blackwell, for only a kiss — not the deflowering of a lady of respectable family, as he himself had apparently done.

Society's rules demanded payment, he thought with a bitter twist. Perhaps it would have set better if he at least remembered it!

Preston interrupted his thought. "Your choice regarding the lady will reflect on you, your grace. Offer," the baron urged. "Do not make Murdoch demand. I believe it's the better way."

Alec uncoiled himself. The baron was right. He was used to having his way, damn it all, and when all did not go his way . . .

Well, in this instance, at least, he had no choice to blame it on the effects of too much wine.

Murdoch was standing with his hands behind his back when Alec approached a scant five minutes later.

"Your grace?" he inquired coolly.

Alec gave a stiff bow. "I should like a word with my" — his lip curled — "bride-to-be.

That is, if it meets with your approval."

Murdoch stared him down. "Do not give me your airs, boy. I want your word that you will treat her as a lady should be treated."

"For God's sakes, man, I am neither a fiend nor a monster." Alec's response was terse and tight-lipped. Maxwell's request prompted in him a faint admiration for the man's protectiveness, though he was in no mood to admit it just now.

"Your word, your grace."

"You have it." Alec's tone was tight. "Now may I pass? And I would like a little privacy, if you please."

Murdoch stepped aside. "She is at the end of the path near the fountain." From the sound of it, he was certain the old man was gritting his teeth. Well, he was gritting his teeth as well.

Alec strode down the winding path. In her blazing gown of red, it was easy to spot her. He knew the exact moment she heard him. She whirled and stared him down every bit as much as her uncle had, he noted with a faint annoyance.

"Lady Maura," he drawled. He executed a deep, exaggerated bow —

And felt the sting of a slap the instant he straightened upright.

His jaw clenched. He leveled a gaze on her that would surely have made many a man fall back.

"What was that for?"

"For saying that . . . that I . . ."

"That you were amenable to my advances?"

"Aye!"

"I fail to see why I should be chastised for speaking the truth."

She glared at him but said nothing.

"Anything else you wish to say, Lady Maura?"

"As a matter of fact, yes! Was it necessary to . . . to . . ."

"To defer to you regarding the details of our night together?"

"Yes!" she hissed.

"I thought it only appropriate, since in all truth I remember quite well what we did with our clothes on . . . but not off."

The way she swallowed didn't escape his notice. He was right, he decided blackly. He was being played like a pawn, and there wasn't a damn thing he could do about it.

"Ah. I see you do remember. Indeed, I recall quite vividly hearing you moan when I bared your breasts. It came the instant you felt my mouth on your —"

Her hand shot up. Alec caught her by the

wrist, thwarting her. His other arm banded around her waist. He shook his head. "You should cease your hostilities, I think. After all, I came to tell you the news."

He could feel the way her chest rose and fell, the way her breathing quickened. He held her fast.

Little by little her eyes inched up to his. "What news?" she asked, her voice very low.

He bent his head so his lips just brushed her ear. "Congratulations, Irish. I came here for a bit of angling and caught myself a bride. And you — well, you've just snared yourself a Scotsman."

CHAPTER SIX

On her wedding day, Maura woke to the sweet sound of birdsong. She lay very still, listening as the birds trilled and whistled and sang to each other just outside the window. A faint wistfulness swelled within her.

The Irish considered it lucky to be wakened by birds singing on the morning of the wedding. But she was afraid she would be forever damned in hell for her actions over the past few days.

With a sigh, she pushed the coverlet aside and walked to the washbasin.

A few minutes later there was a knock on the door. It was Pansy, wife of the innkeeper, Jack. He was a stoop-shouldered man of perhaps Murdoch's age. From the day Maura and Murdoch arrived, Pansy and Jack had treated them with warmth and generosity, seeing to their every need. It was almost as if they were friends, not guests.

Maura reminded Pansy of her eldest daughter. She'd told her as much that first day. Maura recalled that now, as Pansy helped her into a silk, blue and white striped gown. She had purchased it on the way, for just this purpose — to serve as a wedding gown.

Maura was tempted to wear the crimson gown she'd worn for courage two days earlier, almost in defiance of Alec. She had a strong feeling he would neither have liked it nor approved of it. He'd done nothing but show his disdain for her since his proposal — if one could call it that. She, on the other hand, had done her best to keep her distance from her impending husband. It was partially out of anger for his behavior that day — and partially out of fear. What if he should look her in the eye and realize what she had done? What she was about to do? If he discovered the truth, it would jeopardize her plan.

No, whispered a voice in her mind, it would obliterate her plan!

And she might never find the Circle.

She hated to admit it, but she needed the duke too much.

Pansy offered to curl and arrange her hair, but Maura declined, winding it into an almost severe knot on her crown and don-ning a cap. Pansy fussed because she had no veil, but Maura replied that there had been no time to shop for one.

Besides, she didn't particularly feel like a bride. Everything had happened so fast, her mind was still whirling. The procurement of the special license; the local parish priest had refused to marry them in light of that very haste.

She had anticipated that. Indeed, she and Murdoch had planned for it. Oh, yes, she had counted on the priest's refusal to marry them. And indeed, everything had played out exactly as she hoped — and Murdoch continued to perform his part amazingly well. When the priest refused to marry them, Murdoch advised both the baron and Alec that he would take upon himself the task of finding an officiant to preside over the marriage.

A marriage that would take place in the baron's beautiful gardens.

Before the hour was out.

When she was ready, Pansy held the door wide and Maura stepped through. But as she did, her gown caught on a splinter in the wooden floor, ripping a small tear in the hem.

"Rats!" she muttered.

Pansy, however, clasped her hands in

delight. "Oh, no, Lady Maura, you should rejoice! Do ye not know it's the best o' luck to tear yer wedding gown on yer wedding day?"

Maura did know, which was precisely why she was so annoyed.

"You and yer new husband will surely have much happiness together."

If luck would come her way, she thought, she and the duke would not be together for long at all. But for the sake of appearance, she turned and thanked Pansy.

Murdoch waited for her downstairs. Her trunk was loaded onto the carriage, and off they went to Lord Preston's home. The ceremony was set for eight-thirty in the morning. Alec had made clear his intent to leave for Scotland as early as possible after the ceremony was performed.

The baron was waiting for them near the entrance to the garden, as well as Deacon O'Reilly, whom Murdoch had arranged to preside over the ceremony.

"I thought the fountain would be a lovely place for a wedding." The baron presented her with a bouquet of white and yellow roses.

Touched, Maura gave him a quick hug. He and Pansy seemed the only ones happy at the impending nuptials.

Certainly Alec was not.

One glimpse of the harsh set of his jaw tied her stomach in knots.

He looked directly at the clergyman. Baldly, he said, "I wonder what price they paid you to hurry the wedding." His gaze swiveled to her. "And what price have I paid for you, I wonder?"

Maura felt as if she'd been slapped. Her cheeks flamed. Behind her, she heard Murdoch suck in a breath as well. She was both furious and fearful. Had he guessed the truth? He was already suspicious, she knew. He might call her bluff. Faith, he might call the authorities!

The baron issued a firm reprimand. "Your grace, please! May I kindly remind you this is a wedding ceremony? Your wedding ceremony?"

"Aye," stated Murdoch in as threatening a voice as Maura had ever heard. "You would do well to remember it."

Maura discovered her hands were shaking. She felt Alec's gaze on her, but she couldn't look at him. She didn't dare.

"Get on with it, then," growled the duke.

Just as Maura stepped up beside him, the sun emerged from behind a cloud. The sky had been gray when they left the inn, but by the time they arrived at the baron's home, it began to clear. Now, the sun shone directly down on her; she could feel its warmth.

A part of her longed to laugh hysterically. Happy is the bride whom the sun shines on. Yet another sign of marital good luck! Another part of her longed to turn around and run, for surely it would never be so.

Alec McBride looked far more ready to murder than to marry.

All at once Maura's pulse was racing. Alec was a shrewd man. His bearing was that of one who would not be deceived or easily persuaded. Lord help her if he discovered the truth now.

The deacon cleared his throat. In a haze she heard his voice. "Dearly beloved, we have come together . . . to witness and bless the joining together of this man and this woman . . ."

Under his breath, Alec muttered a foul word.

Maura's head jerked up. Her body turned to stone, her blood to ice.

The deacon must have heard as well. He stumbled over the words, paused, then began again, this time in a rush. When it came time for Alec to say his vows, he bit out, "I do."

Those same words clogged in Maura's

throat. But she remembered what she had to do, remembered her promise to her father. "I do," she whispered. But, in truth, the oath was to her father — and her clan.

Alec slipped a plain gold ring on her finger, and then it was done. Finished. Dimly, she heard the deacon pronounce them man and wife.

Slowly she let out her breath. Relieved beyond measure, she started to turn away. Alec caught her elbow.

"Haven't you forgotten something?"

A devilish little smile curled his lips.

Maura's lips parted. She did not trust that smile, oh, not a whit!

"I've yet to kiss my bride."

Her eyes widened. Why, the wretch!

And there was no escaping it. One hand on her back, the other curled around the nape of her neck, he kissed her with breath-stealing boldness, long and hard. He used his tongue, curling it around hers. Though she longed to squirm away, pride held her immobile. When he finally released her, his expression was one of blatant satisfaction.

Maura pressed her lips against the back of her hand. It was a travesty, that kiss. She wanted to level a jab at that squarely shaven jaw; at the very least, a slap upon his cheek.

But he still held her. Maura didn't try to

jerk herself away. Something in her sensed he would snatch her back, so what was the use? Aware that the others had turned away, she released her anger in the only outlet left to her. "Why did you kiss me like that?"

"What! You did not like it? I thought you would be pleased that I showed my . . ." There was nothing but mockery in that small, deliberate pause. ". . . ardent adoration for my new wife."

He released her. The oaf! Did he think he was such a prize that he must gloat? Her body stiff, her shoulders rigidly erect, Maura clenched her jaw so tight her teeth hurt. She started to turn, but he tucked her hand into his elbow.

A brief wedding breakfast followed. Alec was polite throughout, but she knew he was chafing, ready to leave.

The baron accompanied them as they walked outside, where a carriage awaited. He offered his congratulations. Alec acknowledged it with a brief handshake.

The baron turned to Maura. "You'll come back soon, won't you?"

Maura's smile was shaky. "Soon." She wouldn't, of course. And though she had known him briefly, she liked him. She truly did, and it left an awful taste in her mouth that she had so misled him.

She waved to the baron from the carriage as she and Alec left for the dock, just a few miles away. Murdoch accompanied them. But soon they would be alone.

She and her husband.

The atmosphere within the carriage was stifling. Murdoch watched the countryside. Maura looked down at her plain wedding band. Unbidden, she found herself twisting it on her finger. Alec said nothing, but she could feel the oppressive weight of his gaze on her.

Very soon they stood on the dock. Maura watched as her small trunk was loaded onto the vessel that would take them to Scotland.

Scotland . . . and the Circle of Light.

All too soon it was time to board. To leave Murdoch. To leave Ireland. Oh, God, it was like tearing a part of her heart out.

Murdoch said something to Alec, then came toward her. Maura flung herself against him. Her eyes squeezed shut. Tears leaked.

"Don't, child!" he whispered on hearing her ragged half sob. "I will see you soon. Very soon." He touched her hair.

Maura nodded, swallowing hard, waiting until she was dry-eyed before she walked to where Alec stood waiting near the gangplank.

On board the ship, she stood near the stern for long, long minutes. She stood until her homeland disappeared from view.

Only then did she turn, her throat achingly tight. Alec stood halfway down the deck, unsmiling, watching her stonily. The sight of him was jarring. How long had he been there?

All at once uncertainty churned in her breast and she could not stop it. God would surely smite her down someday for what she had done. Had she led herself into a trap of her own making? No. She refused to believe it. Her sacrifice was worth the cost. Worth any cost if she found and returned the Circle of Light, home where it belonged. She would barter with the devil himself if it would gain her the Circle. A shiver went through her at the thought.

Perhaps she already had.

CHAPTER SEVEN

The crossing across the North Channel was rough. Waves splashed high, spraying over the bow. Maura had been in small boats many times before, rowing around the bay when she was young. But this was different. She stood on deck, looking out, bracing herself with her feet, as if she'd been born to the sea.

Perhaps a quarter of an hour passed, then Alec came up beside her. "For pity's sake, don't stand there," he growled. "You'll fall overboard."

"Then you'd be rid of me," she said lightly. "I should think that would suit you well, your grace."

He neither agreed nor disagreed. "At least hold onto the rail."

There was something odd in his tone. Maura looked over at him. Her brow furrowed . . . suddenly she realized why he was so pale.

"Oh, dear. Are you of a delicate constitution, sir?" she asked brightly. How odd that for a descendant of a pirate, her newfound husband was a bad sailor. It was all she could do not to crow.

Alec shot her a venomous look. "You needn't delight in it," he muttered.

"Oh, but I do not delight in it! I merely inquired out of concern for my husband. It is a wifely duty, is it not, to see to the care and comfort of one's husband?"

The little witch! Alec grappled for a handkerchief to press to his mouth. It was true the open sea affected him so. But she didn't inquire out of concern. Why, the chit was gloating!

Wait, my Irish beauty. Wait until I am home in Scotland. At Gleneden. Wait until I have you all to myself. Then we shall see how tart your tongue is.

Ah, yes, wait until he was home.

The ship docked at the port town of Stranraer. The duke's coachman Douglas was there to meet them. After a quick luncheon they were off. The vehicle was small, built for speed, yet still comfortable and well-sprung.

What was not comfortable was Alec's regard as he climbed in and took his place opposite her, tossing his hat on the seat. His black hair was tousled; it should have made him look younger. Perhaps it did. But it also made him appear dangerous. His eyes, so icy and pale, drifted over her. It was as if he could see right through her, into her mind. Her very heart. She wondered almost frantically if he'd discovered the truth already. Yet how could that be?

Maura quickly averted her gaze. The carriage rolled forward and gathered speed. She stared out the window at the countryside. Yet all she could see was Alec's grim visage as she took her place beside him that morning at the wedding ceremony, his jaw bunched hard.

He was angry. Wary. Suspicious. He felt he'd been duped.

And he had.

At length she pretended to sleep. Before she knew it, she began to doze. At some point she was half aware of being tugged down upon the seat. Someone placed a pillow under her head and drew a blanket up over her shoulders.

She woke much later. She felt leaden, almost drugged.

"That was quite a nap you had," came Alec's drawl. "Didn't you sleep well last night?"

That was enough to rouse her into full wakefulness. The incline of her chin high, she sat up. She smoothed her skirts, re-pinned her hair, and resolutely ignored him.

His soft laughter tipped her chin even higher.

Twilight fell, settling over the treetops. Her heart began to pound. She turned her head toward Alec. She fought to make her voice even.

"We are on McBride lands, are we not?"

He looked at her oddly, then gave a nod. He pointed through the window to her left. "Gleneden Hall is several miles to the north-west."

It was uncanny. Maura had known the instant they were on his lands. As they crested a small rise, she caught a glimpse of a building in the distance. Not a castle like McDonough . . . She saw aged timbers, stone chimneys, and a slate roof that pro-tected the massive structure — a structure that appeared as dark as its owner.

A haze of mist began to drape over the earth, seeping into the hills and trees, when she saw lights from inside his home flicker, there one minute, gone the next, as the car-riage traveled through dense forest.

An unearthly chill stole over her. Her father was right. She was right. The Circle was here. Somewhere. Somewhere close. Her ears buzzed; an odd sizzle flashed inside her. With aching heart, she remembered the night her father died, his words.

It calls to me. The Circle calls to me. It cries out to come home.

Oh, God. Now she knew what her father meant. How he had felt!

For she felt the very same — as if the Circle called to her.

The carriage door opened. Maura wasn't even aware they'd stopped. She rose and started down the steps. Her knees threatened to buckle. The long hours in the coach had taken their toll — as well imparting a strange eeriness. Alec caught her around the waist and swung her around and to the ground.

Huge wooden doors were thrown wide. Maura stood as if mesmerized. This, then, was her home — at least for the time it took to find the Circle. She found herself pierced by a pang of dread. Gleneden Hall was massive. In her eyes, it appeared dark and foreboding.

Alec led her up a series of stone steps. At the threshold he caught hold of her elbow. Startled, Maura looked up at him. His expression matched his half smile. Both reflected an almost smug satisfaction. Instinct made her start to step back; before she knew what he was about, Alec swung her up and into his arms and carried her across the threshold, past the doors and into a vast great hall.

He kicked the massive wooden door behind them closed. "Welcome to your new home, Irish," he murmured, just before he lowered her slowly to the floor, one arm curled possessively around her waist.

A host of servants lined up to greet their master. Catching her hand, Alec raised it high, introducing her as the new duchess. Maura winced. She was certain she'd never forget those stunned looks, though they were quickly replaced by smiles. The only name she truly remembered was Mrs. Yates, the housekeeper.

When they were finally alone in the massive great hall, Alec's smile, however, was anything but welcoming.

He tipped his head to the side. "Well, well, well," he said softly, "it's right into the belly of the beast you've come, isn't it, Irish?"

The scathing look she granted him was blunted by the tremor of her lips.

"What do you think of your new home?"

"Well, I've hardly seen —"

"Did you expect more from a Scottish duke? A grand palace perhaps? My lovely lady, my duchess, my wife. I do hope your new home fits your expectations."

Maura ignored his mockery. She craned her neck to gaze at the massive timbered ceiling, the peak at least four stories high.

"Impressive, isn't it? It's the original great hall, what was initially built as a hunting lodge for Robert the Bruce." Alec stood in the very center of the enormous great hall, his hands behind his back. Tall, so very much the proud duke.

"King Robert II of Scotland created the first Duke of Gleneden for my family's support throughout the wars for Scottish independence. It's said the first duke and the Bruce were distant cousins. In fact, you may find this interesting, Irish. The Bruce's second wife, Elizabeth, was the daughter of the Earl of Ulster. It's possible that you and I may claim the same lineage, back through the ages."

"You are smiling, your grace. You find that amusing?"

His half smile widened. "You are quick to take offense. Your nature is a fiery one, is it not?"

Maura's jaw clamped tight. "You have not known me long enough to know my nature, your grace."

Deliberately, she turned her face aside,

letting her gaze drift around the room. Alec gestured. "The stag heads mounted on each side of the doors to the formal dining room are courtesy of my ancestor Duncan, the twelfth Duke of Gleneden. The head of the gray wolf on the wall beside the far window" — he waved a hand to his left — "was taken by the tenth duke in the 1600s."

Maura couldn't help but remember the howl of the wolf on the night her father died. Tingles went up and down her spine.

"The boar on the wall above you is a much more recent trophy, from one of my hunts as a boy," Alec continued.

"The belly of the beast indeed." Maura couldn't resist a jibe. "The McBrides are great hunters, it would seem." She looked him straight in the eye. "Any seafarers in the family, my lord?"

If he was discomfited, he showed no sign of it. He shrugged. "None that I know of."

"I suppose not. Too plebian, I would imagine."

The way he arched a single, black brow hinted at reproach. "You are not only quick-tempered, but quick to judge."

"As are you," she needled sweetly. She took a deep breath. "The fireplace is quite extraordinary."

And it was. It was enormous, its expanse

124

in keeping with the proportions of the room.

"Limestone?" She walked toward it.

"Indeed."

"The family coat of arms?" Reaching out, she touched the carving on one side, the armored helm of a soldier. There was a matching one on the other side.

He nodded. "Argent on a —"

"Fess gule." With her fingertips Maura traced the broad, horizontal band across the width of the shield. "Three mullet of the field." Within the band, she touched each of the five-pointed stars. "The argent, the shield of white, signifies purity and sincerity, I believe, the red for military might. Am I right, your grace?"

Both his brows shot high. "You are. But why do I suspect you already knew that? I am quite relieved to know I've married a woman whose education has not been neglected. Indeed, my brother Aidan, who served Her Majesty for a number of years in India, will be delighted to discover I've wed a woman who is able to correctly identify the symbols — and with the proper terminology."

It wasn't meant as a compliment. It was simply his turn to needle her.

Maura ignored the jibe, still taking in the room with its timbered roof and whitewashed stone walls. But numerous comforts had clearly been added over the years. She glanced down at the handmade carpet beneath her feet.

"Aubusson?" she inquired.

"Persian. Sixteenth century."

Richly colored tapestries hung on the walls. Whether they were French or Dutch, she couldn't be sure. She wasn't about to ask Alec, with his superior airs, that was for certain. One depicted a hunting scene — why, who would have thought?

A medieval lute caught her eye. She paused before an ornate, gilded pier table with a marble inlaid top. The worth of this piece alone, she speculated, would have fed and kept in comfort everyone on McDonough lands for at least several years. A spark simmered within her. She couldn't help the thought that ran rampant through her mind. How much had been pilfered by the Black Scotsman on his raids? Prizes claimed from other vessels and taken for his own?

A group of furniture was clustered around the fireplace. Two divans with plump flowered cushions. Several roomy, claw-footed wing chairs with matching footstools. She seated herself in one, but her back was ramrod straight.

"You are right, your grace. It's all quite

impressive." Her first impression had been wrong. She wanted to hate it, to declare Alec's home as forbidding as its master. But she couldn't. Despite the rich furnishings, with the fire burning in the hearth, the rustic feel gave it a charm that was warmly inviting. "And though I've yet to see all of it, I doubt my opinion will change."

"Alec. You must call me Alec. After all, we are husband and wife now." He moved to a table under the window where a silver tray filled with shimmering crystal decanters and glasses had been placed. "Wine?" he inquired. He half filled a delicately etched goblet.

Maura couldn't seem to take her eyes from his hands. His fingers were long. Graceful yet strong, bronzed from the sun. So intensely masculine she felt her mouth grow dry. "I think not," she said finally.

"Lost your taste for it, eh?"

Their eyes locked. He was toying with her, the cad! Damn him for reminding her!

He started to drink. Stopped, then slowly lowered the glass. He stared at her in taut silence until Maura wanted to scream. Then, in a voice almost deadly quiet, he said, "Do you think I don't know what you did?"

Maura blanched. Composure was impossible. Her breath hung suspended in her throat, but her mind was racing. Was it the fact that she'd drugged him? Or the fact that their marriage —

He approached, so that they stood at opposite ends of the sofa. "Why so coy, your grace?"

Maura ran her tongue over her lips.

"You're not smiling, my lady. I should imagine you would be gloating. You've managed to marry yourself to a duke."

Oh, but he was arrogant! If he wanted to be provoked, she would oblige! "A wealthy duke?" she dared.

"Yes." It was a statement of fact — he did not brag. "You've gained a great deal from this marriage. But that was the point, wasn't it? And as you'll find out anyway, yes, I'm titled in England, too."

She should have realized sooner. Why, he thought she'd married him for money! How laughable!

She ran a finger along the elaborate stitching on the arm of the chair. "With estates . . . where?"

"Two others in Scotland, two in England. And a town house in London."

"I've never been to London," she said sweetly.

"Well, if you're thinking of taking up

residence elsewhere, Duchess . . . do not."

"And why not?" She was inclined to be as lofty as he.

"Because I wish to keep you close. It's as I stated before. Because you are my lady. Because you are my wife. Because you are my duchess."

Hah! Maura longed to roll her eyes.

"Are you hungry?"

His sudden change in tack startled her. "Famished, actually," she admitted guardedly.

"I have some business to attend to in my study, but it shouldn't take long. I'll have Mrs. Yates show you to your room and have a tray sent up." He paused. "And then . . ."

Wrapped in his silky tone was something that sent Maura's gaze skidding up to his in alarm. She was on shaky ground, and he knew it. His expression — the light in his eyes, that rakish hint of a smile — confirmed it. He relished her nervousness, damn him!

"What?" she asked faintly.

His slow-growing smile added to her unease.

"We will share our first night of marital bliss."

He drained his glass, set it on the tray, and strode through a doorway she hadn't noticed until now.

Maura didn't know whether to laugh or cry. If she hadn't already been sitting, she'd have surely collapsed.

My lady, he'd called her. *My duchess.*

But she wasn't his lady. She wasn't his duchess.

She wasn't even his wife.

CHAPTER EIGHT

Alec installed himself in front of the fireplace, long legs crossed together at the ankle, one arm dangling over the side of the chair, the one with the wine. Every so often he raised it to his lips. Before long Mrs. Yates appeared. He declined the meal she offered to bring, but stopped her when she would have left.

"My wife is established in the duchess's chamber?"

"Aye, your grace. Aggie is helping her unpack her belongings."

"Thank you, Mrs. Yates. You'll see that the staff fulfills any requests that she has from now on?"

"Of course, your grace."

The housekeeper bobbed a curtsy and left. Alec decided wryly that there would be a good bit of gossip in the servants' quarters tonight.

He stared into the fireplace. It wasn't lit,

for the day had been warm. He took another swallow of wine, pondering. No, not pondering, he decided with a rare touch of self-deprecation. He was brooding. And he was a man who brooded but rarely.

Lord above, he was married. Married! The very thought set his teeth on edge. He chided himself bitterly for his lack of self-control.

It wasn't that he was averse to marriage. It wasn't that he was determined to remain a bachelor. He was attentive to his title and his duties. He would never disregard his responsibilities. Family was important to him. After all, he'd been raised in a warm, loving family. He wanted an heir someday, with a woman with whom he wanted to spend the rest of his life. He wanted a child — children! — however many he was blessed with. Children who would know the same happiness here at Gleneden as he.

Which brought up the question . . . how the hell was he going to explain his sudden marriage to his family? Perhaps it was a blessing that none of them was expected at Gleneden soon. His mother had written that she planned to spend the entire summer in Brighton.

So what was he to say? That it was love at first sight? he thought mockingly. More like lust at first sight.

All those hours in the coach with her today . . . She appeared so innocent when she pretended to sleep. She hadn't fooled him in the slightest. He knew she was awake. Then when she finally did sleep, she looked so uncomfortable, her head angled against the side of the coach. He'd finally tugged her down upon the seat, while he'd have very much liked to tug her down upon him.

He jerked his mind away from the thought. She affected him more than she should have. Far more than he wanted. He fingered his cheek, the place where she'd slapped him. Slapped him. He'd been slugged before, by his sister Anne. By Aidan. When they were all children. But he'd never before been slapped!

He was still astounded that the lovely Lady Maura had dared.

His mouth thinned.

Or perhaps he wasn't. Alec considered himself a good judge of character; he wasn't easily fooled. He wasn't swayed by Maura's maidenly display of tearful regret that day in the baron's study. He suspected she was a woman of spirit, a spirit that spilled into what could only be called headstrong and strong-willed. It wasn't a cowering little miss he'd wed.

He fought to curb a rising fury. He didn't like his hand being forced. And, he reflected blackly, it was the manner in which this marriage had come about! He couldn't shake the feeling that he'd been manipulated. Too late he saw through her ploy. The beauteous lady wanted to marry a rich man. What better way than to find her way into his bed, and be caught together in the morning? She had calculated well, a master in her role as temptress.

Oh, aye, he had been tempted by the sultry beauty, irresistibly tempted. He had played his role, never guessing that he was being played.

And he had lost. Well, he told himself scathingly, he'd fallen ripe and right into her hands. Never mind that he'd been all too willing to take what the little vixen offered. Never mind that the last thing he expected to bring home to Gleneden was a bride — a calculating one at that! The two of them had bested him. Maura . . . and her uncle Murdoch.

Seething, he drank a toast to the two of them.

His gaze lifted to the ceiling. He took his time. An hour had passed. He chided himself bitterly for his lack of self-control, then poured another glass of wine. He was on edge. He wanted her. But he didn't want to want her.

Perhaps a half hour more passed. He'd made his intentions perfectly clear. He was almost tempted to let Maura stew — and wait, long into the night.

Almost, but not quite.

No, he decided.

A grim little smile curled his lips. After all, his bride was expecting him.

And what a shame it would be to disappoint her.

He drained the last of his wine. His boot heels echoed as he climbed the steps. Upstairs, in the newest wing, the corridor was laid with carpet. She wouldn't hear his approach. She'd been installed in the ducal suite, the duchess's chamber, the chamber his mother had never used, for she always slept with his father. Always, until the day he died.

He raised a hand, poised to knock on her door.

His jaw bunched suddenly. Bloody hell! he thought. What need was there to announce himself in his own home?

He turned the handle and stepped inside. The door clicked shut behind him. It appeared his bride hadn't heard him. She was bent over a drawer in the armoire, the round shape of her delectable little rump clearly visible. It appeared she hadn't heard him, or else she didn't care. Oh, but she would care if she knew the thoughts that were running wild through his mind.

Tonight's game belonged to him, he decided with a measure of satisfaction. He would enjoy seeing her squirm. He would enjoy turning the tables on her and teaching her a well-deserved lesson. He'd been a fool in Ireland, allowing his desire for her to control him. She had fooled him once; he wouldn't allow it to happen twice. Something inside him relished the idea of making her think he would bed her tonight.

He wouldn't. Not yet. He was too angry for that, too full of resentment. He was going to make her wait. Discomfit her. Keep her off kilter a bit. Make her wonder when . . .

"Good evening, Irish."

She whirled. Her hand went to her throat. He'd startled her, he realized. But her recovery was quick.

"I didn't hear you knock," she said coolly.

"That's because I didn't."

He allowed his gaze to travel over her slowly. Her nightgown was fashioned of plain white cotton, its only adornment a bit

136

of lace about the sleeves and hem.

Was her simple attire meant to convince him she wasn't a fortune-hunter? He didn't believe it for an instant. He'd been a blind fool in Ireland! She had set the trap and he had taken the bait. And now she had what she wanted. A title, his name, money, security for the rest of her life. She'd surrendered her virginity for a life of ease. And it wasn't as if he could cast her out, he thought with a bitter twist.

He advanced farther into the room, while Maura, aware of his presence, reached for her robe. Oh, so now the modest maid had reappeared!

She jerked the sash of her robe tight. It only served to accentuate the smallness of her waist, clinging to the shape of her breasts — of which he could see the points of her nipples. He was unwittingly amused. Her attire was of little consequence. No, her simple gown didn't matter — did she realize the provocation she presented? Silk and lace would have made her no less desirable. Or perhaps she did know. Perhaps it was just another calculated move on her part. Perhaps she simply didn't care.

Her expression declared her irritation. Oh, the haughty duchess indeed!

"Your room suits you?" His tone was

politeness itself.

"Very much, thank you." She was coolly dignified, the little cheat! "It was kind of you to allow Aggie to help me unpack. And I've not yet had the chance to explore. Is that a dressing room?" She gestured toward the door next to the armoire.

"No." It was amazing how one single word could give such immense satisfaction. "It's my bedchamber. And most convenient, Irish. I can visit your bed whenever I like. And you can visit mine whenever you like."

Very deliberately he stripped off his coat and tossed it on the chair next to the mirror.

Her eyes narrowed. "I wonder, then, your grace, what you are doing in my room. We are both aware that ours is a marriage compelled —"

"But it is a marriage nonetheless." Casually, Alec began to unbutton his shirt. It landed atop his jacket. "And I promised you a night of marital bliss. I merely wish to set about the bedding of my bride with husbandly vigor. I promise you, you'll not be disappointed."

Defiance flared in those amazingly colored green eyes. "A boast, Scotsman?"

"A fact, Irish."

She glared her disdain. But her tongue

came out to wet her lips. She did that when she was nervous, he noted. As well she should be. Despite that, she did not shirk. No, she displayed no sign of giving way.

"You have already seen to the plucking of the fruit, your grace. It can be plucked only once."

One corner of his mouth slanted up. He found her choice of words amusing.

"Therefore," she continued, "you need not feel any obligation to provide me with a night of marital bliss, as you call it. I relieve you of the necessity. Besides, it was a long journey, was it not? I find I am quite fatigued."

"A pity, for I am not." He made the declaration with great pleasure.

Maura had maintained her stance near the armoire, her shoulders squared. Alec eyed her with shrewd consideration. "You availed yourself of me that night," he reminded her smoothly. "Am I not entitled to the same enjoyment? Am I not allowed to avail myself of you?"

"I would remind you, your grace, you already have."

Alec sat on the side of the bed and patted the space beside him. "But I remember so little of our night in bed together! I apologize most heartily for that. Never again will

I drink to such excess. Now, Duchess, do you see why I find the prospect of a night with you so . . . invigorating? I am eager to make amends for my lack of appreciation that night. Did I give you pleasure?" He allowed no chance for reply. "Given your virgin state, I pray that I did. If my performance was clumsy, I am determined to make amends. To please you. To embrace my role of husband to the fullest extent, particularly in the arena of conjugal relations. Given the haste of our wedding, I admit that I never gave it much thought, but I believe husband and wife should share equal enjoyment in the marriage bed. I do hope you agree. Now, come sit beside your husband."

Their eyes collided. Maura's lips compressed. A taut silence stretched out.

Alec's tone was very soft. "Come, Duchess, or I'll come get you."

Something blazed in those beautiful green eyes. Still she remained where she was. Either she was full of reckless daring or a fool to believe he wouldn't follow through. Despite his previous decision to the contrary, he was just about to do exactly as he promised — proceed to the bedding of his wife — when she walked stiffly around the end of the bed and sat.

A full three feet away from him.

He would allow her that, he decided. For the moment, at least.

A tense silence cropped up again.

Alec studied her profile in silent speculation, navigating his next move, aware of a storm of feelings building inside him. Throughout the mounting silence, Maura maintained that air of distant coolness.

A battle of wills? he wondered. Or a battle of wits?

He considered. She'd been a virgin, but that hadn't stopped her from acting the seductress, and the certainty served to fire his temper . . . as well as his desire. All at once he was determined to make her want him so much she could taste it. Crave him with a heat that met his own.

Because one thing had not changed. Despite his feelings of betrayal, he burned for her as much as he had the night of the masquerade. Dislike it, he did. Deny it, he could not. Her hair was down, a curtain of thick black waves around her shoulders. She stirred him. Stirred him unbelievably. Stirred him as no other woman had ever done.

She also spurned him as no other woman had ever done. Which was not wise. Not wise at all. Didn't she realize it posed a challenge to any man? An affront? A purely primeval call to prove otherwise? Her youth was no excuse. She didn't realize what she did to a man. Her flirtation . . . and his reaction to her the night of the masquerade merely confirmed it.

Alec's move was quick and decisive. He glimpsed a fleeting alarm as he banded one arm around her waist and caught her chin between thumb and forefinger.

"You cannot deny me, Irish. And I will neither deny nor curtail my desire — our mutual desire. Or have you forgotten so quickly? You surrendered your virginity to me. Don't you remember?"

"I . . . A vague remembrance, perhaps. It's just as I told my uncle. I had far too much wine. We — We both did!"

"And prior to that point, you gave no sign you found me distasteful. Quite the contrary. You flirted quite outrageously with me. You were most eager in the garden. Or will you plead ignorance there, too?"

Her lower lip thrust out. A rather delicious pout that made him want to cover her lips with his and tug it into his mouth. Raw desire slipped over him, surging heavy and thick between his thighs, swelling his shaft until he was granite hard, uncomfortably granite hard. If she placed her hand on that stretch of his leg, she would feel it. He had the urge to do exactly that simply to glean her reaction.

"You lead me to conclude you are amorous only when you imbibe. Perhaps I should ply you with spirits again one night — we make an excellent whiskey here at Gleneden — and resurrect the seductress I met that night."

Her eyes flew wide, but her tongue was as acerbic as ever. "I've no taste for whiskey. And at the moment, no taste for you, Scotsman."

"You are young, Irish, but quite old enough to know exactly what you were doing — enticing a man, luring him on. And you excel at it, by the way."

As he spoke, he deftly unknotted the knot of her robe and pushed it from her shoulder, baring white, silken flesh. He heard her sudden intake of breath.

"What happened to the woman I met at the masquerade?" He trailed his fingertips back and forth, tracing the neckline of her nightgown. "Where has she gone? You played the bold pirate, Irish. Now play the loving wife."

"How can I play the loving wife when I am not the loving wife? Any more than you are a loving husband."

There was a flash of something in her eyes, something that made him want to challenge her. To tame her, while wanting to taste her and savor her all at the same time. He'd been right about her. She possessed a will of iron.

But so did he. And he was not to be dissuaded. He would not be dismissed like a green young boy!

"I think you need a reminder," he said suddenly. "Perhaps it will jog your memory of our first encounter and rekindle your desire. Perhaps it will jog my memory of our union."

She started to shake her head.

"You appear determined to forget. And I've enough experience to know when a woman returns my advances. Which you did, and most ardently. Must I reacquaint you?"

"Your grace —"

"I've paid a heavy price for you, Irish. Am I not allowed to enjoy it? Am I not allowed even a kiss?"

"It's not a kiss you want," she cried.

And it wasn't. Her eyes were enormous. The little cheat! Why this sudden reluctance? She had lured him in. With words, with her eyes, with her body. And yes, he'd gone willingly. Through his own fault, he'd paid the price, a heavy one at that — the price of a dukedom. But she had toyed with him once, and he had learned from his experience.

"I make no bones about it," he stated bluntly. "Is it any wonder? I would like to experience again what continues to escape my memory! I apologize for my drunken state that night. It's most odd, however, given that too much wine or any other spirits usually renders a man . . . incapable."

And by heaven, he was going to make her want him — want him the way he'd wanted her the night of the masquerade. Oh, she pretended now that she felt nothing, but he knew better. He recalled the softening of her lips, her tempting eagerness. That was branded into his brain. And now, well, perhaps he should give the lass a taste of her own medicine. He would make her pant and writhe and cry out her longing for him. He would bring her to the point of rapture, then deny her completion.

Catching her hand, he brought her to her feet. Her gaze flickered away, then returned. First the coquette. Now the maid.

He was not a man of quick temper. But the chit had managed to spark it, and once roused, it was not easily doused.

Did she truly believe he was such a fool?

He'd fallen victim to her ruse once already. He would not do it so easily again. And if she was convinced he was a puppet whose strings she could pull at whim, she was mistaken.

Alec caught her up against him. She lifted her head the same instant his mouth came down on hers. His fingers slid beneath her hair, molding to her nape, even as he molded her lips to his. He would leave her in no doubt that he would not be a pawn. His tongue ran along the seam of her lips. She kept them tightly closed. So she would spurn him, would she, now that she was his wife and had what she wanted?

Something inside him hardened. No, he decided. No.

With a sound low in his throat, he brought her closer still. She was wedded tight against him, her breasts mounded against his chest, slim thighs soft against the tautness of his own. She sucked in a breath, and Alec pounced. His tongue parted her lips, stealing around hers as she sought to tuck it back; he took it into his mouth and sucked hard. In some faraway corner of his mind he registered the faint sound she made. But he was in no mood for more trickery. Why did she persist at playing the innocent?

His arm tightened. The pressure of his

mouth was fierce. He kissed her with raw possessiveness, as if to imprint her with his mouth and his will.

He felt the way she twisted against him, trying to free herself. She didn't want his kiss, his touch.

Finally he released her. He raised his head, but he was not finished. He was going to see what was his. A few swift moves and her robe and gown were on the floor.

She stood before him naked.

When she sought to shield her breasts, he caught her by the wrists — how fine-boned and fragile they were — and held them at her sides.

Some distant part of him registered that she turned her face away. Her bravado was crumbling. No doubt she thought him hard and heartless.

Her skin was alabaster white. She was slender as a reed, her legs long and shapely. Yet even feeling used, he experienced a sharp stab of lust. He envisioned those long legs wrapped around his hips, his rod buried deep and hard.

His regard was long and thoroughly un-hurried. Vaguely he registered her distress, for even as he battled the pangs of aware-ness, his mind was elsewhere.

She was exquisite. Christ, it made no

sense. How could he have made love to a woman like this and have no recollection? How? Christ, he must have been feeling the effects of too much liquor more than he thought. Surely he would have remembered beauty such as this.

Doubt crowded his chest. His mind blurred as he struggled to resurrect that night. Perhaps in the dark . . . clothing pushed aside . . .

His jaw clamped tight. His breathing was hard. Quick. He fought a scorching battle with red-hot desire that threatened to overcome reason. Releasing her wrists, he stared down at her, deliberately clamping his hand around one breast. She flinched.

His hand fell away. So, she thought him hard and heartless. So much for bringing her to rapture, he thought with a twist of his lips.

Abruptly, he snatched up his coat and shirt. "I'm going to my room, Irish. Come find me if you discover yourself lonely."

CHAPTER NINE

It is a marriage nonetheless . . . I merely wish to set about the bedding of my bride with husbandly vigor . . . I promise you, you'll not be disappointed.

Like the ringing of bells, Maura heard his voice, tolling through her mind.

It cost her much to admit that the encounter had left her nerves scraped raw. Shaken, her heart still pounding violently, she threw on her nightgown and practically leaped into bed.

She didn't deceive herself. Alec McBride was a formidable presence. He exuded power. Self-confidence. He was not a man one could underestimate, she conceded silently. Not a man one should underestimate.

She was very much afraid she had made a grave miscalculation.

Alec left her in no doubt as to his feelings about this marriage. He resented it. He believed she'd married him for his wealth.

Which was all well and good, she thought shakily. But what if he found out Murdoch had paid the deacon? What if he discovered that Deacon O'Reilly was no deacon at all? Oh, once upon a time he'd been a clergyman. But that was before he was caught pilfering from the church funds and stripped of all privilege.

What if Alec discovered their marriage was a sham?

The thought sent panic tracing through her. When Alec left tonight, she'd never seen eyes so cold and icy. She had only sought to make her way into the house of the Black Scotsman. She hadn't counted on the man himself.

He was shrewd. She hadn't expected him to stroll into her room as he had. That, she acknowledged with a faint hint of panic, was a mistake on her part. She'd cautioned herself not to let down her guard. But she certainly hadn't expected him to strip her naked, the wretch!

It wasn't wise to provoke him, she scolded herself soundly. She must learn to curb her tongue. But he himself provoked her reaction, with his goading little speeches. The man was beastly and arrogant! How dare he barge into her room unannounced!

You are the interloper here, charged a niggling little voice in her mind.

She stared up at the ceiling. She could still hear his voice.

I promised you a night of marital bliss.

She had been lucky tonight. Whether or not he truly intended to follow through, she couldn't be sure. She thought he didn't. There had been too much anger in his kiss. Too much angry pride, she acknowledged shakily.

Her emotions were wildly erratic. She was both excited and afraid. At least she was here. In Scotland. Murdoch had warned her, however. *If you dig a grave for others, you might fall into it yourself.*

Alec McBride might well prove her downfall. One false move and all would be lost.

Maura didn't deceive herself as to his behavior. His message tonight had been clear. This was his home and he would do as he pleased. She was his, and he would do as he pleased with her.

It was his way of telling her he would not be manipulated.

But she could not yield, she thought. She must endeavor to stay out of his bed. She had to believe she could. As angry as he'd been over being forced to marry her, he was still a gentleman. A rather wild and wicked one, and there was the rub.

He believed their marriage had been consummated, or he would never have consented to wed her. And now she was charged with the task of keeping him convinced they were truly wed, without arousing suspicion that they were not.

That angry pride might well prove an advantage. A way of keeping him from her bed. But how long would it continue? She must somehow find a balance so she could hunt for the Circle without him knowing it. She must charm him just enough that he would not become suspicious, yet all the while keep him at bay. If he discovered her virtue intact, he would discover the truth.

He would discover her ruse.

An hysterical laugh bubbled up inside her.

How very impossible it seemed!

It didn't help knowing that all this had occurred as a result of her machinations. She'd thought herself so clever when everything had come off without a hitch in Ireland.

But they were in Scotland now, and she was no longer sure of anything. And one thing was becoming excruciatingly clear.

Alec McBride was no fool.

It was late before Maura finally slipped into

the land of dreams. But they were not pleasant dreams. Quite the contrary.

She was racing through the forest, darting
between the trees. Shadows loomed all
around. Someone was behind her, calling.
Giving chase. Her pursuer grew closer. The
Black Scotsman, she realized. His image
loomed in her mind. He wore his pirate's
garb, a feathered hat over hair that was
black as the night. Beneath a dark, heavy
moustache, his lips pulled back. Chilling
laughter spilled forth, for he was almost
upon her now. On his hand — his right
hand only — he wore a black leather glove.
It snatched at her, that black-gloved hand,
yet she eluded him.

Then all at once she saw the Circle of
Light. It was small. No larger than the span
of her fingers spread wide. It hovered, floating and aglow, slowly turning, the most
beautiful myriad of colors reflected on
beaten silver. And somehow she knew that
she had only to touch it to reach safety.

Almost there. Almost there. With a cry she
stretched out her fingertips, just as the
black-gloved hand of the Black Scotsman
seized hold of her skirt. Then she was falling. Falling a very great distance.

Down into the arms of a wild, wicked
Scotsman with eyes like chips of icy blue . . .

"Wake up, Irish. Wake up."

She woke with a strangled gasp. Alec sat on the bed beside her, gently shaking her shoulder.

The strangest thought popped into her mind. Alec on the bed was not dangerous.

Alec in the bed was quite dangerous indeed.

He stopped when he realized she was awake. "Good heavens, Irish, you've frightened half the staff with your shrieking."

Maura was still half dazed. "I — I was dreaming."

"Yes, I gathered that." His gaze resided on her lips. She felt her face heat up, remembering the way he'd kissed her last night.

The way he'd made her stand naked before him.

And now he regarded her again, this time with his head cocked to the side. "What were you dreaming about?"

She certainly had no wish to tell him.

A finger beneath her jaw, he brought her gaze to his. "What were you dreaming about?"

"A pirate," she admitted grudgingly. "A pirate was chasing me."

"A pirate, eh? Why, I wonder why that could be." A rather wicked gleam flared in his eyes. "Handsome, was he, your pirate?"

Something — a good night's sleep per-haps? — had lightened his foul mood of the night before.

The lack of a good night's sleep had soured hers. "No," she said with acid sweet-ness. "He was quite the most wretched, ugly pirate you could ever imagine."

One corner of Alec's mouth slanted up — a wicked smile without doubt. "And were you rescued from this wretched pirate, Irish?"

Maura frowned. It was discomfiting that he was fully clothed, while she lay beneath the blanket wearing only a nightgown.

"I think not. I fell into the arms of yet another pirate. And I believe he meant to torment me rather than rescue me."

"Oh, surely not. Let me hazard another guess. This other pirate in your dreams. I'd wager he was indeed quite handsome."

She compressed her lips.

"Yes," he said lightly, "I see I am right. I knew I would be, of course."

What audacity! She fixed him with a glare. "And why would you assume that?"

"Simply because I'm quite familiar with the workings of the female mind."

"Are you, Scotsman?" It slipped out before she could stop it. "So you are quite familiar with the fairer sex? You know, it's rude to boast of your conquests to your wife of but a day." No doubt he would brag of his prowess again!

One black brow hiked a fraction. "I was speaking of my sister Anne. When she was a child, she and my cousin Caro could be quite melodramatic."

"Well, I am neither a child nor melodramatic."

As she spoke, she shifted a little so she could face him. But the movement unwittingly dragged the loose round neck of her nightgown down.

Alec said nothing. His eyes settled on her bare shoulder. Maura dragged the sheet back up to cover it.

Their eyes met.

"Shall I stay and help you with your bath?"

Her look of shock must have pleased him. His devilish half smile widened. "No? Another day, perhaps." He paused. "You know, Irish, if your dreams are always so noisy, you'll give me no choice but to have you removed elsewhere."

At least then he wouldn't be in the next room. It was her turn to smile. "Wherever you can find room, your grace."

"On second thought, your grace" — he turned it neatly back around — "perhaps you should simply share mine. Then I would be there to shush you when you are in need of shushing."

Maura's smile froze.

"Or to comfort you, Irish, whatever the case might be."

She turned a look on him designed to blister.

"Indeed, perhaps it's simply because you had to spend the night alone in a strange place that you had such a horrid dream. That's easily remedied, don't you think?"

All of a sudden she wasn't feeling quite so smug. Oh, the wretch! Surely he didn't mean it. Oh, surely not!

"Are you always such a slugabed, Irish?"

Maura yanked her eyes from his face to the bedside clock. She was shocked to discover it was nearly ten o'clock in the morning.

"How long before you're dressed?"

"Not long," she said quickly. She certainly didn't want to bring up the subject of baths and bathing again.

"Excellent."

He rose, started toward the door, then turned back.

Maura froze. She'd started to climb out of bed, and now was terribly afraid that nearly the entire length of one leg was visible.

She knew it for certain when his gaze

lingered on her thigh, then traveled leisurely up to her face. "I thought we might go for a drive. Oh, and wear something serviceable for the outdoors. The sun is out now, but our weather can be a bit unpredictable at times."

Maura blinked. "Your grace?"

"You aren't the sort who wails at getting a bit damp, are you, Irish?"

"Certainly not."

"Do you have a sturdy pair of boots?"

"Yes." She hid her dismay. She had planned to begin her quest for the Circle this very day. "But there's no need for you to bother yourself with me. No doubt you must have many other obligations, especially given you've only just returned home. So I'm happy to explore for myself —"

"Oh, I wouldn't dream of allowing you to go anywhere alone just yet," he said smoothly. "It's a lovely day, too lovely to stay indoors." He pulled out his pocket watch. "If I have breakfast sent up, can you be ready in an hour?"

"Oh, long before that! No later than a quarter of."

"A woman who does not spend half the morning in her toilette! It seems we shall deal together very well, then."

Maura glanced at him sharply. Did he

mock her? She couldn't tell. But his mood was definitely improved.

At five minutes before the hour she rushed down the main stairs. Alec stood at the bottom, gazing up at her, hands behind his back. Both his brows were raised high as he glanced pointedly at the grandfather clock in the entrance hall.

"The house is immense. I took the wrong staircase and lost my way," she said breathlessly. "I'm afraid I wasn't watching when Mrs. Yates showed me upstairs last night." It was a bald-faced lie. She'd poked her nose into a few of the rooms, that she might gain a feel for where to begin her search for the Circle.

"We can't have my bride wandering around and around, now, can we? Why, you might starve to death and the authorities would blame me."

There it was again. She detected mockery — or did she? Alec's tone was light, and now she couldn't tell, for he'd tucked her arm into his elbow and was leading her away. "I'll acquaint you with the house and grounds when we return," he was saying. "As I said, it looks to be an excellent day for an outing, but one never knows when the occasional rain shower may appear."

Outside the main entrance, a boy waited with a small gig. Alec climbed on the seat and offered a hand to pull her up. He was right, it seemed. The sun had disappeared beneath a bank of clouds.

Once she was settled on the seat, he snapped the reins. Maura turned and glanced back over her shoulder. It was amazing how much different his home looked in the daylight, set back within a haze of green, surrounded by trees, with bursts of color everywhere. Deep red fuchsias, hyacinths blushed with pink. There were dozens of mullioned bay windows in the house. She'd been too rattled to notice last night, but the one in her room was particularly inviting, dotted with cushions. Now, she could well imagine sitting there, snug and warm inside, watching while wind and rain whipped the trees.

The horse trotted along the lane. On both sides sheep dotted the pastures. Behind a stone fence, a border collie raced apace with the gig. A pang shot through her. No doubt McDonough Castle had once looked like this — trees, varying shades of green, masses and masses of flowers. But now there was very little green, flowers bloomed but seldom, no matter how much it rained. Here, nature flourished.

160

On McDonough land, nothing flourished as it should have.

Before long the lane forked to the right. Behind a scattering of trees, water glimmered.

Alec had noticed the direction of her gaze. "That's the loch closest to Gleneden Hall," he said. "It's quite fine in the summer."

"I can imagine." The loch looked to be long and narrow, she noted. Despite the clouds that had begun to gather overhead, she imagined how it might appear in the sun, a sheen of rippling sapphire. Beyond, green hills undulated.

"May we stop here on the way back from wherever it is we're going?" she asked.

"Perhaps. If we had had an earlier start, there would have been plenty of time." He slanted her a glance from the corner of his eye.

His meaning was clear. "What!" Maura returned tartly. "Will you drag me from bed each day at the crack of dawn?"

An offhand, lazy smile curled his lips. "My dearest Maura, I would much rather drag you *into* bed."

She felt her face flame scarlet. Her breath halted in her throat as a shocking image filled her mind — that of Alec sprawling naked on the bed, tugging her down be-

161

tween the vise of his thighs. Every inch of her naked skin touched his. Her breasts on his chest, her legs molded the entire length of his, one knee nested against his.

She tried and failed to clamp the thought shut. Never mind that they had already lain together naked, though not in such a blatantly erotic way as the one that filled her mind, praise heaven! Even more shocking, in her mind's eyes her expression was warm and seductive as she willingly offered her lips —

Never mind that such was the very thing to be avoided at all costs.

"There's also a path through the forest from the house to the loch," Alec said. "I'll show you another time."

Maura scarcely heard. His thigh slid against hers at every little jostle. It was distracting. She couldn't help it. She was helplessly aware of it. Of him. Everything about him.

He had dressed much as a working gentleman might. Dark boots encased his calves. His breeches were tight, leaving no doubt as to the shape of muscle beneath. The breeze molded his shirt against his chest, reminding her of the night at Lord Preston's. It was open at the throat, revealing a dark tangle of hairs. Every inch of him was long and hard and taut. Ah, but then she already knew that from the night spent in his chamber when she'd had to divest him of his clothes. Oh, yes, now there was a sight that would linger forever in her mind! Long limbs, netted with curly black hair, thicker and darker on the broad wealth of his chest . . . and lower as well, where it grew wiry and dense around —

Squeezing her eyes shut, she banished the image. But still the night of the masquerade remained with crystal clear clarity.

In the gig, the wind whipped his hair; he wore no hat. She could almost feel those jet-black strands against her lips once more. Nor did he wear gloves. He handled the reins with capable strength, his fingers tightening when necessary, gentling as he gave the horse its head.

Her heart gave an odd little flutter. Her gaze was riveted on his hands. She felt her face heat. His fingers were lean and strong. Those hands had touched her, bared her breasts, shockingly intimate. Remembering the way he'd made her touch him, curling her fingers around —

She must have made some sound. He glanced over at her.

"What's that, Irish?"

"I . . ." She sought to dismiss her awareness, and managed to drag her gaze away from his hands. To the east lay the forest. To the west . . .

"I smell the sea."

"Indeed." They rounded a bend, and a broad expanse of water came into view. "Shall we go down to the beach?"

Maura nodded.

He guided the gig off the road, jumped down and secured the horse and carriage. By then she had already climbed down herself. Tugging up her skirt — she'd forgone her petticoats when he'd advised wearing something suitable for the outdoors — she followed him through a fringe of tall grasses. She stopped at the edge, peering down. The beach was perhaps a hundred feet below.

"You aren't frightened of heights, are you, Irish?"

Maura's head came up. A challenge? "Certainly not! I grew up near the sea. High above the sea, I might add."

"Somehow I didn't think you'd be afraid." A half smile curled his lips. Their eyes met. "My brave, fearless Irish wife. Let us go, then."

Maura would have led the way, but Alec stopped her with a shake of the head. "Let me go first. The path is steep and rocky, and wide enough for only one." His smile turned devilish. "That way I'll be there to catch you if need be, like the pirate in your dream this morning."

Oh, but he was a rogue! She considered it a challenge, one she would not lose. The path wound down the hillside, but sure-footed as a goat, she followed him down. She was feeling triumphant when the pebbles began to give way beneath her feet.

Alec turned at that moment, and catching her hands, pulled her upright, saving her from falling on her bum.

But he didn't let go. Instead a long arm slid around her waist. With him a foot below her, caught up against him like this, they were literally face-to-face. His gaze drifted slowly over her features, dwelling for ages on her lips.

Maura's heart lurched. Her breath thinned to a wisp. She had the oddest sensation that he wanted to kiss her. Oh, but then a sudden gleam in those beautiful blue eyes appeared, a wicked gleam, of course. She had the feeling he knew precisely the effect he had on her. Oh, bother! What the devil was wrong with her? She was being utterly ridiculous. He had made his feelings toward her perfectly clear. He did not welcome a wife. He did not welcome her.

Alec swung her that last foot to the sand. "There. Delivered safe, sound, and unharmed."

Maura stepped back hurriedly. The beach here was wide, skirting the headland to the south. She pointed that way. "What lies beyond? Another beach?"

He nodded. "Much of the coastline here is a series of headlands and coves."

"Can we walk there?"

"If you like."

She caught her skirt up in her hands and trudged along beside him. The wind as they came to the headland was fierce, whipping strands of her hair across her face, even beneath her bonnet. She tried brushing them back but finally stopped fighting it. But the winds calmed once they neared the cove.

Despite the gray skies, it was stunningly beautiful. The beach surrounding the cove was but a narrow strand, dotted with boulders and trees here and there. Gentle waves lapped the shore.

Hands on his hips, Alec glanced around. "Lord, I haven't been here in ages." A faint smile rimmed his lips. "Aidan and I used to come here and race each other across — to this day, my mother doesn't know it. And while we were here, we'd pretend we were

166

pirates." He pointed to an outcropping of rocks. "There's even a cave behind those rocks."

"And I suppose you were the fierce pirate captain."

He grinned suddenly, a grin that made her breath catch. "Of course. I'm the eldest."

Maura stilled the clamor of her heart. "By how many years?"

"Two."

"Well, then," she concluded dryly, "I rather suspect it wasn't so much that you were older, but simply that your brother was smaller than you."

"Well, there is that."

Fluffing her skirts, she sat on a rock shaped rather like a chair. "Is that why you came to the masquerade dressed as a pirate?" she asked daringly.

"Perhaps." Brazenly, his gaze slid down and settled on her breasts. "Certainly I never expected to find one in kind."

Maura ignored the jibe — and crossed her arms over her breasts. "It seems the perfect place from which to sail a pirate's ship. Perhaps one of your ancestors was a pirate?" She held her breath.

"Now there's a tale I've never heard. Though supposedly there's treasure buried somewhere near Gleneden. Oh, and let me not forget! There are also rumors of a family curse, though I've no idea precisely what this curse is supposed to be."

She gazed at him steadily. "Why aren't you wary?"

"Of what?"

"A curse should never be taken lightly, Scotsman."

He didn't hide his amusement. "Be serious."

Maura's lips compressed.

"Good heavens, you are serious."

She thought of the Circle. "There are things in this world that cannot be explained, sir."

"Like pixies and faeries and banshees?"

A shiver shot through her. Through the window in her mind, she remembered the moment her father had passed to the afterlife. It wasn't the cry of a banshee, but the eerie howl of a wolf.

"Next you'll be telling me you believe in ghosts!" He glanced at her, then laughed outright. "My word, I cannot believe it! Only the Irish would believe in such things!"

Her eyes flashed. "Do not amuse yourself at my expense, Scotsman. And do not insult me or my countrymen."

He held up both hands, a gesture of

defeat. Ha! She suspected Alec McBride was a man who would never admit defeat.

"No insult intended, Maura. But I've told you of my family. Now tell me about yours. You said you grew up near the sea."

"Aye."

One dark brow quirked up a fraction. "The whole of Ireland is surrounded by the sea, Irish. Where in Ireland did you grow up?"

"Inishowen."

"And your schooling?"

Maura hesitated. Caution warned that she must be judicious with what she revealed. She didn't want him looking closer and delving into her background. She knew he already considered her a fortune-hunter. "My father was my tutor."

"And did you then attend a school for young ladies?"

She shook her head.

Both his brows shot up. "An earl's daughter? And no finishing school?"

Her chin climbed high. "A title does not always command riches such as yours, your grace," she said quietly.

Their eyes caught. "I meant no offense," he said softly.

"None taken." Nonetheless, her tone remained stiff with pride.

"Any brothers? Sisters?"

"No. My mother died when I was very young. My father, more recently." An ache settled around her heart. There had been no time to mourn. To grieve over the loss of her father. Through some miracle, her voice remained steady. "So you see, there's just me." Hastily she amended the statement. "And Uncle Murdoch, of course. He was my mother's only brother."

"Is your uncle married?"

His interest was keen. Too keen for curiosity? she wondered.

"No," she lied. "When my father died, I took up residence with Uncle Murdoch."

She pushed herself to her feet and stood, looking out to sea. Alec rose and stood beside her. All at once her insides knotted. She swallowed a rush of awareness. His nearness was distracting. Disturbing. Not even an inch separated them. She was keenly aware of his height, his size. She heartily prayed that he would move.

He did not. Instead she felt his gaze on her profile, but she didn't acknowledge it.

"Such avid concentration," he said. "May I ask what you are thinking about, your grace?"

She was thinking that he shouldn't be calling her "your grace," for one thing. "You may ask, but that doesn't mean I must answer."

"Oh, come, we are husband and wife. May I not be privy to your thoughts? *Should* I not be privy to your thoughts?"

"Only if I am privy to yours," she said lightly.

"Touché," he said dryly.

Maura glanced up at him. "Very well, then. There's a promontory near my home. Sometimes I would climb there. It took nearly half a day since it's very near the most northernmost part of Ireland. You cannot imagine . . . It has the most unparalleled view."

"I think I can imagine." She had no idea that Alec's gaze was trained solely on her.

"The sea was all around," she went on. "To the north. The east and west. It was like being on top of the world, and I used to fancy I could see clear to the Arctic. It rained sometimes, but still I stayed. Because when the sun came out, there was always the most glorious rainbow. It looked like it stretched around the world." A faint wistfulness crept into her voice. "It was like nothing you've ever seen before."

"Oh, but you've not yet seen a Scottish rainbow."

"The sky is too gray here for a rainbow

proper," she informed him primly. As if to prove it, she gestured upward where the entire sky was locked in cloud cover.

He gave a raucous laugh. "You're touting the beauty of an Irish rainbow? On that soggy bog of an island?"

Maura wrinkled her nose at him.

Together they turned and started toward the headland. The wind gusted furiously now, stinging her eyes so that she could scarcely see. She led the way up the rocky pathway to the lane carefully, with Alec close behind. One particularly fierce blast sent her reeling back. His hand at her back was all that kept her upright. Once again he rescued her.

The rain began the instant they were seated in the gig. It pummeled them like ice. Maura grabbed the strings of her bonnet. They ripped through her fingers and her bonnet sailed away. Her cloak flapped high, like the wings of a gigantic bat.

It seemed to take forever to get back to Gleneden, though it was little more than a mile or so. Near the entrance, a groom took hold of the bridle. Lifting her down, Alec held her hand as they climbed the stairs.

Once they were behind closed doors, he turned to her. "I'll boast no more about our Scottish sunshine. Now, why don't you have a bath, a nap if you like, since you didn't sleep well last night. Or if you wish, I can show you your new home."

Her new home. Guilt prodded her. Gleneden would never be her home, but for the time it took to find the Circle. "I'd love to see the house," she said quickly.

"We're both in need of dry clothing. I must sign a few documents with my estate manager as well, so it may be half an hour or so. Shall I knock on your door when I'm ready?"

She detected a slight derision on his part. At least he'd asked this time. She walked away, concealing her excitement. This would give her the chance to determine where to begin her hunt for the Circle.

CHAPTER TEN

It was Mrs. Yates who came to fetch Maura. She explained that Alec awaited her in his study; he was still conferring with the estate manager. An endearing woman, Maura learned that Mrs. Yates had been with the household since she was a young girl. She proudly informed Maura that she was appointed housekeeper when Alec's mother — the Dowager Duchess since Alec had wed — had been a bride herself.

Another needle of guilt. Alec's mother was still the Duchess of Gleneden.

Alec was bent over a map spread out on a monstrous-sized table, along with another man. When he saw Mrs. Yates and Maura by the door, he beckoned Maura inside.

He straightened. "Maura. Mr. Campbell, may I present my wife, Duchess of Gleneden. Maura, this is my estate manager, Malcolm Campbell. We don't hold it against him that he was born into the Campbell

Clan, but neither do we let him forget it."
Alec's tone was wry.

Mr. Campbell chuckled. "Och, and ye
know, yer grace, 'tis lucky ye are to have a
Campbell who will deign to work fer ye."
The man turned to Maura and bowed his
head low. "Yer Grace."

Maura held out her hand and shook his
soundly. "Mr. Campbell, a pleasure."

Alec glanced at her. "Stay if you like,
Maura. I shouldn't be long."

"Of course," she murmured.

She walked to the bank of windows across
the room, pretending to stare at the courtyard. Deliberately, she kept her back to the
men. Foolish, unexpected tears burned the
back of her throat. She fought to stanch
them, to compose herself. Seeing Alec tease
Mr. Campbell, the comfortable air between
them wrought painful — yet, oh so endearing! — memories of Murdoch and her
father. Like Murdoch, Mr. Campbell was a
tall man, though he carried more girth than
Murdoch's rangy frame.

And her father . . . oh, Lord, how she
missed him! Remembering the night of his
death was like a knife through the heart. A
twisting ache rent her breast when she
thought of him. The hurt was still too fresh,

the emptiness in her soul a yawning, gaping wound.

As for Alec, she remembered the way he'd teased her the night of the masquerade. She had yet to see his teasing air return, not until now, with Mr. Campbell. Of course, his aim had been to entice her into his bed, but she couldn't fault him for that, now, could she? Not when she had played the coquette in equal measure.

It brought home her deceit even more, the way she had tricked him so she could come to Scotland. How she regretted her deceit! But it couldn't be avoided. She must continue to be strong. She couldn't allow such feelings to get in the way.

A pair of strong hands descended on her shoulders. Maura started. She hadn't heard Mr. Campbell leave.

"Are you ready?" Alec asked lightly.

Maura turned. She kept her head high, her gaze downcast — not that it mattered, she soon discovered.

She was aware of him peering down at her. "What is it?" he asked.

"What is what?"

"Are you crying?" He sounded incredulous.

"No." Maura gritted her teeth.

"You are." With the pad of a finger, he

swept up a trail of wetness and held it before her, as if it were a trophy.

"Look. You *are* crying."

The oaf! Did he think she needed evidence? "I am not, Scotsman. I am done crying."

For an instant his expression was utterly perplexed. Why, she wondered, were men always so astonished when a woman cried?

He persisted. "Why were you crying?"

She said nothing.

"If you're unwell —" he began.

"I am not," she said. When he showed no sign of moving, she waved a hand. "I — I was thinking of my father," she admitted haltingly. "His study was much like this." In truth, it was. Warm wood covered the walls. A large desk, leather chairs. The difference was that Alec's was meticulously maintained, and furnished just as meticulously. Her father's was minimally maintained, whenever she or Jen managed to get round to dusting it, and sparsely furnished. Last year they'd sold off a valuable painting to see to the tenants' wintering.

There was a yawning silence. "I'm sorry," Alec said finally. "I'd forgotten. You mentioned it earlier. And I remember now that your uncle said something about your father being the late earl."

It was a supremely awkward moment.

"If you like, we can certainly postpone —"

She shook her head. "There is no need. I am perfectly fine. I should hate to lose my way to the dining room again and die of starvation."

He smiled slightly. "We can't have that now, can we?" He pulled a handkerchief from his pocket and handed it to her.

Maura wiped away the traces of tears, blew her nose, and passed it back to him.

"I suppose my nose is bloody red now, isn't it?"

He paused, as if he didn't know what to say.

"Go on," she muttered. "Just say it. It's bloody red."

He smiled, the first true smile she'd seen since they'd arrived in Scotland.

"I was going to say charmingly pink, but that would be an inaccuracy. Yes, it's bloody red."

Oddly, that seemed to lighten the air.

He extended a hand, indicating that she precede him. "Shall we?" he murmured.

They were just stepping out the door when a sudden shaft of sunlight chanced to catch Alec's face. Maura's breath caught, for he reminded her of a god come to life. His hair was thick and richly black, cropped so a lock fell forward onto his forehead. His brows were just as black, the arch pronounced; a perfect frame and foil for eyes so startlingly light blue given the darkness of his hair. His nose could only be called patrician, his jaw squarely sculpted. His mouth was beautifully masculine, unsmiling at the moment. Each feature in itself was one of perfection. In sum, Alec McBride, Duke of Gleneden, was a man of arresting masculinity, so strikingly handsome as to be unforgettable. Was it any wonder that flirting with him the night of the masquerade had been so easy?

Be careful, cautioned a voice in her mind. It wouldn't do to find herself smitten with Alec McBride. Aye, he was a most fetching man to look upon. But other than the night they had met, and today, if she were honest with herself, she'd found his character rather despicable.

She had but one goal here in Scotland, she reminded herself.

To find the Circle of Light and bring it home — home to Ireland.

Nothing or no one would stop her from honoring her promise to her father — and with that vow came courage and resolve.

Several hours later Maura's head was spinning at the size and arrangement of the house. It was shaped like an E, with the centrally located great hall giving way to long hallways that angled into several wings. She counted no less than six staircases, including the grand staircase in the hall. This was the oldest part of the house; dating from the time of Robert the Bruce, as Alec had told her yesterday. Numerous additions such as the north and south wing had been made throughout the centuries, with comforts added and rooms changed so that, in truth, things were never outdated.

The central wing was for entertainment and formal events. It included the ballroom and music room, as well as the library. The north wing was designated for family. In it were the duke and duchess's suite, other bedchambers, Alec's study, the schoolroom, and various rooms generally used for the family. The south wing was primarily designated for guests.

Maura couldn't help the avenue to which her mind strayed. There were antiques, vases, numerous items of extreme value, she was certain. How many, she once again wondered furiously, had the Black Scotsman acquired during his pirating days?

And where would such a man hide the Circle of Light? She disguised her cursory search as curiosity. In one bedroom, she opened a glossy, almost gaudy chest from the Orient and peered inside. A quarter hour later she peered into the drawer of an elaborate French secretaire. In another room, she slipped a toe beneath the edge of an intricately stitched Turkish carpet and cast an unobtrusive glance beneath.

Or so she thought.

She was startled to see Alec leaning leisurely against the door frame, arms crossed against his chest. "What are you looking for, Irish?" he asked, his tone rife with amusement. "I mentioned a curse this morning. Have you decided I'm concealing hidden treasure? Odd, but at a family dinner in London earlier this year, we talked about that very thing — that if there were treasure here at Gleneden, Aidan and I — and Annie, too — would have discovered it long ago." He held up both hands. "But if you know some Irish superstition or spell that will make it magically appear, I invite you to find it. Indeed, I will applaud you if you find it."

Maura muttered an old Irish curse.

They ended strolling down the long corridor that led back toward the great hall. Alec clearly took great pride in his heritage. He was pleased by her numerous questions and interest. There were portraits on each wall, the family through various generations.

Maura stopped before the one just outside the ballroom.

"That was painted several years before my father became ill," Alec told her.

She smiled at the chestnut-haired young girl, standing near her father, who looked ready to burst into laughter.

"My sister Anne," Alec said. "Or Annie, as we call her. And yes, she is every bit as vivacious as she appears." Maura felt a momentary wistfulness. There was an air about Anne in the portrait that made her want to laugh along with her. She'd have liked Anne, she decided.

Alec gestured. "My brother Aidan."

There was no mistaking the pair as brothers. Both were extremely tall, of matching height. Aidan's hair was a shade lighter than Alec's, whose jaw was also more square, his build lean but powerful.

Maura blinked at Alec's mother. Dainty and dark-haired, she wondered how such a tiny woman had borne such towering sons. It was clear Alec and his brother came by their height from their father, a deep-chested man with ruddy cheeks and chestnut hair. The artist had captured a closeness, a sense of genuine love, and for an instant Maura experienced a fleeting regret that she would never meet the rest of his family.

It also made her wonder how Alec had come by his disagreeable nature.

She glanced at him. "Your father," she ventured. "Forgive me for asking, but what illness did he suffer?"

Alec shook his head. There was no denying the pain that shadowed his expression. "That's the thing," he said. "Countless physicians saw him. They argued and fought as to the cause. They disagreed on his treatment. My father was healthy and robust. Yet he simply woke one morning, deathly sick, unable to gather the strength to rise. He remained deathly sick for over a year. Each day, every day, we feared might be his last."

Maura felt herself sway. Sheer strength of will kept her upright. Just like her father. Oh, sweet heaven, just like her father. Perhaps it was a blessing that he had suffered but a single day.

"To this day," Alec said quietly, "no one can really say what illness claimed my father."

Maura knew. A fierce certainty took hold. It was the curse. The curse that plagued the clans McDonough and McBride — the Clan McDonough as punishment for failing to guard the Circle of Light.

And the McBrides for stealing it.

They moved on to view several more portraits. All at once a queer sensation seized hold of her. It was as if some force outside her body made her turn to the opposite wall.

She nearly cried out.

It was like her dream reborn.

A man with a black feathered hat stared down at her, over hair as black as midnight. His eyes were blue, hard as rock; they gleamed as if to mock her. As if he knew something no one else did. As if he knew something she did not.

Her heart pounded quick and hard, almost painfully. The Black Scotsman, she realized. Beneath a dark, heavy moustache, his lips pulled back in a leer. It was like being drawn back into her dream. She could swear that eerie laughter spilled forth. On his hand — his left hand only — he wore a black leather glove, clamped over his sword. A chill spread over her, a chill that seemed to ice the very air in her lungs.

Alec stepped up beside her.

Maura heard herself whisper, "Who is he?"

"That is James, the seventh Duke of Gleneden. Nasty looking fellow, isn't he?"

Evil was the word that came to her. She stared at that black-gloved hand. A shiver went through her, a shiver she felt in her very heart. It was as if she could feel that hand wrapped around her throat, choking the life from her.

"I would have to check the family annals, but I believe he endured some sort of family tragedy. He had but one son, I think. Luckily for that," Alec said dryly, "else I wouldn't be here with you now."

The curse again.

"I would love to look at the family annals sometime," she said. "Such things can be fascinating reading. One should take pride in one's family origins, don't you think?"

"I quite agree. When I was young, no doubt I could have told you his wife's name, if he had brothers or sisters, all of those things. I'm afraid I've forgotten some of it," Alec admitted.

Perhaps it was true, then, that the Black Scotsman had concealed his identity even from his family. Or perhaps Alec wouldn't own up to having a black sheep in the family.

Dragging in a deep breath, Maura turned away. She could no longer bear to look at James, seventh Duke of Gleneden.

Her breath was still quick and hard. She

fought to calm her heart. She fought to regain vision of the Circle of Light, the way it appeared in this morning's dream. Silver and glowing. Floating on a bed of nothingness. Reflecting every color in the world.

Somehow she had to find it.

And pray it would end this curse once and for all.

When it came time for supper, she donned the crimson taffeta gown she had worn the day after the masquerade, when she and Murdoch met with Alec in the baron's study. The color, she had discovered, lent her strength.

Nor was Alec's demeanor disagreeable. Quite the contrary. He was as amiable as he'd been this morning, and supper was not the ordeal she had feared it might be.

Yet she was under no illusions as to Alec's behavior. She had the uneasy feeling that during the afternoon, while they were together, he'd been digging, prying into her background. She prayed he was satisfied with her answers; she was fairly sure she had given him no reason to doubt her.

After dinner he shared with her tales of his travels. He'd been to America. To the Continent. To Egypt to visit the tombs of ancient pharaohs.

Maura found herself listening with rapt absorption, her elbows on the table, one hand supporting her chin, not caring that she displayed poor manners. Prior to coming to Scotland, Dublin had been the extent of her travels, she thought wistfully.

The evening passed far more quickly than she'd anticipated. After the last dish was removed, Alec slid his chair back and rose to his feet and extended a hand. Maura hesitated. A hasty glance upward revealed his regard was ripe with amusement.

Taking a deep breath, she placed her hand in his and rose.

"A glass of wine in the rose parlor, Irish? Or perhaps the great hall. It's quite cozy to sit before the fire with a glass of brandy."

She shot him a telling glance.

"No? I thought you had your fill of tea during dinner. You must have been feeling more poorly than I thought the day after the masquerade."

"Pray do not make light of me, your grace."

He chuckled, the sound low and oddly pleasing.

Maura's heart skipped a beat. His laugh . . . the way he looked at her, his blue eyes so warm . . .

She swallowed. "Actually, I believe I

should like to retire."

His brows shot high. Maura held her breath. Dear Lord, she prayed he didn't perceive it as an invitation. "So soon?" he asked. She had no chance to respond. "Ah, but I forget," he murmured. "You didn't sleep well last night. In that case, allow me to escort you upstairs."

He offered an arm. Maura had no choice but to take it. Her fingers rested lightly on his sleeve. Even through the layers of cloth, she could feel the taut muscle beneath. He was silent as they climbed the stairs and turned down the corridor that led to her room . . . and his. She was too nervous to say a word. Would he follow her in? Claim his husbandly rights? He'd toyed with her last night. She wasn't a fool. He'd wanted to discomfit her, and he had.

And now his air of self-confidence left her no less uneasy. He resented her. He resented this marriage. He'd made that very clear at the ceremony. But today his attitude had changed and it seemed he'd accepted the circumstance with no further consideration.

Maura knew better. She envied him his composure as they stopped at the door to her room. He opened it, but remained where he was, wearing the half smile that was becoming so familiar . . . a smile that both disarmed her yet left her wary.

She released his arm. She wasn't quite sure what to do, what to say. Her poise had deserted her, as had her tongue.

His head lowered. She looked up sharply. It gave her a start to find him staring straight at her mouth, his eyes dark with some emotion she dare not ponder. For a heart-stopping moment she was convinced he meant to kiss her.

The bottom dropped out of her belly. Shadows from the wall lamps played across his features. Everything inside her twisted into a knot. Oh, Lord, she thought help-lessly, he was so handsome she could barely breathe. She wanted . . . oh, but she wanted him to —

His knuckles grazed the slant of her cheek. "Thank you, Irish, for a most pleasant day." Lifting her hand, he brushed his lips across her fingertips, then turned and walked away.

Inside her room, Maura closed the door, then slumped back against it. Unwittingly, she lifted the back of her hand to her mouth — the very place his lips had kissed, she re-alized — then snatched it away. Airy as his touch had been, she felt as if she'd been branded to the bone.

She was trembling, she realized. Her heart was thudding so loud it echoed in her ears like a drum. Heaven help her, but she was a fool. She hadn't planned on this. She hadn't expected to be so attracted to him. She hadn't expected to be attracted to him at all! she thought wildly.

But she was, far more than she had realized. Far more than she should have been. And she had been from the start. The admission shouldn't have come as a surprise, but it did.

She had wanted to feel the heat and pressure of his mouth against hers. She'd wanted him to kiss her the way he had the night of the masquerade, long and slow and heated.

All the more reason to guard against him.

For she had learned something that day. Alec was a man of many sides. Those pale blue eyes could be icy and cold, or heated and seductive. Filled with cool deliberation or fiery anger.

She didn't quite trust him. Again she had the feeling she had been weighed and tested throughout the day. Which left no conclusion but one.

Alec McBride was perhaps even more dangerous when he was charming . . . than when he was not.

CHAPTER ELEVEN

Two days later Maura rode a dappled gray mare to the village just south of Gleneden, past the church to the graveyard. She tied the reins to a tree, then glanced around.

Murdoch stepped out from behind a stout oak tree.

Maura ran to him, throwing her arms around him. Murdoch had followed almost directly in her wake. It was part of the plan they had conceived, a way to stay in touch should she find the Circle.

When he was able, he stepped back, searching her features. "Lady Maura! What's wrong, girl?" His welcoming smile vanished. "It's the duke, isn't it, child? I knew he was a blackguard! I swear, if he has mis—"

Maura shook her head, blinking back tears. "No, no, Murdoch! I'm fine. Truly I am. He's not the sort of man to harm anyone."

And as soon as she'd said it, she realized

that he wasn't. She knew it instinctively. He had remained polite and charming, but she sensed his distance. She sensed his watchfulness. In turn, she tasked herself to be prudent and cautious, ever vigilant, lest she further arouse his suspicion.

Neither of them allowed it to show on the outside, but Maura knew that Alec was as wary of her as she was of him.

"Have ye learned anything, Lady Maura? Have ye found anything?"

She shook her head. "Not yet. The house is large, each wing built in different centuries." She hesitated. "It may take longer than I expected," she admitted. "But the Circle is there, Murdoch." She told him about the portrait of James, the seventh Duke of Gleneden. As she spoke, a shiver slid down her spine. "Alec said he endured some sort of family tragedy. And I know why." Her tone turned bitter.

"The curse?" asked Murdoch.

Maura nodded. "I searched through the family annals — I told Alec I was fascinated by such things. But there was little about him. The date he married, and the date of his son's birth and death." She scowled. "For such a scoundrel, he lived to a ripe old age. Why, he was nearly eighty years old when he died. I wonder when he ceased his pirating days."

She was silent for a moment. Her eyes grew dark. "Murdoch, the Circle is here. I know it. I can feel it. It is uncanny. I cannot explain why, but somehow I just know it is. I — oh, I know it sounds silly, but it's just as Papa said. As if I can hear the Circle calling to me. Crying out."

Murdoch squeezed her shoulder. "Ye need not convince me, child," he said gently. "I have faith that you will find it."

Maura smiled at him, then held up a finger. "Wait," she said. "Wait." She went to her mare and untied two small sacks. Dropping to her knees, she untied one and brought out two large candlestick holders with a flourish. "Look!" She licked a fingertip and rubbed it against the base. "Pure silver! I brought this pair and another, a tray and a gilt-edged vase as well. Sell them and take the money home to Nan."

"Lady Maura!" Murdoch couldn't hide his distress. "What if the duke discovers they are gone?"

She scowled. "He will not. The Black Scotsman stole from us. And these will never even be missed. I found them in the garret." Which she had. Well, the candlesticks, at least, so it wasn't entirely a lie. The candlesticks were in the garret. The tray and the vase had come from a bedchamber in the old wing.

Murdoch took the sacks, his expression sober. "I know that look, lass. Take care that ye are not too bold."

Maura knew what he meant, that she should take no more risk than she dared.

They arranged to meet in the same place two weeks hence. She gave him a hasty peck on the cheek, mounted the mare and rode back to Gleneden.

Outside the stable, she handed the reins to a groom. Whistling a merry little tune, she rounded the corner, only to bump headlong into a form as solid as a granite wall.

Strong heads steadied her. "There you are," Alec said smoothly. "Where were you?"

"Just out for a bit of a ride." How lame that sounded!

"Along the road?"

"Through the fields mostly."

"No wonder I didn't see you, then. I just came from the village —"

Maura's heart lurched. Mercy, what if he'd seen her with Murdoch!

"— but once I was home, when I went to find you, no one knew where you were."

"Why were you looking for me?" She sought to quiet the quick, hard pounding of her heart.

"We've spent no time together today, your grace. I thought we might walk down to the loch."

Your grace. Maura felt her skin grow hot. Must he call her that? It was intentional, she was sure, in order to discomfit her.

Which, of course, it did.

"Have you been there yet, Irish?"

"No. You told me you would show me a path through the woods."

Alec took her arm. "I did, didn't I?"

They walked past the north wing toward the forest. They hadn't gone more than a half mile when Maura stopped short. "Oh, look!" she cried. "How lovely." She pointed to a stone bridge that crossed a small brook. A vine-covered archway led into a small open clearing. "What is that? A well?" A timbered roof, almost a miniature of the one in the great hall, covered a round stone well.

"Yes. It's always been known as the wishing well."

Maura had already started across the bridge. She paused near the well, glancing around. "It's lovely here, so quiet and tranquil."

Alec propped a hip on the stony wall of the well. "A matter of opinion. My mother finds the well charming. It was bricked up for years, even in my grandfather's time, I believe. My mother had it opened again when I was a boy." He pointed to a stone bench on the other side of the clearing. "A bit solitary for my taste, but she finds it peaceful and sometimes comes here to read."

Maura laughed. "I was just about to say that very thing!"

The well was perhaps six feet across, built up to about the level of her hips. She peered far down into the round opening, down the moss-laden sides that ended in shadow. "It's dry," she said in disappointment.

"I'm not surprised. I can't imagine why anyone would want to make a wish here, since one never knows when it will fill with water." He smiled slightly. "My sister and my cousin Caro used to wish upon stars. I often wondered why they never came here."

"Perhaps they did," Maura said.

"Possibly," Alec said wryly, "but I think perhaps they simply wanted to stay up long into the night and bedevil their nurse or the rest of the household."

He paused, as if in fond remembrance, Maura suspected.

"When the well does fill with water," he said, "by the next day it's completely gone.

It's the oddest thing, but I believe it's been that way for a number of generations."

"Well, I find it just as charming as your mother," Maura announced.

"Do you, now? Why do I have the feeling you merely wish your opinion to be contrary to mine?"

"Your statement, sir, not mine," she retorted.

And one he chose to ignore. He held out his hand. "Come. The loch isn't far. Just over the next rise."

Maura hesitated. She didn't want to take his hand. She didn't want to touch him. Her response to him was too unpredictable. She couldn't control it. The thought sprang wildly into her head that she couldn't control him.

"Your grace?"

He beckoned with the tips of his fingers. The glint in his eyes was almost a dare.

He knew, damn him. He knew full well what he did to her.

Maura's chin came up. Almost defiantly she placed her hand in his. Perhaps just as defiantly, his fingers curled hard around hers.

They walked in silence for a time, following a winding pathway through the forest. Sunlight played hide-and-seek through the treetops.

But all was forgotten when she caught her first glimpse of the loch. Wooded hills rose on the opposite shore, their shadows reflected in the brilliant blue of the loch below.

She ran down the grassy hillside, exclaiming in delight. "A boathouse! Oh, and look at the dock!" She ran out farther, perching her hands on her hips, then pointing across to the hills. "The trees near the shoreline, the ones with the lovely, arching branches. Are they downy birch? And Scots pine higher on the hills?"

"They are." Alec seemed pleased that she knew. "I'm glad to see there is something in Scotland that pleases you, Irish. You should see it in the autumn, when all the leaves are brilliant and gold. And in the springtime, with primroses and violets everywhere."

Ah, but she wouldn't be here in the autumn. Or the springtime.

Maura ignored the insistent little voice in her head. Plunking herself down near the end of the dock, she tugged off her slippers, peeled off her hose, hiked up her skirts and dangled her toes in the water. Feeling like a child again, she was unaware of the way Alec's gaze alighted on her darned cotton stockings.

He sat down, long legs stretched out

before him. Laughing, Maura aimed a splash at him with the bottom of one foot.

He ducked.

"What, your grace! You're not the sort who wails at getting a bit damp, are you?"

This time he couldn't evade the spray of water she sent his way.

With a peal of laughter, Maura leaned back on her hands. "Is there a boat in the boathouse?"

"Aye. And you are not to venture out alone in it," he said sternly.

Maura pulled a face. "And you, your grace, are behaving like a stodgy old man."

"Am I? Lovely as it is, my sister Anne and my cousin Caro once spent a very frightening night here on the loch when a sudden storm blew in. If you were alone, Irish, and I could not find you, I might think you'd been spirited away by a selkie."

"By what?"

"A selkie. We Scots have our legends, too, you know. A selkie is a creature of the sea, with a seal-like skin. When he — or she — cast off their skin, they assume human form. A selkie-man is said to be a dashingly handsome creature, with extremely persuasive powers over women."

"And would you be jealous, your grace, if I were to find myself smitten with a selkie-man?" She dipped her toes in the water, watching it dimple.

"I would be very jealous, Irish. And it occurs to me that perhaps you are a selkie-woman, come to bewitch me. You did tell me you grew up by the sea."

Maura bit back a laugh. "You are hardly bewitched! You find me an annoyance rather than bewitching."

"I was quite bewitched the night of the masquerade. And if you were to try, you might bewitch me once again."

Maura's pulse began to clamor.

"And far more easily than you think," he added softly.

A dare or a jest? Her breath caught halfway in her throat. Unsettled by his lengthy regard, she wasn't quite sure what to make of his comment.

"But I would appreciate it if you would let someone know where you are." He referred to her absence that morning. "I should hate to lose you so soon."

Maura was annoyed. "I do not take kindly to being told what I may and may not do. Will you place me under watch if I refuse, your grace?"

"Tempt me not," he said pleasantly.

"Then tell me not."

A slow smile crept across his lips, "I will

tell you this, then, Duchess. If I wished to keep you under lock and key" — his tone was buttery smooth — "it would be in my bedchamber."

Judging from his half smile, Maura decided it best not to pursue the subject. Ignoring him, she donned her slippers and hose.

Alec offered a hand up.

They were just crossing the stone bridge when he glanced over at her. "It occurs to me I've been remiss as a husband."

He stopped her in her tracks. Maura's gaze flew up to his. She could think of only one thing in which he had been remiss.

His smile was sly. Damnation! It was as if he traversed a road that led directly into her mind, the rogue!

"Our wedding being as hasty as it was, it occurs to me you had no time to assemble a trousseau."

Maura blinked. "What?"

"A trousseau. It's a bride's —"

"I know very well what it is," she interrupted. She might as well be blunt. "I have no need of one. I'm an Irish country lass at heart —"

"Who is now the Duchess of Gleneden."

A pang of guilt shot through her. Well, she wasn't, but . . . "Nor am I the sort to put myself on parade like some silly young debu-tante."

"Well, of course there's no need. You're a married woman now. But it would please me if you allow it to be my gift to my bride." He went on, "I've business in Glasgow, and several other matters to attend to. If we start on our way early tomorrow, we can take the train from Tay into Glasgow. It's an excel-lent place to buy what you need. Whatever you fancy. Anything you fancy."

Maura kept her dismay at bay. With him gone, it was the perfect opportunity to search for the Circle!

"Truly, I prefer to remain here. I've hardly had the chance to feel at home here at Gleneden."

"And you have years and years for that, Irish! Besides, what would people think if I left my bride so soon after our wedding? Someone might say I was a neglectful hus-band."

Or that she was a neglectful wife.

She took a deep breath. "I really prefer to remain here at Gleneden."

"Why?" It appeared it was his turn to be blunt.

Maura thrust her chin out. "I know what you are doing," she said, her voice very low. "You are testing me. You think I wed you so that I could become a duchess, for the possessions I might gain. But I don't want your title or your wealth. Or anything it can buy. In sum, sir, I won't spend a single shilling of yours."

A little voice in her mind reminded her of the candlesticks and such that she'd given Murdoch only that morning. That was different, argued another voice. That was payment for what the Black Scotsman had stolen from the McDonough. That was for the people of McDonough. Not for her. Not for her own pleasure. She wanted nothing for herself.

"Now that," Alec remarked dryly, "is simply being foolish. You are a duchess. You must dress accordingly."

"A pity you find me so lacking, sir. I am sorry to embarrass you so." The scathing look she bestowed on him was blunted by the tremor of her lips. The admission cost a bit of pride, but she held her head high. Stupidly, she felt the sting of tears burn the back of her throat.

"I said no such thing, Irish, and you know it. It is not a lack of breeding you suffer from."

He gazed down at her. Gentle as his tone was, she sensed impatience. She chafed at his superior height — and at her inability to read what was in his mind when he saw so keenly into hers.

"And precisely what is it that I suffer from?"

"Merely this, Duchess. I wed a lovely Irish rose. But I've discovered my Irish rose has many thorns."

Maura's lips tightened. "And I have wed a prickly Scottish thistle."

Alec lifted his gaze heavenward. "Ah," said he, "a wife with both beauty and wit. What more could a man ask for?"

"I will not lie. It is how I feel." Even as she said it, Maura cringed inside. What a hypocrite she was. "I prefer to remain here at Gleneden."

Alec had leaned a hip against the top of the bridge, his legs crossed leisurely at his ankles, his arms across his chest. A breeze ruffled his dark hair across his forehead, lending him a boyish look.

But there was nothing boyish about the rest of him. His shirt was unbuttoned, revealing a wedge of dark, hair-roughened chest. Maura felt her mouth go dry. He said nothing, merely gazed at her, and all at once she recalled the feel of her lips trapped beneath his the night of the masquerade. So warm, so hotly persuasive. Sternly, she checked the thought.

"Did you hear me, sir?"

"I heard you," he said mildly. "Nonetheless, you may wish to make an early evening of it. We'll be leaving at dawn, and I should hate to have to come help your maid in getting you dressed, particularly when I would much rather assist you in getting undressed. But" — a slow smile crept along his lips — "I am happy to render assistance in either case."

The cad! So he thought he had won, did he? He delighted in tormenting her. Everything about him — his almost lazy demeanor, that devilish smile that now curled his lips — proclaimed his smugness. She chafed at his self-righteousness.

Yet clearly he could not be persuaded otherwise.

"Very well, then, Scotsman. If it's my company you wish in Glasgow, you shall have it."

He offered his arm. "Excellent. I'm glad I was able to persuade you. I should hate the thought of being in Glasgow pining for my wife."

Pining, was it? Ha!

She smothered a biting retort just in time.

Better to risk one battle, she reminded herself, than lose the war.

CHAPTER TWELVE

Upon their arrival at the train station in Glasgow, Alec handed his wife into a hack, while a young boy stowed their two bags. Alec couldn't help but smile while the horses clopped along the narrow streets. Maura's pretty little nose was pressed against the window. She reminded him of a child who was making her first visit to the city.

"It's very old, isn't it?" she said.

"Glasgow?"

"Aye."

"It is. The Romans built fortresses here in the first century, and the city itself in the sixth or seventh, by St. Mungo. Some legends claim he was related to King Arthur."

"And rather smelly, too." She grimaced.

"It's become a city of industry. The shipyards have brought both wealth and pollution. It's much like Edinburgh, in that there is an Old City and New City. I must say, I prefer Edinburgh. Now there's a city to take your breath away. Edinburgh Castle stands guard high over the Firth of Forth. It's quite a sight to behold."

"I wish I could visit there, then."

"I'm sure you shall. And London, too."

Maura was well aware she wouldn't visit either. As soon as she had the Circle of Light in hand, she and Murdoch would be off to Ireland and Castle McDonough.

When they arrived at the hotel, the doorman greeted Alec. "Your grace! Lovely to have you as a guest again."

"Thank you, David. And this time I've brought my wife."

"Then may I congratulate you both!" The doorman bowed low over the hand she extended. "Your grace, I hope your stay is a pleasant one."

They were shown upstairs to a grand suite. It was immense, with lavish, textured walls and billowing brocade draperies. A sitting room adjoined the bedchamber, where three steps led up to a wide four-poster and tester.

"I hope the room is to your liking, your grace."

Maura felt herself grow tense.

"I'm sure it will be, Edward."

The door closed.

Alec turned, glancing over to where his wife stood near a small side table. Her bonnet dangled from her fingertips. Her shoulders were stiff and square. He was well aware that she was on the defensive.

"Perhaps, your grace," he said to her, "a better question would be whether or not the room is to your liking."

Maura turned. "This is my room?"

"Indeed it is."

"And yours?" she queried.

Alec inclined his head, aware of the two lines of worry that gathered between piquant black brows. "I believe the bed is more than large enough for the two of us."

Their eyes locked. Hers flitted away, then skidded back to his. Her chin went up a notch. "Is the hotel filled to capacity, then?"

He shrugged. "I've no idea."

"Then perhaps another room may be secured."

She masked her anxious panic well. Alec, in turn, was both annoyed and angry. He held it at bay.

"Why? It's not the first time we've slept in the same bed. Not even a fortnight has passed since you were quite eager to share my bed. Of course, now that you are my duchess, that zeal does seem to have

208

passed."

There was a protracted silence. Maura said nothing.

"I am known here at this hotel, Irish. I won't have it bandied about that my wife and I are on such terms that she must have her own room." A slight edge crept into his tone. "We may not sleep together at Gleneden"— not yet, he thought — "but we will tonight."

Maura took a breath. "I thought it was understood. You wanted my company, nothing else."

"As you reminded me our first night at Gleneden, I've already seen to the plucking of the fruit. Why, then, are you so ill at ease? I am fully capable of keeping my desire under restraint."

Maura gritted her teeth. Damn his persistence. Damn his arrogance!

"I do, however, continue to wonder where my bold, amorous pirate has disappeared — and when she will reappear."

"And if she does not?" Her tone was honeyed.

He slanted her his most disarming smile. "Well, then, I shall simply have to go about making her reappear."

Maura's guard went up threefold. So did the beat of her heart.

"Now come, Duchess, let us go out for a stroll."

She blinked. "I thought you had business here."

"And so I do, so let us be about it." He walked smoothly to one of the double doors and held it wide. "After you, your grace."

Maura was left with no choice but to precede him.

Their "stroll" consisted of exiting the hotel and turning to the right at the corner. She sucked in a breath. Her gaze slid from one side of the street to the other. There was no question it was a street of exclusive shops. When he tried to lead her into the nearest one — the sign above said MADAME ROUS-SEAU — Maura hung back.

"Your grace," she said tartly, "I thought this was settled yesterday. There is nothing that I require. My wardrobe is quite satisfactory."

Alec's eyes narrowed. "Irish, I would advise you not to cross me," he stated bluntly. "Once I've made up my mind, there is no changing it. I agree it may cause many a head to turn, but if you will not enter Madame Rousseau's shop — my mother, a woman of utmost fashion, favors it above all others, even those in London — then you leave me no choice. I've no aversion to pitching you over my shoulder here and now."

He didn't particularly intend to follow through, but her expression made him itch to carry out the threat.

Several people passed by. Maura remained where she was, her gaze damning him with emerald fire. Faith, but the chit was stubborn!

"Which shall it be, Duchess?"

"You wouldn't dare," she said from between her teeth.

"Are you prepared to take that chance?"

Maura's mouth opened, then closed. Alec read in her expression a mounting uncertainty.

"It is not a demand I make," he pointed out. "It is merely a question that requires one of two answers, either yes or no. Now what shall it be, your grace? Will you enter under your own power? Or will you enter under mine?"

Maura glared.

"I see in your eyes the inclination to do me bodily harm," he said lightly. "Pray do not. At least not here. I should much prefer that it occur" — there was an unholy gleam in his eyes — "in private."

The ice reflected on her lovely features should have frozen him solid, but she

211

entered the shop.

Behind the counter was a petite, fashionably dressed woman of perhaps fifty or so. Only a few streaks of gray at her temples declared her age. Slanted dark eyes lit up with pleasure as soon as she saw Alec.

"Your grace! A pleasure to see you!"

She must have been quite a beauty in her day, Maura decided. She quickly revised it when Madame Rousseau stepped out from behind the counter, as slim as she must have been in her youth. At the sound of her voice, several girls slipped from a curtained area, carrying tape, scissors, and pins.

"Madame," Alec greeted. Lightly, he kissed her fingertips. "May I present my wife, Duchess of Gleneden."

Madame gave a little curtsy. "*Enchanté,* your grace," she said with a laugh. She glanced back at Alec. "Oh, but many a heart will break when it is learned that the Black Scotsman has taken a wife!" Her manner became brisk. "How may I help you today?"

Alec slid an arm around Maura's waist and brought her close. "Madame, would you allow me to confer with my wife in private for a moment?"

"*Mais certainement.*" Madame bowed her head and gave a low curtsy. She clapped her hands, and her assistants disappeared behind the curtained area. "Please ring ze bell whenever you are ready."

"I thought we settled this yesterday." Maura was tense, her tone very low.

"Did we?"

"We did," she said levelly.

"We did not," he countered smoothly. "I concede, however, that you continue to amaze me. And you continue to bemuse me, as well. A woman who completes her toilette in minutes. A woman who abhors shopping and spending her husband's money! You are quite unlike any other."

Maura wasn't sure if that was a compliment or not. She chose to take it as one. "Thank you," she said crisply. "Now may I return to the hotel?"

He ignored the question. "Irish, you have the chance to spend whatever you like, on whatever you want, on as many gowns as you want. Most women would be in heaven."

"As you just said, I am not like other women. And I hope you don't mind my frankness, Scotsman, but it seems rather reckless of you to give a woman carte blanche in a shop such as this."

Alec couldn't believe it either. He took a deep breath. He didn't understand it. He didn't understand her. This was what she wanted, wasn't it? She'd put herself in his bed in order to gain the right to proclaim herself Duchess of Gleneden. And now with his fortune in hand — all that it could buy — she shunned it! In the same way she shunned sharing his bed!

Or did she play at being coy in order to persuade him he was wrong? Either way, he was both angry and affronted.

"A bargain," he said suddenly. "What if we make a bargain?"

She eyed him warily. "What sort of bargain?"

He caught her elbow when she instinctively stepped back. He chuckled. "Not that sort of bargain, Irish."

Maura moistened her lips. "What, then?"

He leaned an elbow on the countertop. "Here is what I propose. Let Madame and her assistants obtain your measurements. Then you may choose one item from Madame's shop — gowns, slippers, whatever you want — any article of female attire that you want. Cost is of no consequence."

She gave a shake of her head. "But there is nothing I require."

"I didn't say to choose what you required, Duchess. I said choose something that you want. Something that will make you happy."

Maura's gaze whisked to the table of silk

stockings behind him, then back to his face. "Are you not afraid I'll send you to the poorhouse?"

He laughed. "You can try. Try as hard as you like."

"And what if I say no?"

"Unless you pick out something you want, I'll buy the whole damn shop."

"What!" she cried.

"I will," he vowed.

She cocked her head to the side. "Why do I have the feeling there is more to this bargain?"

"In turn, I will choose one item as well. Once we return to Gleneden, you will reveal your choice, and I will reveal mine. But once we are home, you must promise you will wear whatever I purchase . . . and whatever you purchase. That is the bargain."

Maura pursed her lips in avid consideration. Alec sucked in a breath, his gut on fire. He resisted the urge to cover her lips with his, trace that delectable pink pout into his mouth and let desire lead where it would.

He settled for tracing the pondering frown between her brows. "Is that agreeable to you, Duchess?"

"If I am to save your fortune, then it appears I must," she grumbled.

A smile grazed his lips. It blossomed into a low, full-bodied laugh. "All right, then." He trailed a finger down the curve of her cheek. "Madame?" he called out. "Her grace is ready for her measurements."

When she was done, Alec got up from the chair just outside the dressing room. "My turn to chat with Madame."

As soon as he was gone, Maura went straight to the table of silk stockings. Picking up a pair, she let them slide through her fingers. Madame had looked at her a bit oddly when she told her what she wanted. And now Maura was giddy with pure delight. She felt like whirling around and hugging herself. Very soon she would have her very own pair of silk stockings.

Alec's voice came from behind her. "I see you're quite taken with those. They're quite fine, aren't they?"

Maura was too busy happily congratulating herself to notice that he wore a cat-who-swallowed-the-cream sort of smile.

They dined that night in the hotel dining room, a lovely room done up in hues of bronze and gold. Candlelight winked off the chandeliers.

Maura ate sparingly. She reached often for a delicately etched goblet — with a generous pour from the waiter — then chanced to catch Alec's scrutiny as she raised it to her lips.

He slanted her a knowing grin.

Maura quickly lowered the goblet to the table.

With every moment, every second, he sensed her growing nervousness. She declined dessert, ducking her hands beneath the table. Every so often her gaze flitted toward the stairs.

Alec swirled his after-dinner brandy, then leaned back in his chair. He was well aware of the reason for her uneasiness.

"Is something wrong, Irish?"

"Yes, as a matter of fact." She raised the back of one hand to her forehead. "Oh, dear. I find I am developing a most dreadful headache."

He tipped his head to the side. "How curious."

"Curious?" she echoed.

"Perhaps it's the wine."

She glanced at him oddly.

"Wine does seem to have various effects on you," he pretended to muse. "If you recall, the night of Lord Preston's masquerade, it piqued your ardor for me quite handsomely." He trailed a fingertip down the line of her jaw. It tensed beneath his touch.

The rogue! He was enjoying this! But she admitted to herself that he was right about one thing — handsome was indeed the very word that came to mind whenever he was near, and equally as much when he was not!

"Your grace, I should hate to ruin the evening, but I fear the ache is growing quite abominable."

Alec had the feeling she was telling him in no uncertain terms that *he* was quite abominable.

"Perhaps we should summon a physician, then."

"No!" she said quickly. "A little rest and I'm sure I shall be right as rain." She pushed back her chair. In an instant he was there beside her, a strong hand cupping her elbow as they reached the winding staircase.

"Irish, perhaps I should carry you. Your headache must surely be making you weak."

On the sixth step, she gritted her teeth.

"Really, Maura, this is most unwise. Lean on me. Save your strength."

She caught sight of him in the mirror on the landing. He was laughing at her, the knave!

As soon as they entered the suite, Maura realized how badly she'd misjudged him.

And how foolishly she'd underestimated him, for his hands were already at the buttons on the back of her gown.

Her head jerked up. "A maid . . . Surely the hotel —"

"No need for one, not when your husband is here. I would consider myself a most inconsiderate one if I left you when you most need me."

Her gown dropped to the carpet, along with her layers of petticoats.

"There, now. That must feel so much better." He pressed a warm kiss on her nape, a kiss that made her quiver inside.

The feel of his mouth on her skin sent shivers of pleasure all over her skin.

"You've developed a chill? We must hurry then and get you into bed."

Deft male fingers tugged at the laces of her corset. Maura sputtered, then gasped as he turned her. "I . . . you . . . wait!"

Her stays landed atop her skirt, her chemise tugged over her head.

No longer confined, her breasts spilled free. Some faint sound escaped her lips as she glanced down and confronted her nudity.

"Hush, Irish. Modesty is not a word that should exist between husband and wife, don't you agree?" A kiss was planted at the rise of each breast even as he stripped her drawers down her legs. "Beautiful, Irish.

Beautiful."

His hands in her hair, he tugged the pins that held it. Her hair tumbled over her shoulders, over his hands. Her shoes were next, her cotton stockings peeled away. "There, you see? No need for a maid after all, not with a considerate husband at hand. Now then, let's get you into bed."

In all honesty, Maura wasn't sure she'd have made it under her own power. She was about to swoon from embarrassment — or shock. Perhaps both, she decided in utter mortification, just as a muscled arm slid beneath her knees and she felt herself lifted. And then all she could think was how he accomplished it with such effortless ease.

Then he did the unthinkable. In seconds his jacket and shirt were off, revealing the powerful plane of hair-roughened chest.

At last she regained her powers of speech. "What if this malady is catching?" she cried. "Perhaps you should sleep elsewhere to-night."

"Nonsense! Unfortunate, I admit, if that proves to be the case." An exaggerated sigh. "But I won't stand accused of being an insensitive husband. And if so, at least we can make our recovery together. And if we are not ill, well, who knows? We may decide to stay a few days longer — our honeymoon

— and languish here in bed if we choose."

Maura's thoughts were a wild jumble. Oh, but he was so pleased with himself! His ploy was utterly transparent, his amusement unmistakable, his audacity boundless. Why bother to mask it behind so-called concern?

And why did she even care, when it was already done?

But it appeared he wasn't done. His hands were at his waistband. A few swift moves and he stepped from his trousers. Her mouth grew dry. He was close enough to touch. His buttocks looked hard and taut. He turned.

Naked.

She could have looked away. She should have looked away.

She didn't. Some crazed madness had come over her that she didn't, and this was the most mortifying of all! Inhaling sharply, she flung herself over, pillowing her face against her arms with a moan. Imprinted in her mind's eye was the image of raw, stark virility.

Alec extinguished the bedside lamp and slid into bed beside her.

"Come, Irish, let me warm you. Let me keep away your nightmares."

A strong hand descended on her hip. A long arm captured her, snared her close, as close as a man and woman could be without being joined. It was as if she lay cocooned within every inch of him.

She struggled to still the frantic throb of her pulse. She was half afraid to breathe, to move, for fear of stirring the part of him that so dominated her mind.

His body radiated heat. Her heart hammered. But Alec did nothing more than stroke her arm and shoulder, a featherlike touch that was oddly soothing. Little by little she felt herself relax, drifting into the world of dreams.

Much, much sooner than Alec had hoped.

CHAPTER THIRTEEN

When Maura woke, the bed was empty. She had slept soundly, more soundly than she expected in light of the fact she lay nestled against Alec the night through.

She was bathed and dressed when he reappeared. They breakfasted in the hotel dining room, then it was off to the train station. Alec's coachman Douglas met them at Ayr. Alec handed her into the coach and settled across from her. He remained coolly polite, if a bit distant. Or did he merely ponder? Regardless of the reason behind his silence, it rattled her nerves. And in her nervousness, she began to prattle.

"It's dreadfully dreary, isn't it? We're in for a spot of rain, from the look of those clouds. Oh, look, there is a peat bog! And you dared to call Ireland a soggy bog of an isle, do you remember? There are no more peat bogs on McDonough lands, you know. One year my father traveled all the way to

Donegal so the castle and our tenants would have fuel for the winter. The weather was horribly brutal that year, I believe. I couldn't have been more than ten or so, but I shall never forget."

Ten minutes later she spied a pony. "Is that a Shetland?" She gave a delighted laugh. "It reminds me of the ponies in Connemara. Have you ever seen a Connemara? Connemaras pulled the carts of peat back to McDonough —"

She broke off. Alec surveyed her, his expression rather vexed.

Maura turned defensive. "What?"

A brow quirked high. "I had no idea I'd wed a mockingbird," he drawled. "I wish your uncle had seen fit to tell me."

"Well, if you weren't so rude as to sit there like a stump of wood and instead make the effort to converse now and again, there would be no need for me to fill the silence," she informed him loftily.

"A spate of temper! Why am I not surprised? You're a fierce little creature, aren't you?"

Maura cast him a virulent gaze. Her chin firmed. She wouldn't let him bait her. She proceeded to gaze out the window the rest of the way home.

Certainly she did not deign to venture a

single word.

Back at Gleneden, she handed her hat to a waiting maid, then requested that her riding habit be laid out.

There was a tap on her shoulder. "I fear your ride shall have to wait." Alec gave a nod. Maura looked beyond his shoulder to discover that the skies had opened up like a floodgate. Rain lashed the windowpanes.

"Of course, living on that soggy bog of an isle called Ireland, no doubt you're used to a little rain."

"You," she declared aloud, "are a wretched creature to torment me so. But no doubt the sky is as moody as Gleneden's master." Directing an acid smile his way, she removed her gloves and handed them to Aggie, the maid. "I think I should like tea in the red parlor."

The little maid seemed puzzled. It was Alec who supplied the reason why.

"I think, Irish, you mean the gold parlor in the north wing, the family wing. There is no red parlor, although there is a pink parlor in the guest wing."

Maura glanced at the maid. "The gold parlor, then, please."

"The gold parlor it is, your grace."

The maid bobbed a curtsy and hastened to do her mistress's bidding. Maura glared at Alec, then turned toward the north wing. The beast was enjoying himself at her expense far too much.

But it impressed upon Maura exactly what she was up against. Since her arrival, her search for the Circle of Light hadn't extended beyond more than half a dozen bed-chambers in the north wing, and a cursory search of the garret where she found the candlesticks she'd given to Murdoch.

Sitting in the gold parlor with her tea, she reminded herself there was no need to be disheartened. Gleneden Hall was simply larger than she had expected. The hardest thing was figuring out where a pirate who had lived two hundred years ago would have hidden the Circle — hidden it where no one might find it in the next two hundred years.

Because no one had.

It was still here.

Somewhere.

That strange sense that it was here had not lessened.

If anything, it was sharper — even more keen — stronger than ever. She felt it every time she passed the portrait of James Mc-Bride, seventh Duke of Gleneden. And every time, as well, it was as though she'd been plunged into a vat of ice. Something gleamed in his eyes, as if he taunted her.

And each and every time, she cursed his black-guard soul. Maura stirred her tea restlessly and replaced the little spoon on the saucer. Her gaze circled the room, coming to rest on a painting of a basket of fruit above the sofa. Poking her head in the hall to make certain no one was about, she scurried back inside to peer behind each of the six paintings in the parlor. No hidden compartments behind any of them. No secret drawers in the long low table behind the sofa. She chafed. If Alec weren't in the house, she could prowl to her heart's content.

Returning to her tea, she glanced out the window. The rain had begun to lessen. The hours of travel had made her long to be outdoors. If the rain stopped and there was enough daylight left, she would walk to the wishing well. Maura smiled. It was not a place of whimsical beauty, but rather one of whimsy. She and Alec's mother had something in common. They both liked it there.

"Your grace?"

Maura glanced up. It was Aggie, and only then did she realize that the girl had called her twice. She winced inside. She wasn't used to being addressed as "your grace."

"Yes, Aggie?"

"His grace requests your presence in your

room, your grace."

"Thank you, Aggie." Did he think she would scurry to his summons? By heaven, he could wait.

A full fifteen minutes passed before she strolled to her room. Alec was sitting in one of the large wing chairs in front of the fireplace. Judging from his expression, it didn't appear he'd been waiting impatiently.

He got to his feet. In one hand was a small be-ribboned box. He tapped it against his chest.

"Did you think I forgot our bargain at Madame Rousseau's?" he asked.

Maura's heart bounded. Her stockings! She snatched at the box.

Alec held it high above his head. "Take care you don't lose it!" he cautioned. "Remember our promise. Whatever you bought, you promised to wear."

"Yes, yes!" She was the impatient one.

"And whatever I chose, you will wear as well. I have your promise?"

"Yes! I promise!"

He handed her the box. Maura ripped off the ribbon, held the stockings to her chest and crowed, "I cannot believe it. My very first pair of silk stockings! My very own!" In the midst of her dancing up and down, he caught her elbow and wheeled her around.

He pointed to the door.

Aggie and half a dozen other maids filed in, each carrying several round boxes, which they stacked near the armoire. When they withdrew, Alec nodded to Maura.

She fell to her knees and tore off lid after lid from box after box. His shoulder propped against the door, Alec looked on. By the time she was done, clutched to her chest and scattered all around, were dozens of sheer, silk stockings. Maura was laughing helplessly.

She looked up at Alec. "Oh, my word, you bought every last pair in the shop, didn't you?"

"I believe Madame said something to that effect, yes."

Alec looked on thoughtfully. Had she asked for everything, he would have purchased little or nothing. But all she wanted was that one simple thing, and that nearly pried from her! Now, he wished he'd bought nearly every last item in every last shop on the street.

For God help him, it was bloody well worth it to see her light up like this.

Tears of laughter streamed down her cheeks when he tugged her up to her feet. She threw her arms around his neck. "Alec McBride, you are quite mad!"

Caught up in some strange awakening deep in his gut, he sucked in a breath. He handed her his handkerchief to wipe away her tears. He'd never seen such joy for something that, to him, was so trifling.

Her reluctance had gained her far more than greed or insistence. She claimed it wasn't money or his title that she hoped to gain. Had her being caught in his bed indeed been an accident? If only he could be sure.

All he knew was that he wouldn't have traded anything in the world to miss the glow on her face in that moment. The light shining from her beautiful green eyes was simply beyond price.

Throughout dinner, every so often Maura allowed her slipper to dangle from her toes, angled her leg out from beneath her chair, bunched up her skirt ever so slightly to admire her stockings.

Over tea, Alec glanced at her. "Irish, are you doing what I think you are?"

"I am doing nothing, sir," she said primly.

He set his cup on the saucer, neatly folded his napkin and laid it beside his plate. The next time she angled her leg out he reached beneath the table and caught the back of her calf.

"So you like your new stockings, do you?"

"I do indeed."

He ran his fingers up behind her knee and gave a full, throaty laugh. "Well, so do I, Irish. So do I." His hand was roving now, almost to her silk ribbon garters. Maura's eyes went huge.

The evening passed far more quickly than she'd anticipated. After the last dish was removed, Alec pushed his chair back. Maura started to do the same. His voice stopped her.

"Wait," he said softly. "Your hands. Let me see them."

She glanced at him, surprised when he turned to face her. "What?" Her hands ducked instinctively beneath the table, into her lap.

He shook his head, his scrutiny suddenly piercingly intent. "Your hands, if you please, Irish."

Maura's heart was suddenly pounding. She shifted so she faced him, then started to lift them from her lap. Lean fingers caught at hers. Turning her palms up, he cradled her hands within his.

"Your hands are scarcely larger than a child's," he murmured.

She swallowed, her throat suddenly dry. Alec's hands, lean and strong, far eclipsed her own.

His expression was shielded from her. He stared so long and so hard she instinctively started to withdraw. As soon as he felt it, his fingers banded her wrists.

All at once she quivered, both inside and out.

He glanced up, his gaze snaring hers. "Why are you trembling?"

"I don't know," she whispered.

Maura looked down where his fingers encircled around her wrists. His hold was strong, yet somehow gentle.

Suddenly he pulled the ring from her left hand, the plain gold band he'd slipped on her finger in Ireland. Almost before she knew it, he'd exchanged it for another.

Maura turned her hand over and stared. The ring was simple but beautiful, a large sapphire surrounded by tiny diamonds that winked in the light.

Her lips parted. "Wh-What is this?"

His expression was solemn. Intent. "For over two hundred years, every Duchess of Gleneden has worn this ring."

"But . . . your mother —"

"Is now the Dowager Duchess. Once my mother came out of mourning, she replaced this ring with another given to her by my father, one she treasures greatly for the sentiment it represents. But as my bride, this ring belongs on your finger." He paused, then said softly, "It looks lovely on you, Duchess."

Lifting her hand, he bent his head and kissed the inside of her wrist. There was a catch in her heart. Somehow it was as intimate as if he'd kissed her mouth.

Suddenly she wanted to cry. Her throat grew hot. The tenderness of his touch, the way he looked at her — it melted her insides. Was she falling in love with him? She couldn't . . . shouldn't!

The truth was like a betrayal. She despised herself. Her deceit. His ring made her mission here all the more unpalatable. She had no right to wear it. Alec would hate her when he discovered the truth — and it was killing her. She hated that she must hide her deceit.

He rose to his feet, their fingers still linked. Taking a deep breath, Maura rose, too.

A glimmer of a smile touched his lips. The serious moment was gone. "What do you say to a glass of wine in the gold parlor, Irish? Or perhaps the great hall. It's quite cozy to sit in front of the fire with a glass of brandy."

"That might prove difficult. Despite the

rain, it was quite warm today and thus there is no need for a fire," she found herself teasing back.

"Then perhaps you're ready for your other present."

Her smile wavered. "But this —"

"Is your wedding ring," he finished, "not a gift. As Duchess of Gleneden, it is your right to wear it."

A maelstrom of emotion churned in Maura's chest. In her mind, a silent conflict warred. Her deception tore at her more and more each day. But, dammit, she had no reason to feel guilty. The Black Scotsman had stolen from her clan. She was here to reclaim the Circle, and she was close — so close! When she thought of all the items of value in this house . . . But a fraction of their worth would feed every family on Mc-Donough land for many a year.

Damn the Black Scotsman. Damn, damn, damn him!

"Are you ready for your other present?"

She had no idea that Alec took note of every emotion that played across her features.

She shook her head. "Your grace, I have what I want — my silk stockings. Many pairs of silk stockings, if you recall." She forced a laugh. "I have no need for anything else."

"You cannot renege. A bargain is a bargain. Yes, you have your choice, but you've yet to see mine, which you'll find in your room." A rakish brow climbed high. "Aren't you curious?"

Aye, she decided. Curious, yes. And most certainly dubious.

"Go," he said softly.

She knew she had no choice. What had she been thinking, to make such a foolish promise? Gathering up her skirts, she gingerly climbed the stairs to her room. With every step came the urge to turn and run. But if she ran, it would be right back into his arms. And if she awaited him upstairs . . .

There would be no evading him.

In her room, Maura went straight to the bed. Laid out upon the counterpane was a sheer lace nightgown. She decided she'd never seen anything quite so lovely in her life. She ran a hand over it almost reverently, the gossamer lace so fragile and delicate she was almost afraid to touch it for fear it would disappear.

"Do you like it?"

The door clicked shut. It was Alec, his voice low and husky. He'd come inside without her being aware of it.

Maura looked up at him. "Your grace, I am not quite sure what to say." Her tone was scarcely audible.

"Do you dislike it?"

She shook her head.

"What, then?"

For the second time that day, tears pushed to the surface. Alas, these were not happy tears.

"You are . . . overcome?"

"Do not mock me, Scotsman." She fought a deep, abiding shame. She might as well tell him what she was about. But she was afraid he'd send her back to Ireland, and she would never find the Circle of Light. "I — I feel like a thief."

"An odd word to use, Irish."

"Why is it odd?" Her tone was very low. "You've made no bones about your feelings. You think I conspired to wed you for your money. For" — she waved a hand — "all of this."

Curling his knuckles beneath her chin, Alec guided her eyes to his.

"I am not a miser, Irish. I will not act like one, nor is there a need for you to think I will. There is certainly no need for you to act like one. You may purchase whatever you wish. I will see that you have pin money. If you need more, there is money locked in the far right drawer of the desk in my study. The key is inside the vase directly behind my desk. Or you may come to me. Now, may we agree that we will not have this conversation again?"

Intense blue eyes searched hers before Maura gave a slight nod.

"Excellent. Now, to the business at hand." With a devilish half smile he glanced at the nightgown. "I must confess, I found this gown exceptionally . . . provocative."

Maura found it exceptionally . . . revealing. She gulped. "Oh, my. It's — It's —" She would burn in Hell for the way she'd deceived Alec. And if she did not burn in Hell for that, she would burn in Hell for daring to don a nightgown such as this!

"Yes. I can see where it might compel a loss of words." He gave her a gentle push toward the screen. "Put it on."

Her jaw fell open. "Wait. You expect me to wear —"

"Yes."

"Now?"

"Indeed."

"Now?"

"The mockingbird has returned, I see. Surely you must have noticed it's night, Irish."

Must he sound so damnably rational? She struggled to keep the desperation from her tone. "Where is the robe?"

"I don't believe there was one. In any case, I wouldn't have bought it. That would defeat the purpose of buying a nightgown such as this."

She could present no argument to that statement, and realized she had little choice. Dammit, he was enjoying this all too well. She snatched it up from the bed and stepped behind the screen.

From the other side, Alec heard several muttered, rather inflammatory curses. At a rather virulent one, he sighed. "Do you need help with your laces?"

"I haven't even gotten to the bloody laces, not with all of these damned buttons to undo!"

"How fortunate I am here, then." He rounded the screen and stepped up behind her.

Maura didn't delude herself. When Alec had prompted her upstairs, she certainly hadn't expected her maid to be waiting.

"The constraints of women's clothing are bothersome, at best. Sheer torture, at the worst. May I suggest there's no need for you to fetter yourself so when you are in your bedchamber — or mine, for that matter." His hands were busy throughout his speech. "There, it's done."

Maura held a hand against her chest, though her gown was certainly in no danger of falling. "May I have some privacy?"

"Of course." Alec disappeared.

A tumult of emotion whirled in Maura's chest. Reaching deep into the pocket of her gown, she pulled out her beloved velvet pouch and put it on the chair. She pulled one arm free of her striped silk gown. Alec was right, she allowed, having progressed to her petticoats. She had promised to wear whatever he purchased. She had hurtled herself into this entire predicament of their so-called marriage without any real — perhaps the better word was realistic — ideas of how to proceed beyond getting herself into the Black Scotsman's home. She'd known at the outset that she had to tread carefully with regard to husbandly expectations. To wifely duties. Alec McBride was an intensely masculine, flesh-and-blood man.

With flesh-and-blood desires.

And she could hardly deny that she, too, harbored those very same desires.

The attraction that began the night of the masquerade still simmered beneath the surface, whenever they were together. Despite his fury at her manipulations, it was still there. Always a constant. She sensed that Alec had contained it, controlled it, fought to ignore it.

She, too, fought the very same struggle.

It was a dangerous dance of deception. A precarious line she must tread. If she pushed him away too far and too often, he would grow suspicious. To his credit, he'd been remarkably restrained, given the explosive heat of their attraction that night at the baron's masquerade. Granted, she had no experience to judge by, but she thought it was explosive.

For her, at least.

Maura slipped the nightgown over her head, then twitched it into place. Pulling the pins from her simple chignon, she shook her hair free, combing through it with her fingers.

There was a beveled mirror behind the screen. She slowly raised her head to look at her reflection. She was shocked at the woman who stared back at her. Her skin shone through the lace. The gown hid precious little of her body. It was so sheer, she might as well have been naked. The lamps were dim; they bathed the outline of her body in a hazy shimmer. With her hair unbound, every inch of her flesh clearly visible, she looked like a woman who had just crawled from her lover's bed.

Or a woman about to crawl into her lover's bed.

She couldn't bring herself to move. Her heart stood still. She was afraid to turn around, to face Alec.

She didn't have to.

All at once he was behind her, tall and powerful. She would have turned, but he stopped her with a shake of his head.

With a single fingertip beneath the tie at her shoulder, he slid it down, baring the skin. A tug, and it separated.

Maura couldn't have moved even if she wanted to. She stared, mesmerized by his reflection, mesmerized by hers. Their eyes locked, hers wide and startled. Alec's burned like fiery blue torches. It was as if he touched her very soul. His right arm curled around her waist, pulling her back against him. She quivered inside, aware of his latent power and strength. He swept aside the black curtain of her hair, exposing the fragile length of her neck, the delicate slope of her shoulder.

Never in her life would she forget the scorching hunger on his features. She saw it in his eyes just before he lowered his head. He kissed her nape, a blazing trail to the tender spot just below her ear. She had not dreamed that she might be so achingly sensitive there. His lips grazed the side of her neck. She tilted her head, granting even more access to the tantalizing touch of his lips.

Her body reacted instinctively. Impatiently. Her nipples thrust against the sheer cloth. They tingled, icy needles that craved . . . something. Something more . . .

She was vaguely aware of the gown pooling at her feet, and then she knew what that something was. His palms cupped the weight of one breast in his hand. His arm slid over her right shoulder, laying claim to her left breast. His thumb brushed against the crown; she nearly cried out.

Maura couldn't tear her gaze from the mirror. It was as if he took possession of her, an exquisite entrapment. His fingers traced circles around both her nipples. His thumb raked lightly across both peaks. Taking it between thumb and forefinger, he squeezed lightly, then palmed back and forth, back and forth, tantalizing until she moaned.

Swamped by sheer sensation, her eyes were half closed. His hands were at her breasts, lean and dark against her pale skin. A rush of sheer pleasure shot through her.

It was wildly erotic as she watched him play her body . . . and watching him watch her was even more erotic.

Lean fingers splayed across her belly, spanning the width between her hips, dark against her pale smoothness. His caresses impelled a shockingly compelling persuasion. Maura held her breath. His fingertips painted a tantalizing path to her belly, paused for one mind-shattering moment —

Then slipped brazenly into the triangle of curls above her thighs.

Every ounce of strength seemed to drain from her limbs. His tongue traced the tendon of her neck. Her head fell back.

With a muffled exclamation, Alec turned her in his arms, flooded with arousal. His legs braced slightly apart, he caught her knee and brought it high around his hip. He held her squarely between his legs. One hand molding the curve of her buttocks, he clamped her tight against him, bringing her up and against the jutting hardness of his erection for mind-spinning moments. Maura clutched at his arms, feeling the knotted tension in his arms as he caught her up and bore her to the bed.

There, they lay together, side by side. Alec's mouth covered hers, staking his claim. Jerking his shirt apart, he rubbed his chest against hers. Her skin was pale, almost translucent; he could see the fragile trace of veins beneath. Dark desire gripped him. He was powerless to control it. He closed his mouth around first one swollen nipple, then the other, sucking hard.

His hand strayed lower. As tall as she was, she was incredibly fine-boned and slender. His fingertips stretched wide, easily bridging the hollow of her belly. A lone finger circled the kernel of flesh hidden in her nest of curls, then stole between sleek, feminine petals. He felt the jolt that went through her. His own need vibrated deep in his chest. Christ, she was hot. Damp with heat. Trembling with desire. And he was burning both inside and out.

Alec felt her lips part beneath his. He gritted his teeth, easing a finger inside her passage a scant inch. Even there she was small, her flesh closing tight around his finger. God, she would fit around his shaft like a second skin. He could almost swear —

Maura sucked in a breath. "Your grace —"

Beads of sweat broke out on his forehead. "Alec," he muttered. "My God, you call me 'your grace' when I've my hand in your —"

"Alec!" she cried.

He captured her lips. His thumb circled

244

that pinpoint of pleasure. She writhed against him, around him. "Yes, Irish, that's the way. Soon it will be me inside you."

Maura's eyes snapped open. Alarm seized her. Her breath came raggedly, her thoughts in jagged bursts. If she allowed this, Alec would discover the truth of what happened — nay, what did not happen — the night of the baron's masquerade.

The truth would out.

She could not risk it. She dare not risk it.

Because then she might never find the Circle.

And all would be lost.

"Alec," she whispered, and then it was a cry: "Alec!"

Something in her voice penetrated through the fiery haze of pleasure surrounding him. His eyes flicked open. He stared directly into hers.

His lips grew ominously thin.

Maura's face was scalding. Her pulse pounded wildly. Her heart in chaos, she looked at him, only to wish she had not.

"Dammit, Irish, what is it?" He was awash with sensation, dying to be inside her. Didn't she realize how close he was to that point of no return? He was a heartbeat away from driving hard and deep, as deep as he could go.

Then he saw the tremor of her lips, and a strange expression flitted across his features. He went a little pale. "What is it? Christ, the night of the masquerade, did I —" the words were ground out. "— did I hurt you?"

"No," she said faintly.

"What, then?"

Maura shook her head. He released her. Sitting up, she crossed her arms over her nakedness. She despised her trickery, her forbidden yearnings.

Alec got to his feet, the planes of his face rigid and tense, his mouth a taut line. Maura glimpsed the raw hunger that still burned in his eyes. She hated herself even more.

His eyes were suddenly icy, as icy as his tone. "Have it your way for now, Duchess. The next time will be mine."

Maura jumped when he slammed the door between their rooms. Her lips still throbbed from being oh so thoroughly kissed. She staved off tears of shame. He would hate her, she was certain, when she revealed her deceit.

The encounter left her quaking inside. Shaken to the core. Fraught with worry. Somehow she was going to have to find a way to stay out of his bed. Somehow she must find a way to placate him, to appease him. How long, she wondered desperately, could she hold him off?

And yet — God forgive her, but she longed to experience what it would be like to make love with Alec McBride. Her heart twisted, for he would never know how much she yearned for it. Once. Just once.

But making love with Alec was the one thing she must avoid at all costs. If she didn't avoid it, all her efforts would have been in vain.

The Circle of Light was here. So very near. That strange sense of certainty had never left her. Once she found it, both she and Alec could resume their lives as they had been before they ever met.

All she had to do was find the Circle — find it soon! Then she could go back to Ireland. Home to Castle McDonough.

And far, far away from Alec McBride.

CHAPTER FOURTEEN

Fast in the grip of a powerful desire, his erection heavy and thick and pounding, Alec rolled to his back and shot to his feet.

Have it your way, Duchess. The next time will be mine.

Out in the hall, he plowed his fingers through his hair and leaned against the wall. He swore, a vile and vicious curse. Christ, his mind was in a fog when she was near. A battle warred deep in his soul. He couldn't think. Hunger still burned. Desire scalded his veins.

Go back in. Take her, urged a voice within. *She is your wife. She is yours. Take her. Why deny yourself the spoils?*

He couldn't, he reflected grimly. He wouldn't. Not like this. Not until she wanted him with a passion that matched his.

Oh, he had no doubt it was there. He'd felt it in the eager parting of her lips, every tremor in her body, the desperate way she clung to him. When he kissed her, he felt so many things! It was as if she fought the same battle as he. Little wonder it rankled that his Irish rose continued to deny her longing.

Why, in the end, was she so reluctant? Why?

His steps took him downstairs to his study. He needed distance between them to cool his blood. A mere wall between them, a single room, simply wasn't enough. The temptation of knowing she was in the next room would be too strong. In the study, he snatched the whiskey decanter and a glass and collapsed into the chair behind his desk, his emotions still raw.

A shadow slipped over him.

His lovely Maura was a beautiful woman. From the beginning, he'd wanted her. She had invited him, lured him. And he had swallowed the bait, only to become a husband and acquire a wife in a way he'd never expected. He'd been so resentful, so angry; he'd told himself he didn't want her. But he did. God above, he did. He gave a bitter laugh of self-reproach. And since she was now his wife, it was entirely natural to take her to bed again, yet something held him back. *She* held him back.

Things had changed since they wed.

When they left Ireland, he was determined to stay aloof. He'd been a fool there, allowing his passion to control him.

And now he found himself at war — at war within himself.

If this marriage had not been forced upon him, he wondered, would his feelings for Maura be any different? Would he desire her any less? No, came his reluctant admission.

But to all appearances, the one woman he truly desired did not desire him. And she was his wife, by God!

He was both furious and perplexed. Was it because she had what she wanted? The title of duchess and a rich husband?

If only he knew! When he kissed her, he felt so many things. How right it felt!

Yet how strong was his pride.

And how strong was hers!

She was like a burr beneath his skin, forever in his mind. It was as if she fought the same battle as he. Need. Temptation. He longed to feel her surrender, not just to him, but to her feelings.

He'd felt her passion. Her craving. As strong, as desperate, as his. He'd felt the need that vibrated in her heart, as surely as it vibrated in his. He wasn't wrong. Or was he? Doubt seated itself deep in his vitals.

He gave a self-mocking smile. Were his emotions so clouded by his longing that he could not trust them?

He had done this to himself, he realized. He'd told himself he could remain indifferent to her beauty. He had denied himself the spoils, because he hated that he'd been duped. His pride wouldn't allow him to admit his desire burned as strongly as ever. Here at Gleneden, those first few times he kissed her, it was to prove that despite what happened in Ireland, he wasn't powerless. He'd wanted to assert himself. To show her that he would not be a puppet. If only his hand hadn't been forced.

Yet what did that matter? She was his wife. He was her husband.

Neither of them could change that.

Nor did it change his desire for her.

And Maura wanted him. Her lips did not lie. Her lips had never lied.

She had trembled in his arms tonight. Trembled with pleasure, he was certain. He felt the precise moment she surrendered — the precise moment of retreat! A half-formed suspicion cut through him — that she was not as worldly as he'd thought. Indeed, he could swear he caught a glimpse of fear — of vulnerability — and that was most frustrating of all. Had he been a brute the night they'd slept together in Ireland?

She denied it.

Truth or lie, he conceded to himself, it had inevitably led to the same conclusion.

Marriage.

Draining the glass, Alec rested his forehead against the back of the hand that held it, staring into the dark. What a fool he'd been, he told himself scathingly. He could no more stay his desire than stop breathing. He had only to look at her and fire scalded his blood.

He leaned back. His mouth twisted. It still grated that she'd married him for his wealth. *Had she?* pricked a needling little voice. Was she a fortune-hunter? She had asked for nothing. Indeed, she disdained what his money would give her!

A ruse? No, he decided. Pride? Oh, aye, indeed. Yet it pleased him — pleased him immeasurably — to see her delight over her stockings. He wondered what she would say when the rest of his purchases arrived. When they had left Madame Rousseau's shop, no doubt Madame rubbed her hands together in glee.

But he must own up to the truth. It was he who had sought her out that night. But then, she had participated — oh, most willingly! He gave a brittle laugh; he was certain it had nothing to do with his appearance.

And everything to do with the fact that he was the Duke of Gleneden.

But it certainly didn't seem as if it was his person or his possessions that she coveted! What then? He examined her motives. What was she after? What had brought her to Gleneden?

He couldn't dispel the notion that the lovely Maura McBride — he was rather startled at how easily her new name slipped through his mind — was up to something. She wanted something. But what the devil could it be, if not his name and his fortune?

Alec smiled tightly. Maura had been shocked at his blatant caress tonight. Her flesh had clamped tight around his finger, so tight he'd had to halt his penetration. So tight that for an instant a fleeting notion ran through his mind.

But that was impossible. If he didn't know better — if he hadn't seen for himself the bloodstained proof upon the sheets — along with Maura, her uncle, and the baron, he could almost believe . . .

Suspicion gnawed at him. He groped for memory. Snatches of remembrance appeared and disappeared, just beyond his reach. He'd always felt that something was amiss about that night. He set aside the glass and pushed both fingers into his temples. Why couldn't he remember making love to her? Why? It was as if his mind had been wiped clean, as if there was a gaping hole. He fought to bridge the gap. He fought to recall every detail. Why the devil couldn't he remember bedding her?

His mind worked furiously. How could the memory elude him so? Why couldn't he remember? He'd shared a whiskey with the baron before the masquerade. In light of being found in bed with her the next morning, he had believed the only thing possible — that he must have been feeling the effects of too much liquor by the time he took Maura up to his room more than he realized. But to be so foxed that he couldn't remember bedding the woman who was now his wife? It nagged at him.

His mind was like a cobweb. Hazy, yet impenetrable.

He tried again.

And this time . . . ah, this time! Sketched in his mind were hot, enflamed kisses. Maura pulling briefly away to pour wine. He'd drained his glass. So had she.

He closed his eyes. Memory sharpened.

Bottoms up, he'd said. And then —

He'd tugged Maura down onto the bed. The taste of her mouth, the curl of his

254

tongue around her nipples . . . every touch returned in vivid recall. He remembered his hand over hers, closing her fingers around his shaft, one by one, her touch almost timid. Vaguely, he remembered thinking it so at odds with her sultry invitation.

Then everything blurred. It was as if his mind had gone blank until he woke the next morning.

A fleeting sensation passed through him. The thought unveiled a vague sensation; he fought to keep hold of it. Another sensation caught hold . . . that of Maura tugging. At his boots. At his breeches . . .

All along he had sensed that something was not right. There was a reason behind it, he was certain.

And that reason had something — everything! — to do with his bride. He held his liquor well. That's what made it so difficult to believe he'd been to bed with a virgin. And he had been fine.

Until that last glass of wine.

His body went utterly still.

Until that last glass of wine.

"Oh, God," he whispered.

It was suddenly all so very vivid. He could see it in his mind; hear the way their glasses clinked. Bottoms up, he had declared.

He swore, a long, blistering oath.

It made sense now. Her shyness whenever he touched her. The way she responded, the way she resisted before ultimately yielding her lips to his.

And now he knew why.

She had drugged his wine, the little witch!

The following morning, Maura helped herself to a dish of Scottish oats from the sideboard. Pouring a little milk over the top, she started toward the table. It was curious; this was the first time Alec wasn't at the table before her. Why, she almost missed his bedeviling presence!

Mrs. Yates came through the door. "Ah, I thought I heard you, your grace! How are you this fine mornin'?"

Maura glanced up at her. She had just pushed her spoon into her bowl. "Excellent, Mrs. Yates." She gestured with her spoon to Alec's chair. "Have you seen his grace about this morning?"

"He's gone to Glasgow again, your grace. He asked me to tell you he'll be back by tomorrow, so you needn't worry."

Maura's heart picked up its beat. She wanted to rub her hands in glee, leap up and crow. Finally, here was the chance she'd been waiting for. The ability to search for the Circle of Light to her heart's content, without having to glance over her shoulder every few seconds should someone walk by. She could poke and probe as she wished, wherever she wished.

"I'm thinking of changing a few things here and there in some of the rooms," she said lightly. "Don't be surprised if you see me wandering about."

The housekeeper curtsied. "Very well, your grace. Should you need any help, just ring for one of the maids," she said cheerily.

Maura flashed a beaming smile. "Thank you, Mrs. Yates. I shall."

By the end of the next day Maura was exhausted. She'd checked beneath every bed and chair, run her fingers into each cushion, feeling for what she knew not, peeked into each cupboard, peered behind every picture and tapestry in the house, searching for anything that might reveal a secret hiding place.

On the third floor in the original wing, there was a large room where the air was thick and damp. The light was dim, the window hangings drawn close and tight. She searched as thoroughly there as she had in every other room.

The room had clearly been in disuse for a very long time. She choked at the dust she stirred up. Lifting her head, she glanced about, aware of a curious sense of . . . well, she wasn't quite sure what it was. She wasn't frightened, just aware that something was very different here. She wrinkled her nose at its musty smell. It was rather inhospitable. If this room were to be put to use, she decided briskly, it would need new paint and new furnishings.

She caught herself. If that were to happen, it would be Alec's wife who would undertake the task. A pang shot through her. She made the admission almost painfully. An empty ache stole over her.

Alec's wife, whomever she might be. She would be the true duchess. Not her. Not Maura O'Donnell. Oh, but it didn't bear thinking about. Yet all at once it was all that filled her mind . . . another woman lying naked and languishing against him, his hand an idle caress upon her shoulder. Alec arousing this unknown woman with his lips, with his tongue and hands, as he had the night he'd bought her stockings.

The day he told her of the selkies, she had teasingly asked if he would be jealous if she found herself smitten with a selkie-man. There was something almost grave when he answered in the affirmative.

Without question, she was jealous when

she thought about Alec with another woman. Fiercely jealous.

So much so that it was almost a physical pain, deep in the pit of her belly, a rending ache she could not bear. Slowly, she straightened, unaware that she had bent over, as if she were in pain.

And indeed, she was. Her heart squeezed. Her throat was thick with emotion. All the more reason not to fall in love with him. No, she must not let herself care for him. She could not let herself care for him.

Alec was far too dangerous to her heart.

All the more reason to find the Circle as quickly as possible and go home.

Ireland was where she belonged. Not here in Scotland. Not with Alec McBride, Duke of Gleneden.

It was then . . .

Oh, mercy, she had forgotten . . . No, she had never realized until now —

She recalled how Alec spoke of his father's lingering battle with death. And she bit back a cry of desolation as she remembered her own father's last day, his last, straggling breath. A sick dread clutched at her.

The curse that plagued Clan McDonough also plagued the McBrides.

It was not pain she had experienced before. This was pain. The certainty of knowing that Alec would die. Far sooner than he should have. No one would know why or when or how . . .

Because of the curse.

Unless she found the Circle of Light.

Only half aware of what she was doing, Maura stumbled outside. Before she knew it, she was standing at the wishing well. Like Alec's mother, she found comfort and peace here. It didn't matter that the surroundings weren't particularly picturesque. She found the little well charming, and walked here every day.

She was stunned to find it half filled with water. Sunlight dappled the surface. How, she could not fathom. There had been no rain today or yesterday. Throughout the clearing, the dirt was dry as bone.

Maura spun around and slumped to the ground, her back against the stone. Her hands were shaking as she pulled her pouch from deep in her pocket. She clutched it fast between her fingers.

Inside was the earth from McDonough lands, the pebbles and dirt she'd gathered when she left home. This was her reason for being here.

Pain like a knife ripped through her breast.

Ireland was where she belonged. Not here in Scotland, living beneath a cloud of guilt and deceit.

She sought to think of home. Of Castle McDonough. Jen. Toothless Nan. Patrick the Woolly. The ancient church high upon the hill where pagans and Christians alike had worshiped.

The place where the Circle had once burned so brightly.

But all she could see was Alec, his gaze icy and blue, damning her for not saving him.

At that same moment in Glasgow, Alec opened a small iron gate and strode down a brick walkway. The house was built of weathered brick, each one very much like the other on the narrow street.

At the door, he rapped the brass knocker three times. Heavy footsteps echoed from within the house. The door was thrown wide.

"Your grace!" the man inside greeted him heartily. He was in his late forties, burly, and stood half a head shorter than Alec. His shoulders and neck were thick with muscle. "Come in, come in, your grace."

"You may dispense with the formalities, Thomas." Alec smiled. "It's just the two of us."

"Habits die hard. I still call your brother

261

'Colonel.' "

Thomas Gates had served with the Highland Regiment under his brother's command. Alec stepped into a small entryway as Thomas closed the door.

"I've always been surprised you remained here in Britain rather than return to India," Alec commented.

Thomas grinned. "I fancy m'pension more than that accursed heat in India."

Alec retrieved two pungent cigars from his waistcoat. "Fancy a smoke?"

Thomas released a hearty laugh. "I do. A bit early in the day, but I have just the thing to go with them."

Inside a small parlor, Thomas filled two brandy snifters. Alec sat back and the two of them enjoyed a bit of small talk.

The cigars had burned down when Alec said, "I hear you've turned down a post with Scotland Yard, Thomas."

Thomas shrugged. "I fancy bein' me own man now." He grinned. "I can be a wee bit more discerning about the jobs I take on."

"Precisely the reason I am here."

Thomas laughed gustily. "I knew it wasn't my ugly face that brought you to my doorstep."

Alec crushed the ashes left on his stub of cigar. "I have a favor to ask of you, Thomas," he said, wasting no more time on small talk. "In light of being your own man now, how would you like a visit to Ireland?"

"Ireland!" Thomas was clearly surprised. "And the purpose of this visit?"

"A few discreet inquiries. You'll be amply recompensed." Alec paused. "Aidan always said there was no better man than you at his back, Thomas. If he trusted you, then so do I."

His host glanced at him sharply. "What! This sounds like a matter of life and death."

"No. But it is most certainly a matter of utmost discretion."

"That's the nature of my work now," Thomas said. "Well, it's actually been that for a great many years," he added with a grin. "And you know I will do anything for the colonel's family. But what might be in Ireland other than an overabundance of wind and rain?"

Maura, Alec decided dryly, would have taken vehement exception to his description of her homeland. Reminded of her righteous indignation over his own characterization of Ireland, a faint smile began to crease his lips. But then he thought of her deception, and the smile never quite made it to fruition. He sobered quickly.

Thomas's own smile faded upon seeing

Alec's somber expression. He frowned. "A matter of utmost discretion," he repeated. "A matter concerning what?"

Alec had gone very still. There was a faraway look in his eyes.

Thomas frowned. "Your grace," he prompted. "A matter concerning . . . ?"

Alec's attention snapped back. "A woman, Thomas. The former Lady Maura O'Donnell." He took a deep breath. "My wife."

CHAPTER FIFTEEN

Alec returned to Gleneden late the following afternoon. He found himself impatient — he refused to call it eagerness — to see his wife. But his estate manager was waiting in his study with papers to be signed.

Atop a day's worth of post was a letter from his mother. Alec hesitated, then tore it open. He felt a niggle of guilt and made a mental note to write her. It was time . . . no, past time that he wrote. He pictured her dainty mouth pursed in astonishment upon discovering he was married. No doubt there would be a subtle inquiry as to when he would produce an heir.

A smile on his lips, he exited his study and hailed Mrs. Yates in the great hall. No, the housekeeper hadn't seen her grace since luncheon.

One of the downstairs maids piped up. "I saw 'er grace on the terrace some time ago, yer grace."

Alec headed outside. Perhaps she'd gone to the loch. Or maybe she'd gone riding. Perhaps to the cove.

Where the devil was his errant wife?

In the midst of that thought came a sight that brought him up short.

He saw her outside the courtyard, down where the slope of lawn leveled out. She sat beneath the shade of an oak tree.

Eagerness. Longing. Desire. All of those things flooded him. He reminded himself that there was much he didn't know. Too much his lovely Irish lass kept hidden. Deliberately concealed.

Yet in that moment none of it mattered.

There was an odd catch in the rhythm of Alec's heart. Only Maura would have sat thusly on the ground, careless and heedless that grass might stain her dress. A group of the servants' children sat in a half circle before her.

Maura's back was to him. Alec advanced silently, holding his finger up to his lips when one little boy caught sight of him.

Lord, she looked sweet. Heat coiled deep in his belly. Her head bent low when a little girl with curly hair and apple-red cheeks crawled into her lap.

The children stared at her raptly.

As did Alec. She told a tale filled with

266

myth and magic. And when she was done, they all cried for another.

She tossed her hair over her shoulder. It was loose and unbound, held away from her face by a ribbon.

He listened as she spoke with her lilting, Irish brogue. "There is a place in this world," said she, "a place where the wind meets the sky, and the sky meets the earth —"

"Scotland," said he, declaring his presence.

"Ireland," declared she, decrying it. She twisted around to glare up at him. "Perhaps you should continue with the telling of this tale, your grace." Her eyes sizzled, but her tone was honey sweet.

Alec glanced at the children. "Oh, I believe Her Grace is much more suited to the telling of tales than I."

Maura stiffened. What the devil did he mean by that?

"And her grace is certainly much prettier than I, don't you think?"

A dozen vigorous nods and giggles affirmed it. Alec planted his shoulder against the tree trunk and folded his arms. "I shall interfere no more, Duchess. Pray continue."

And she did, ignoring him. As for Alec, he was only half aware of the story. All the

267

while she spoke, his gaze wandered over her. When the story finally ended, she glanced at her audience. "Would any of you like a sprinkling of fairy dust?"

Shouts and hands went up.

Her laughter was like the tinkling of little silver bells. Reaching into the pocket of her gown, she withdrew a velvet pouch. Alec vaguely recalled seeing it on her bureau a few times.

She reached in, pretending to pull something out. Then she waggled and waved her fingertips. "There! You wear a cloak of fairy dust, my doves. It will protect you and keep you safe and warm and happy!"

"Another story, your grace," begged a little girl. The stable master's youngest child.

Maura dusted off her hands. "Tomorrow, Greta. I promise."

Alec lent his wife a hand up and onto her feet. "What of me? Am I not worthy of a sprinkling of your fairy dust?"

The children dispersed.

"I believe you are well able to see to yourself," she told him tartly.

"Ah, Maura, you wound me."

She snorted, tugging her hand away.

They began the walk back toward the hall. "I apologize for my abrupt departure and return to Glasgow," he said smoothly. "I hope you can forgive me. It was a matter I neglected to attend to before we left there."

"You needn't apologize, and there is certainly nothing to forgive. I understand that you must tend to your affairs."

"A forgiving wife. I consider myself blessed. I trust you had a pleasant day?"

"I did."

Her tone was such that Alec was a trifle affronted.

"Tell me of it, Irish."

"I fear there is little to tell."

"Oh, come, there must be something."

Suddenly he stopped short. Maura turned to face him. His expression was odd.

Something leaped in her breast. "What?" she said. "What is it?"

"My good woman, there are cobwebs in your hair." He flicked them away with his fingers. "Fairy dust?" he inquired.

Annoyed, Maura longed to slap his hand away. Damn the man! Must he be so observant?

Nor was he done. "And I believe" — he plucked something from the folds of her gown — "yes, I was right. There are bits of fern in your skirt. I expected a few blades of grass. But not ferns. Most assuredly not fairy dust in either case."

Did he tease? Or did he mock? With him,

she could never be sure.

She wet her lips. "I was at the wishing well this morning."

"But there are no ferns there. There is nothing there, save the well."

"I strayed from the path several times." If she was defensive, she couldn't help it. In truth, she had searched the area around the wishing well and all the way down to the loch. "I played with the children this afternoon. Oh, and this morning I spent a little time in the garret. I imagine that's where I picked up the cobwebs."

"The garret?"

Maura was irritated. Must she account for every moment of the day? By heaven, she would not.

Particularly when she'd met Murdoch that morning.

Last night she'd crept into Alec's study. The money Alec had told her about — the money hidden in his desk — was precisely where he'd said it would be. She took nearly all of it and tucked it in the pocket of her robe. She'd given it to Murdoch to take back to Castle McDonough. By the time he returned to Scotland, she hoped her search would be over. Her deceit was wearing on her. With every day that passed, she feared that Alec would discover why she was there.

That could not happen. It would not happen, she assured herself.

Now, if only she believed it!

Maura lifted her chin. "There are some lovely pieces of silver in the garret. I thought to have them cleaned and displayed in one of the parlors."

Blue eyes flickered. "You needn't sound so defensive. After all, you're mistress of the house."

Maura eyed him. What did he mean by that? Oh, good heavens, she was being ridiculous. She *was* the mistress of the house.

For the time being, at least.

"Oh, and by the way," he said, "I stopped by Madame Rousseau's shop. I was pleased that she had a number of gowns completed. By now they're surely tucked away in your armoire."

"I have my stockings, your grace. If you recall, that is all I desired from her shop."

"How fortunate that I wed a woman such as you. There is no need to be frugal, however. And I should be remiss in my duty as husband if I did not wish to shower my bride with gifts."

They stood near a brick wall near the herb garden. The scent of mint teased her nostrils.

The scent of man took precedence as Alec took a step closer.

"I've just noticed we are quite alone, Irish."

Ah, she knew she had cause to be suspicious! The gleam in his eyes made her guard go up. Because of a slight slope in the ground, her eyes were almost level with Alec's. "And so we are," she said briskly.

"I suggest we give each other a proper welcome, then."

Maura's heartbeat skittered.

"Tell me, Irish. Did you miss me?"

She wasn't quite sure what he was up to. She was at a loss for words. "I . . . certainly. Certainly I did."

Alec took a step closer. His gaze fastened on her lips. "Despite your feelings the night before I left?"

"Y-es."

"Your tone leaves me doubting," he said huskily. "Convince me."

Bother, but she couldn't think with him so close! "What?"

"Convince me you're happy I'm home."

"I am happy you're home." The words came out stilted. Alarm skittered up Maura's spine. Less than the width of a hand separated them.

Alec shook his head. "That is hardly the

welcome I hoped for. Come, darling, will you leave me in despair? I ask but a kiss."

Darling? Maura nearly choked. Yet his air was that of a tiger stalking its prey. A very hungry tiger.

Oh, and how she would much rather be the hunter than the prey!

Taking a breath, she leaned forward on tiptoe and brushed her lips against his cheek. She braved no more, for he smelled of soap and sandalwood, and suddenly all she wanted was his mouth on hers, banishing all thought and care. All but the yearning that wound through her whenever he was near — and when he was not!

A lean arm slid around her waist, catching her close. She was forced to steady herself by splaying a hand on his chest.

"That was hardly convincing," he chided. "What must I do to lure my wife back into my embrace? What must I do to entice her willingly and without question?"

Maura's breath thinned to a wisp. Moored in her breast was a sea of uncertainty. Something in his air was unsettling.

"Put your arms around my neck, Irish. Kiss me the way you kissed me in Ireland. Cling to me the way you did then."

She could hardly speak. "You toy with me," she said, her voice very low.

"Never. Do I not stir you as you stirred me that night in Ireland? What has changed since then, I wonder?" His gaze roved her features.

Maura fought to keep all expression from her face. The only way she could manage was to lower her eyes, which then focused directly on the sculpted smoothness of his lips.

"Ah, Maura, you leave me no choice but to convince you."

Her insides were churning. She could scarcely breathe, let alone talk, yet somehow she managed. "And just how might you do that, Scotsman?"

"One kiss at a time," he whispered just before his mouth closed over hers.

Indeed, it took but one kiss to plunge her into desire. And aye, her arms stole willingly around his neck. His mouth parted hers; warm breath mingled with hers. His kiss was burning. Masterful. Persuasive. It made her come all undone, weak in the knees and wanting. Yet there was something in his manner that warned her to beware —

She tore her mouth away. "Why?" she cried. "Why do you continue to kiss me like that?"

"Why do you let me?" he countered.

"You didn't want me as your wife," she

reminded him unsteadily.

"That doesn't mean I don't want you in my bed."

Everything inside her seemed to shatter. It was a blow to the center of her heart. "Am I to be flattered, then? You were hardly the eager bridegroom."

"While you were certainly eager to make yourself my bride."

Maura blanched. "May I remind you it was you who . . . who . . ."

"Claimed your virginity?"

"Aye!" Little wonder that she faltered. Her feelings — her thoughts — were scattered in every direction. She dared not meet his eyes — on several counts. For one, embarrassment flooded her every pore. Secondly, she feared he'd glimpse the lie on her face. Guilt rode heavy on her soul. She couldn't let it sway her. It couldn't be helped. It didn't change what the Black Scotsman had done those many years ago. The Black Scotsman had stolen the lifeblood of every soul on McDonough lands forever after. It didn't change her reason for placing herself at Gleneden. Oh, Lord, she was digging herself ever deeper. She had to make Alec believe it. She had to make him believe her! Because if she didn't, then all her effort would be for nothing. She couldn't leave, not without the Circle.

"I want you in my bed, Maura." His tone was very deliberate. "I daresay that with the exception of that one night in Ireland — that one night," he stressed, "you endeavor to stay out of it."

Maura's face flamed. Her heart lurched. Honesty commanded a high price, a price she could not pay. It was wearing on her, wearing her to the bone. She hated that Alec would surely despise her deceit, and it was killing her.

She had been right to be wary. Aware that he watched her closely, she had the wildest sense he peered directly into her soul.

"Am I wrong, Maura?"

She looked away.

"Look at me, Maura."

She tried to withdraw her arms. He only held her tighter.

"Why? You said I didn't hurt you," he reminded her. "Did I?"

She shook her head.

"Did I please you?"

She bit her lip. She didn't trust herself to speak. She constrained her vision to the plane of his cheek.

"If I did not, I apologize. I understand a woman's first time can be difficult. I regret if that was the case."

Maura cringed inside.

"It is embarrassing to admit I have no recall. I beseech you, share with me what memories you have of our first union. Perhaps I might remember then. Perhaps I might exchange those memories with new ones."

Maura's gaze jerked back to his face. Her pulse skittered. Oh, Lord, she thought in sudden panic, did he know she had drugged him? She had the awful sensation he did.

"You wanted me as much as I wanted you. That, I haven't forgotten, Irish. Yet now you make me doubt my skill as a lover. If not, permit me the chance to change your reluctance."

She was trapped. Caught in a web with no way out. "You mock me, Scotsman."

"I merely question what continues to elude me. But I admit, I am puzzled by your behavior."

"How so?" She could barely force the words past the tightness in her throat.

His gaze never left her face. "You dance away," he said softly. "You dance back. It's almost as if I wed another woman entirely."

Maura felt her cheeks flame. She curled her fists against his chest and pushed herself away.

But there was nowhere to go. His stance

was wide, his shoulders broad. He was every inch the haughty duke. He was like a fortress of stone that could not be breached.

"Come here," he said softly.

She shook her head.

"I'd enjoy a bit of a tussle." There was a pause. "In bed or out," he added silkily.

Maura knew her eyes were huge. "Alec —"

"I'm a man, not a boy, Irish. I'm acquainted with the pangs of desire. I'm well acquainted with the desire in you, Duchess. Your lips do not hide what you seek to hide. I've tasted the passion in you, in every kiss we've ever shared. In the heat of your body, the dew between your thighs, every breathless little sigh into my mouth. I cannot rob what you give freely."

Her composure was fraying. She felt as if she were in a maze, twisting and turning, unable to find the way out.

"How long, I wonder, will you continue to deny me?"

"I — I do not deny you."

"Oh, but you do."

Maura stepped back. Her hand went instinctively to the pouch in her pocket. She gripped it, pulling it out, curling her fingers around it, willing it to give her strength.

"May we continue this discussion tomorrow? It has been —"

"Ah, yes, I know. A tiring day. Or perhaps the ache in your head has returned." This time he did mock her. "Run, Irish. Run away once more. But it won't be long before I catch you."

Maura swallowed. But when she turned, her slipper caught in the hem of her skirt. She would have gone down if Alec hadn't snared her elbow.

And somehow her little velvet pouch slipped from her grasp and fell to the grass.

Alec bent down and caught it in his palm. His expression changed to one of curiosity as he felt the weight within it. "Perhaps I'm the one who needs a sprinkling of your fairy dust."

He nudged the strings apart. Maura tried to stop him but then everything inside her froze. It was as if she watched from some far distant place as Alec opened the pouch and turned it upright.

The contents spilled into his palm. Dirt and stones sifted through his fingers to the ground.

And he laughed. *He laughed.*

"Well, if that isn't the damnedest bit of fairy dust I've ever seen."

CHAPTER SIXTEEN

Maura made a choked sound. Stricken, her gaze lifted to his. "Damn you, Alec Mc-Bride. Damn you —" There was a tiny break in her voice. "— you bloody Scotsman!"

It was suddenly too much to bear. Only half aware of what she was doing, she picked up her skirts and ran toward the hall. She leapt over an exposed root. Behind her she heard a curse. Alec had not been so adept. A quick glance confirmed his stumble.

Inside, she bolted toward the back stairway, her feet flying ever faster.

Run, Irish. Run away again. But it won't be long before I catch you.

The words merely fostered her flight. He was still behind her, but he was gaining, his tread on the stairs heavy and swift.

Her breath came in ragged spurts. The door to her room was open. She bolted through, then tried to close it.

Too late. Alec shouldered it wide, then

jammed it closed with the heel of his hand.

He turned. Maura stood in the middle of her room, her eyes full of angry accusation.

"Maura!" His tone reflected his consternation. His bewilderment. He advanced to where she stood. "What the devil is wrong? Why did you run? It was just a handful of pebbles and earth." He reached for her.

She batted his hand away. "It wasn't," she nearly screamed. "It was a piece of my home. A piece of my heart!"

"Maura! I don't understand."

She flung herself at him then, thumping his chest with her fists. "It was Ireland. My father's lands. My lands."

"McDonough lands?" Realization began to set in. Alec caught her wrists.

Maura wrenched herself free. "Aye!" she cried. "You've robbed us again. But I swear, you've robbed us for the last time, you bloody Black Scotsman!"

All strength drained from her limbs. She sank to the floor. Utterly desolate, she hugged her arms around herself and began to rock back and forth. Her shoulders heaved but she made no sound.

Alec stared down at her helplessly. Something tightened in his breast. It hurt to see her like this.

"For God's sake, Irish." Sinking down to

his knees, his arms closed around her. He pulled her close. Even then she tried to resist. His beautiful, spirited Irish rose . . . When she curled her hands into fists, he brought her closer, wedging them against his chest. He held her captive, firm but not hurtful.

"Maura . . . Maura, listen to me." His murmur stirred the hairs at her temple. "I'm sorry. Set your mind at rest, sweet. What, did you think you'd never return to Ireland? You'll see your people again. You can return anytime you like. You have only to say it and it will be done."

He meant to reassure her. But it appeared his words had the opposite effect. It was as if she curled into herself. It wasn't something he could see. But he felt it.

And then she broke into dry, jagged sobs.

It was like a knife to the throat. A slash upon his heart.

Throughout the storm that raged within her body, Alec held her. Held her until she lay limp against his shoulder, his throat oddly tight.

For a long, long time they remained like that — Alec's arms around her, Maura's cheek pressed into the hollow of his shoulder.

She gave a small, breathy sigh.

In turn, Alec caught one small, feminine fist and pressed a kiss upon her knuckles.

She stirred against him.

Alec lifted his head to look at her. His half smile ebbed.

Her hair had come undone. It showered over her back and shoulders, a black, silken rope. Alec sucked in a breath.

With a subtle tightening of his arm, he brought them both to their feet.

Within the span of an instant something changed. Everything changed. Passion supplanted protectiveness. Desire unseated comfort.

The very air between them was charged with fever-pitch awareness.

Slowly, he lowered his head. Their lips touched . . . clung. Her hands curled against him. With a small sound in her throat, she angled her head to meet him fully.

He deepened the kiss by degrees. Lingeringly. Her lips parted beneath his; she opened to him like a flower beneath the summer sun. Every fiber in his being surged to explosiveness. He tamped it down, when all he longed for was to be inside her, driving deep and hard. His mind was buzzing. It felt like he'd waited a lifetime for this kiss . . . for this woman.

This time he was the one who dragged his

mouth away.

Her head ducked low. Her breath was shallow and quick. Her hair sheltered her face. He pushed it aside, tucking the silken strands behind her ear. His thumb traced down her cheek.

"Open your eyes, Maura. Let me see you." Within his tone lurked a quiet command.

Her gaze climbed slowly up to his mouth. It rested there for long, immeasurable moments before lifting to his eyes.

Their eyes cleaved.

There was no evading him now.

Pinned beneath the power of his gaze, Maura felt herself sway. Her anger had drained. A stark, painful longing cut through her. She was weary, so weary of being forever on guard against him. Weary of fighting her own treacherous longing. She wanted to yield. She wanted to be caught. She wanted to be held. She wanted to be his.

She wanted to belong to Alec McBride, the Black Scotsman.

"I did not lie when I said I want you in my bed." He delivered the words with unmistakable deliberation. "I want you, Irish. I want you now." He scoured her face intently. Even with her cheeks stained with tears, to him she had never been more beautiful. "Tell me you feel the same."

"I do," she whispered tremulously. And then again, this time echoing a vibrant need: "I do want you, Alec. I do."

The words had scarcely left her mouth than he lifted her; her toes left the floor. She felt the knotted hardness of his bicep as he swung her around, high in his arms. But it wasn't to her bed that he directed his steps.

It was to his.

He closed the connecting door between their rooms with the heel of his boot. Their mouths still fused, he lowered her to the floor. His fingers were busy undoing the buttons of her gown. He caressed every inch of flesh bared to him.

In some faraway corner of her mind she realized she should stop him. There was too much at stake for her to abandon her cause without care. Without conscience.

But in that moment she didn't care. Resolve unraveled. Decision was impossible. Kissing Alec was an insidious pleasure, she decided hazily. An almost sinful pleasure. It lured like a drug. She wanted more; she couldn't get enough of him.

His mouth pulled slightly away. He cursed the encumbrance of clothing even as he attacked and dispensed with each layer.

Frustration prompted his declaration.

"I swear I am going to burn every gown you own, Irish." He dragged her bodice from her shoulders. A kiss was dropped on the swell of each breast, thrust high by her corset. "From this moment on you need not bother with the nuisance of clothing. I decree it."

"What, do you fancy yourself king, sir?"

"Aye, and you are my queen. My pirate queen."

"And you my pirate lord." Maura's laugh was breathless.

The last of her petticoats dropped to the floor. Alec bent low and began to peel away her stockings. He stroked the back of one knee, glancing up at her. "Lovely. A gift from an ardent admirer?" He glanced up at her.

The caress made her shiver inside. "Perhaps you should tell me, your grace."

"Oh, aye." He chuckled. Silver lights danced in his eyes. They were beautiful, so clear and blue, almost crystalline. "A most ardent admirer."

Maura's heart turned over. It felt wonderful, to tease with him like this. Alec was on his feet now. He fell silent. Those beautiful blue eyes roamed over her, every square inch of her. And now they burned with a hot, molten glow.

Maura felt a blush rise, from the bottom of her feet clear to her face. Only then did she realize it was still daylight; late afternoon sunlight seemed to cast a halo over her nudity.

Filled with nervous modesty, she tried to step close. Alec shook his head.

"Not yet, my love. Let me look at you."

My love. Oh, if only he meant it!

Maura held her breath while his eyes journeyed slowly down the length of her. A decidedly rakish smile curved his lips. "A pity I have no patience."

She blinked. "What?"

His smile widened. "It wasn't so very long ago, my pirate queen, that you confided you loved to dance naked around the fire. I admit, this is a sight I should like to see."

Maura smothered a groan. Alec laughed and shrugged free of his shirt. "You are discharged of the request," he told her. "At least for today."

He shed his clothing with equal haste to those he'd shed from her. Maura's pulse began to pound as he bore her to the bed. A push and his trousers slid down his legs.

Sunshine spilled through the windows, bathing him as it had bathed her, and for a mind-shattering instant he stood there, the sunlight behind him gilding his frame.

It left nothing to the imagination.

Her heart tripped. Her mouth went desert dry.

Alec McBride, Duke of Gleneden, was not a man one could ever ignore. There was about him an intensity of presence that commanded attention, whether one willed it or not. From the very first time she spied him at Lord Preston's masquerade, towering over all others, she had experienced that pulse of sheer, explosive energy.

Nude, the man was even more impressive.

His form was perfectly proportioned, all sleek, fluid length as he stretched out beside her. Her heart bounded forward. Alec's desire was . . . well, just as impressively — just as abundantly — proportioned. Oh, yes, she was well aware when that element of his desire sprang taut and free against her belly. Indeed, she sucked in a breath of shock.

Alec's smile faded.

"Look at me, Irish."

Maura's cheeks were fiery hot. Her gaze trickled to his. With his thumb, he traced the shape of her mouth.

"I told myself I didn't want you, Irish. I told myself that I didn't need . . . this."

He shocked her by pressing the ridge of his hips against the flat of her belly.

Lean fingers slid beneath her hair, curling around her nape. "I was a fool, Irish. I was wrong. So very wrong." His voice plummeted to a whisper. "You stir me. You torture me. You slay me."

Each word might have been an echo of her own.

He kissed her, slowly at first — oh, so slowly! And then with mounting fervor — with fevered hunger, a soul-blistering kiss that left them both vying for air.

"You are exquisite."

Alec's hand climbed the rise of her ribs. Laid claim to one breast, toying with the peak, splaying his fingers wide. With a muffled exclamation, he fed her nipple into his mouth.

Shivers washed over her skin. Her breasts puckered and swelled. He allowed no embarrassment, no time for anything but sweet, sheer sensation. Her fingers shaped the back of his neck, coiling in his hair.

Alec raised his head. His eyes were burning.

His hand trapped hers, bringing it down . . . down ever more. Maura's heart plunged into a frenzy. Her gaze ventured the very same path. The tips of her fingers raked the hair-roughened plane of his chest. His belly. Clear to the mass of dark coarse hair that surrounded his shaft, thrusting. His hand engulfed hers. With the pressure of his fingers, a subtle tightening, he closed her fingers around him . . . Maura was stunned. Her eyes widened. If anything, he swelled harder. The knowledge that she aroused him so was heady. Thrilling. Yet spinning through her mind was the question of how she . . . how could they . . .

And then even that was lost when he touched her, there between her thighs, a bold possession that sent a shock of sensation deep in the pit of her belly. He traced the lips of her channel, executing a rhythm that drove her half wild. He circled the secret little nugget buried within her nest of curls. In some distant part of her, she was stunned; it was as if her body searched for this blatantly erotic caress.

Her lungs emptied in a rush. "Alec," she gasped. "Alec —"

His mouth trapped hers. "It's all right, sweet. Let me. Let me touch you. Let me please you."

Maura writhed. She melted against him. Around him.

"Aye, lass, that's the way. Don't hold back. Just let it happen. Just . . . let it happen."

Her breath sheared. Something inside her gave way. Swamped with sensation, her body pulsed its release. She was dimly aware of crying out.

When sanity returned, Alec was braced above her.

His knees spread her wide. Her gaze was riveted to his rod, thick and fever hot, the swollen tip buried within damp feminine folds.

Maura flinched. She couldn't help it. She buried her face against the side of his neck, aware of a deepening pressure. She could feel herself being stretched. Widened. Instinctively she sought to clamp her thighs together.

"Alec —" His name was half choked. "Alec, I . . . we did not —"

"I know. I know." His head turned ever so slightly. "Do you trust me, Irish?"

She drew a shuddering breath. "Aye," she said helplessly. "Aye!"

He pulled himself out. The head of his rod glistened.

Maura drew a ragged breath. Her gaze was drawn to his face. His features were taut with rigid strain. The cords on his neck stood out.

Only then did she realize the restraint he exercised. Raw emotion filled her throat. Something inside her caved way.

"Alec!" she cried. "Alec!"

Alec was just as affected as she was. He hissed in a sizzling breath. Sweet Jesus, she was hot. Silky and slick around the head of his cock. He tried to be slow. He tried to hold back. But when she offered up tremulous lips, it was more than he could stand.

With a hoarse sound of need, he plunged forward. He felt the tearing of her virgin flesh. His lips swallowed the tiny little gasp she made. Something purely primitive, purely possessive, pounded through him. She belonged to him. She was his. His.

Embedded as far as he could go, he kissed her lips. Her cheek. The hollow at the base of her throat. His hands caught hers. Their fingers threaded. Twined.

Their bellies pressed. Sealed. Their mouths clung. Her breath belonged to him — as his belonged to her. With every breath, with every heartbeat, he plunged closer to her womb.

"Maura," he said raggedly. "Maura."

His thrusts pierced deeper. And then he was lunging, with tender fierceness. Each plunge bringing him closer to her womb. Closer to the edge. With every breath, with every heartbeat.

She made a tiny sound. Of need. Alec kissed her mouth, the arch of her throat. And then she was burning. There was fever in her veins. A blaze in her heart. And then she felt herself pitched into a void, exploding in a raw, sizzling climax.

And this time she was not alone.

CHAPTER SEVENTEEN

Sprawled above her, Alec was still gasping for air when reality set in. His suspicions had just been confirmed.

Maura was — had been until this very day — a virgin.

He eased to his side, waiting until his pulse slowed before he rolled to his feet. Without a word, he went to the washstand and filled a small basin. His blood was still boiling hot. But not from passion. Not from desire. In its stead was a furious betrayal.

Wetting a cloth, he returned to the bedside, slipped a hand behind Maura's left knee and tugged it up.

Her thighs tensed. She made a faint, jerky movement.

Alec's fingers tightened ever so slightly. Wordlessly he shook his head.

The cloth touched tender woman's flesh.

The sound she made was half strangled. His gaze immediately swung to her face.

"Are you all right?" He brushed aside a tangle of dark hair from her cheek.

"Aye," she said faintly.

Alec resumed his task, carefully wiping away the inside of her thighs — the traces of their union. His head was down. Intent. His ministrations were a stark contrast between the gentleness of his touch and the iron cast of his jaw. Maura's face burned. Somehow this seemed far more intimate than the straining pressure of him inside her, hard and deep — as deep as he could go.

At last he rose. As if his nakedness were of absolutely no consequence, he picked up the washbasin and set it on the stand. Without breaking his stride, he continued on into her room. Still puzzling why as she grasped for the sheet, he returned and dropped the night robe draped over the screen in her room into her lap. Maura donned it, while Alec reached for his own from the armoire near the window. He turned, granting her an all-encompassing view, a scant five feet away.

Maura struggled not to look, yet in the end she capitulated. His organ was soft now; a trace of her blood still lingered.

She sucked in a breath.

Alec smiled tightly.

He gestured toward the fireplace.

"Sit, if you please." His tone was ever so pleasant.

Holding her breath, Maura moved to sit in the nearest wing chair.

In some faraway realm in her mind she registered his tone of utter politeness.

She soon discovered her mistake.

She eyed him warily as he moved to stand before the fireplace. Her pulse picked up its rhythm. Clothed or unclothed, she was more heart-stoppingly aware of this man than ever. Her gaze was unwittingly drawn to the wedge of dark hair on his chest, revealed by his robe. She tried to stop it — to no avail. Knowing he was naked beneath the robe was both exciting and unnerving. He made her heart leap all over again. Maura hadn't reckoned on that. She'd thought that being with a man would banish all reserve.

When her gaze finally climbed to his face, he smiled tightly. Not until then did she realize he was keenly aware of her scrutiny. Indeed, he seemed to take a certain pleasure in it.

Her tongue came out to moisten her lips. Wicked was what he was. Wickedly attractive. Wickedly beautiful, as well, she conceded. His legs and buttocks were all muscle, the plane of his back and shoulder cleanly defined and sculpted.

"My darling Maura," he said smoothly, "I find myself puzzled. Perhaps you can help me; indeed, you are surely the only one who can help me. It seems I've accomplished a highly unusual feat — that of claiming my wife's virtue — why, not once, but twice."

Maura quivered inside. His anger lay veiled in silk.

"Nothing to say, my love? How fortunate, then, that I recall what you said, Duchess, the night of our arrival here. You informed me that I had already seen to the plucking of the fruit — that it can be plucked only once. You — please forgive me if I do not recall your exact words — you seemed to particularly relish informing me that I needn't feel compelled to provide you with a night of marital bliss."

Again, that tone of polished civility. Maura winced inside. His wording, she knew, was quite accurate.

Hands linked together behind his back, his gaze — his tone — stabbed at her. "You relieved me of that particular obligation, as you put it, Duchess. How is it, then, that a journey that began as a fetching little pirate in Ireland landed you here at Gleneden — once again in my bed — and once again, a virgin's blood upon the sheets."

Maura drew a shuddering breath. "Alec —"

"Am I a lucky man? Or a foolish one, taken in by my wife's claim that I had wronged her? At least I know why she spurned my advances once we were in Scotland — she wished to hide the fact that she had never lain with me — with any man! No, she couldn't risk being discovered!" He gave a black laugh. "Perhaps I am lucky. At least this time I remember it."

Maura braved a glance at him. A mistake. There was a storm alight in his pale blue eyes. Only then did she realize how furious he truly was. She almost wished he would bluster and rage, instead of this frosty cold facade.

She eyed the door to the hallway. Then the door to her room.

"Don't even think of it," he growled.

Silently she bequeathed on him an ancient Irish curse.

"I gather you had a hand in my lapse in memory?"

Maura's lips pressed together.

He was impatient. "I know I was drugged, Maura. You may as well tell me how it was achieved."

She confined her vision to her robe,

smoothing the folds.

"Look at me, Irish." His tone was almost dangerously soft. "How was it accomplished?"

She was tempted to tell him to go to the devil. Almost . . . but not quite. "A mix of herbs. From Toothless Nan." Her chin climbed high. "To make you sleep."

An unending silence. Then: "Toothless Nan? Toothless Nan?" he exploded. "What is this? Have I been spirited back to the Middle Ages?"

Maura's eyes flashed. "Toothless Nan knows of such things — of potions and herbs! By heaven," she said feelingly, "I should have summoned Nan instead of a physician the day my father died!" Even as she said it, darkness settled over her like a shroud. It wouldn't have helped. Nothing could have prevented it. Nothing could have saved him. Nothing. He would have died anyway.

Claimed by the curse. Held captive by the curse.

It did not help that Alec's mind veered in the same direction. "Your father," he said curtly. "Is he truly dead?"

Maura was stunned. "Do you think I would lie about my father's death?" Bitterness etched her words.

Alec walked to the end of the fireplace, then back. He stopped, crossing his arms over his chest.

"And your mother? She was not acquainted with the baron's late wife, was she?"

"My mother was laid to rest when I was a wee one."

"And you had never met the baron before then?"

She shook her head.

"It was just a ruse to get you into the masquerade?"

"Aye."

"So it was no accident you sought me out."

"You seem to have all the answers, your grace. What do you think?"

A muscle ticked in Alec's jaw. This was not the time to challenge him.

She continued, "If you're looking for someone to blame, your grace, you need not look any further."

"So you lied about who you were?"

She surged upright. "I did not lie! I am Lady Maura O'Donnell. My father was the earl!"

Alec clenched his teeth. McBride, he thought. She was no longer Maura O'Donnell. She was Maura McBride.

"And Murdoch, your uncle?" he demanded. "By heaven, he allowed you to come here alone? He abandoned you not knowing what kind of man I am? What I might do once we were alone?"

Maura thought of Murdoch, not so very far away in the next village. She cautiously decided that was best left unsaid.

He regarded her — regarded her until the silence that spun out was suffocating. "You're hiding something," he said softly. "What, I wonder? What role did he play in this?"

Maura couldn't help it. Her gaze veered away, while Alec's sharpened.

"Out with it, Irish!"

"Murdoch is not my uncle," she said finally. She chose her words carefully. "He is . . . has been with my family for years."

"He's been with your family for years, eh? I suppose next you'll be telling me he's the family butler!"

Her eyes flew wide.

Alec swore. "Sweet heaven, he is, isn't he?"

He didn't need Maura's affirmation to know it was true. Her features told the tale all too keenly.

"You tricked me into marriage," he charged. "Why, Maura? Did you relish making a fool of me?"

"Think what you will, but it wasn't like that. It wasn't like that at all."

Alec gave a self-mocking laugh. "Then how was it? By God, I don't know what to believe! You deceived me, Maura. You tricked me into marriage. You've lied — by God, I cannot begin to guess how much. Why me, Duchess? Why did you purposely seek me out that night? I'm entitled to an explanation."

Maura looked away. Rather, she tried to. He captured her shoulders. "Oh, no. There'll be no turning away this time."

The air between them was sizzling. "Aye," she cried out. "Aye, I deceived you. Aye, I tricked you. But I did not relish it."

"And what just happened? The two of us together, Maura? Was that part of your plan?"

Her heart squeezed. A wrench of shame went through her. He couldn't know the guilt she felt. But she knew that if it happened all over again, her choice would have been no different.

His mouth twisted. "I see that it wasn't. Why then, Maura? Why?"

There was a stifling heaviness in her chest. She braved the biting demand in his eyes as best she could.

"I needed to find you. I — I needed to

come here. To Scotland. To Gleneden."

"And I was the means?"

"Yes! Yes! It was the only way I could think to come here. To stay and not arouse your suspicions. To search for the Black Scotsman —"

"The Black Scotsman!" He made a sound of impatience. "It's just a name conjured up by some silly young maids —"

"No. Not you, Alec. The pirate. The first Black Scotsman. The real Black Scotsman." The instant she spoke his name, it was as if her veins filled with ice.

His eyes narrowed. He tugged her down on a small settee, his expression grim. "What the devil is this? Maura, you make no sense."

"What the devil, indeed." Her tone was fervent. "The portrait downstairs. James, the seventh Duke of Gleneden. The one who wore the black glove. You said it yourself — that he was a nasty fellow — and he was, Alec. Far more than you realize."

Alec made no remark.

"You didn't know, did you? That he was a pirate. No one knew."

His eyes narrowed. "Nonsense. My lineage is honorable. Respectable —"

"Oh, stop! I daresay all families have skeletons in the closet."

"If no one else knew he was a pirate, what makes you so certain he was?" He was thin-lipped and abrupt.

Maura suddenly shivered. "I know, Alec. *I know.* And my father did, too. That's what brought me here. That's what brought me to you."

She recounted the myth then. How the Circle of Light brought fortune and favor to those of the Clan McDonough.

How the Black Scotsman plundered the seas, concealing his identity.

How he stole the Circle of Light.

She told of how death came to Randall O'Donnell, the lord who had lost the Circle of Light to the Black Scotsman. Pain bled through to her voice. "It happened just this way to my father, and my father's father before him. Death, without warning. Death, so unexpected, since the time of Randall O'Donnell, grandfather to my grandfather!"

Alec's lips pressed together. "This is what you meant when you said I'd robbed you?"

"Aye."

Alec said nothing.

"You don't believe me?" she cried.

"An enchanted Celtic relic come down through the ages? One that no one has seen — provided it even exists! — for nearly two hundred years? Maura, you've begun to believe in the tales you tell the children."

Her eyes grew stormy. "You would not doubt it if you saw my homeland."

Alec thought of Thomas Gates. Very soon he would know.

"My family was cursed when the Black Scotsman stole the Circle of Light, because we failed to protect it. Yours was cursed as well. Cursed by Randall O'Donnell as he sailed into the night. Cursed when the Black Scotsman stole the Circle of Light!"

"Look around you, Maura. Does it look as if we've been cursed?"

"And can you say with certainty that no ill has befallen your family?"

"No more than any other."

"What of your father? You told me how he suffered, Alec. How you watched him die little by little, more and more with each day."

"That had nothing to do with your Circle of Light. And aye, my mother lost three children. But that, too, was fate." He made a gesture of impatience. "Chance. Destiny. It wasn't because of any curse."

"You said your sister and cousin were caught out on the loch one night. Everyone was frantic. They might have died, Alec."

"But they didn't." He dismissed it. "It was a freak storm."

"I promised my father, Scotsman. I promised him I would find the Circle of Light and bring it home — home so our people would no longer suffer — so the land is green and fertile and flourishes as it once did. Help me," she implored. "Help me, that I may return home and put an end to this curse once and for all."

Alec got to his feet. "You may have married me to find some ancient Celtic relic that may or may not exist. But that doesn't change the fact that you are my wife," he declared with a touch of arrogance. "I told you earlier you could return to Ireland whenever you wished. I would never begrudge you that. But this is your home now, Maura. Gleneden is your home."

Maura's heart pinched. Her head bowed low. "No," she said painfully. "Ireland is my home. Ireland . . . not Gleneden."

There was a thundering silence.

Alec's eyes flickered. "It no longer matters how or why we married. It cannot be undone. I am your husband. You are my wife."

She shook her head. "No," she said. "No."

Catching her elbows, he brought her to her feet. "What the devil! Do you mean to tell me there is more you've withheld from me?"

Maura's nerves were screaming, but her

heart went very still.

"Aye," she said faintly.

His expression was forbidding. Utterly fierce. She closed her eyes to shut out the sight of it.

But there was no solace. No sanctuary. No hiding anymore.

She swallowed. "Alec," she whispered. "We are not wed."

CHAPTER EIGHTEEN

The silence that followed was brittle. Brutal.

He released her.

Her eyes opened. There was no evading his. He stared at her, his features fierce. The touch of his eyes was an icy blue, as chilling as the northern seas. One look from those icy blue eyes sent a shiver running through her — but hardly one of delight.

Maura felt cut to the bone. It was all she could do to brave such chilling regard. Alec was again the peremptory duke.

His mouth was a taut, straight line. "Explain yourself, if you please."

Her pulse clamored. She discovered she was shaking inside and out. Damn the man, but he could be quite intimidating when he chose!

"Deacon O'Reilly . . . Murdoch found him. You were right, you see. We — I — paid him to perform the ceremony. But he had no authority to preside over our wedding.

Over any wedding. He was stripped of all privileges in the Church when he was discovered stealing from the church fund."

He offered no reply. Maura had the fleeting sensation he didn't dare speak.

That he was furious, there was no question. His lips were ominously thin. His quiet fury was almost worse than if he'd shouted. She had never realized that quiet could be so unnerving.

She swallowed. "It was never meant to come this far."

Alec's regard skidded to the bed. It was no accident his gaze lingered on the stain where they had lain. "Clearly," he bit off, "it wasn't."

Maura winced at his icy barb. "I thought it would be easy to find the Circle. I thought to return to Ireland long before this. A week, at most. I — I thought you could explain my departure by saying I died in the crossing back to Ireland."

His eyes seemed to sizzle. The silence spun out. Maura stood still while he walked pointedly around her to stand at the window, his profile forged in iron. She had the feeling he was gathering himself in hand.

At length he turned. "Well, then," he stated coolly, "there's nothing else to be done, is there? We'll marry. At once."

Maura was stunned. "What?"

"As soon as it can be arranged."

Her head was spinning. "You want to marry me?"

"It's not a question of want. It's a question of needs-must."

She stiffened. "Why, thank you, your grace, for that reassurance."

His tone turned sharp. "It must be done, Maura. You know it as well as I."

"I know of no such thing. You think that because you are the Duke of Gleneden, that I must heed you. Well, I think not, Scotsman." Anger overrode caution. It banished all else. "You may be master of Gleneden, Alec McBride, but you will not master me. You forget, I am not your wife, nor will I ever be your wife."

"You refuse my proposal?"

"That was a proposal? I perceived it as a demand. Besides, do you expect me to be flattered? I came to recover the Circle, which was stolen," she stressed, "by your ancestor, the bloody Black Scotsman."

"So you would bed down with me yet not marry me?"

Maura flinched inside. Must he make it sound sordid?

"Ah, but it was never supposed to happen, was it?"

"Aye. All the more reason we must forget." Her tone was very low. Her reality was painfully acute. "I belong in Ireland. My clan needs me, now more than ever since my father is dead." A faint bitterness crept in. "And you certainly did not hide your aversion for our marriage when we stood in the baron's garden. I should think you'd be glad we are not wed. That I am not after your title or riches or any of your —" She broke off.

His gaze homed in on hers. "What, have you spirited away the silver?"

Maura swallowed.

"Dear Lord, you have, haven't you?"

Her chin lifted. "A few pieces from the attic. Some of the rooms. The pin money you said I might have. Nothing you will ever miss. We need the money far more than you."

"Let me guess how you accomplished this." His brows lifted. "Murdoch?"

There was no point in lying. "Aye, he is near. So you see, he did not abandon me after all."

The air was charged and crackling. He gave a bitter laugh. "Oh, but this is rich! My own wife — who was really never my wife — is a plundering thief!" He paused. "But I will soon know the truth for myself,

Irish. Whether or not your lands are as barren as you say."

"What the devil does that mean?"

"Oh, come, sweet. You cannot deny the circumstances of our 'marriage' warranted suspicion . . . and warrant confirmation."

Maura was still grappling with a dawning awareness. She would soon know the truth herself.

Her eyes never left his face. "You sent someone to Ireland? You sent someone to spy on me?"

"I would hardly call it spying, Irish. I consider it more of a mission to ascertain the truth."

She was too furious to speak.

Alec's gaze slid down her body. "You do realize there now exists the possibility that you may soon carry my heir?"

"Your heir! Need I remind you we are not wed?"

"Precisely the reason we should be." His tone was clipped and abrupt. "Or does Toothless Nan have a potion for that, too?"

Maura caught her breath. Oh, but that was cruel of him. "Then my heir will grow up in the land you so fondly call that soggy bog of an isle."

He looked at her. "Has it occurred to you that I have every right to pitch you out this very day?"

A jolt went through her. She felt herself pale.

"Yes, Irish, I see that you do."

Her anger eroded. Her lungs burned, yet it was as if she were frozen in place. She could only watch numbly as he shoved his legs into his trousers, then reached for his shirt.

Despair shattered her. "Alec." His name was half strangled. "Alec, please do not! Aye, I deceived you. Aye, I lied! But I beg you, please let me stay and find the Circle. Help me find the Circle. Then I will be gone. Out of your life forever."

He shoved his feet into his boots, stood and started toward the door.

"Alec. Alec, what are you doing? Where are you going?"

His features were grim, his voice clipped and distinct. "Since you are not my wife, I certainly don't expect that you care where I go — or what I do."

The door slammed, and then he was gone.

Maura erupted into tears.

Alec planted his hands on the back of the chair in his study. Lowering his head, he squeezed hard, struggling to control the heat that still swirled in his body. He inhaled deeply, but it did little to quell the upheaval inside him.

Maura was right. He told himself he should be glad she wasn't his bride. She had schemed. Lied. With no qualms whatsoever. It was just as he'd said. He had every right to cast her out.

But it gave him no satisfaction knowing that he'd been right after all. That his so-called marriage to the lovely Maura happened because she wanted something from him — the chance to search for some mythical object that no doubt had ever existed!

But his fury vied with a heart in torment.

I belong in Ireland.

No. She belonged here. With him.

But she had refused his proposal. Refused it! Refused him!

He was stung to the marrow of his bones. His mind — his very soul — was in turmoil.

He could almost believe she was an Irish witch. He was bewitched. Bedazzled. Beguiled.

As if she'd cast some spell over him!

It would also account for her belief in such nonsense as the Circle of Light, he decided with black humor.

Just when he'd begun to trust her, he learned the truth.

It wasn't him she wanted, but this damned

Circle of Light. How she could believe in something so absurd, he had no idea.

But she had trembled against him. Burned for him in passionate surrender.

The thought nearly brought his rod rising once again.

With an impatient exclamation, he headed outside to the stable. He needed a good long ride to clear his head.

Before he knew it, he was at the cove where he'd taken her that first day at Gleneden, and climbed over the rocks to where he could sit. He recalled telling her how he and Aidan played at being pirates when they were young.

Never in his life would he have guessed that his lovely bride believed in a pirate called the Black Scotsman — and his ancestor yet!

Never in his life would he have guessed that she had come to Gleneden to seek out a treasure this pirate had claimed.

What was it she had said?

A curse should never be taken lightly, Scotsman.

For a fraction of a moment an eerie tingle danced along his spine.

He shook it off and stared out across the water, listening to waves lap at the shoreline. He watched the sun blaze on the horizon, then plummet beneath. For an instant it was as if he saw something he'd never seen before — a hazy silhouette of a pirate's vessel, cutting through to the south and west.

To Ireland.

A long time later he got to his feet and mounted his horse for the ride back to Gleneden. He recalled Maura's face when he told her he had every right to pitch her out.

Her expression had been utterly stricken, her beautiful green eyes shadowed and dark. It was an image that would not leave him.

He searched the stormy seas in his heart. He would help on her foolish quest for her precious Circle. Oblige her until her belief was laid to rest. And then . . . and then . . .

He didn't know.

All he knew was that the very thought of letting her go tore at his heart as nothing had ever done before.

Her room was dark when he let himself in, shortly before midnight. Quietly, he approached the bed.

Maura stirred. "Alec?"

His gut twisted. He silently cursed himself, for her voice carried the thready sound of tears.

He sat. Through the dark, his gaze captured hers. With the back of his fingers, he grazed the softness of his cheek, the merest caress.

"After we search for your Circle, it is your wish to return to Ireland?"

He was careful to keep all trace of emotion from his voice.

Her lashes swept down. "I must," she said softly.

His thumb brushed across her lips. "Then so be it."

He rose and started toward the door between their rooms.

"Alec?"

He half turned. "Yes?"

She slipped from beneath the covers and walked to him. Slender arms stole about his neck.

"Thank you," she whispered.

Alec went very still as she raised herself on tiptoe and kissed his mouth — the contact almost fleeting.

But it was a kiss that seared him to the core of his being.

Maura withdrew her arms. Her bare feet eased to the floor. Alec gave a slight nod of acknowledgment.

He wondered if she would ever know it cost him heaven and earth to walk away.

Four days came and went. It was a time of

rising temperatures, of rising heat . . . of rising passion.

Ready to ignite at any time.

For Alec and Maura were equally aware of the other. Having tasted of the other merely sharpened their hunger. And living together under the same roof, knowing the other slept at night with but a single wall between them . . .

Tension simmered, smoldered.

Alec called himself a fool a hundred times over. Why hadn't he insisted that Maura marry him if she wanted to continue her search?

Yet if she despised him for it . . .

He couldn't stand the thought.

Nor did he want her under those circumstances. If she stayed, it must be of her own free will.

Nothing less would satisfy either of them.

Thomas Gates had sent a note that the unexpected arrival of his sister and her children had delayed his trip to Ireland — to McDonough lands. Alec wondered if he'd reacted too hastily in engaging Thomas. No, he decided. He needed the truth.

So it was that his mood was unsettled.

Maura, however, was utterly driven. Intent. As if she could not wait to be away from him. But not for the reason Alec believed.

It was no longer just because of her promise to her father that she wanted so desperately to find the Circle.

It was for Alec, too.

She dreaded what might happen if she did not. Fear clutched at her. She feared for Alec's safety. She had to find the Circle so the curse that bound their families together would finally be broken.

She couldn't bear the thought that something terrible might befall him.

She relived the night he'd come and sat on her bedside. The immeasurably gentle way he'd caressed her cheek. Every time she thought of it, her heart turned over.

She reminded herself that when she found the Circle, she must return to Ireland.

And never see Alec again.

All the more reason to resist him.

All the more reason to deny her own traitorous longing.

The search now renewed, she was grateful for Alec's help. He knew Gleneden as no one else did. But four days of searching in the hall and outside turned up nothing.

Maura was undaunted. Even though the servants had emptied the shelves in the library, she returned there one morning.

Alec came upon her sliding her hands over the paneling beside the fireplace.

"Looking for hidden passages? Secret stairways?" he inquired.

She shot him a murderous look.

"Maura, for heaven's sake, have done with it!"

She spun around to face him. She was insistent, her conviction unwavering. "It's here," she cried. "I just haven't figured out where."

"My ancestors were honorable people."

"And so are mine. Certainly none of mine were pirates!"

"Well, let me think. Suppose you are right. Why would my pirate ancestor — provided I do have such a rogue in my lineage — have hidden such a treasure? Wouldn't he display it? He certainly wouldn't hide it."

There was a mutinous tilt to her chin. "Perhaps not something so precious as the Circle of Light. Everyone would know then that he truly was a plundering pirate. Everyone would know the Black Scotsman was the Duke of Gleneden. I have thought on this a great deal, Alec —"

"I'm quite aware of that, Irish."

Maura scowled at him, but went on. "I imagine he would put it somewhere where he could savor it —"

"The mythical object that no one in this century or the last has ever seen. Whose existence cannot be proven —"

"I don't expect you to care," Maura cried. "It's here. Somewhere. I feel it with every breath. I know it's here at Gleneden."

"If you feel it, if you are so certain, then why haven't you found it before now? Why are we still searching for it?"

"You don't believe me, do you? You don't believe it's here. You don't even believe the Circle exists."

"Forgive me for not being blessed with the superstitions of the Irish," he snapped.

Angry hurt flooded her. Her eyes spitting fire, she started to charge past him.

Alec caught her elbow. "For heaven's sake, Maura, I'm sorry. I shouldn't have put it like that."

Her chin climbed high. "Why not?" she said stiffly. "You are free to speak your mind, and I am entitled to my own beliefs, am I not? Pray forgive me for turning your household upside down, your grace. And do excuse me. I believe I should like to be alone for a while."

"Maura," he said softly. "Maura . . ."

She refused to look at him. Chafing, impatient, he sensed her composure unraveling and let her go.

Perhaps she was right. Perhaps she needed a little time for herself.

CHAPTER NINETEEN

Early in the afternoon, Alec decided to look in on his wife . . . blood and thunder, he'd yet to stop thinking of her as his wife!

She hadn't appeared for luncheon, and . . . well, he was worried about her. Oh, who did he fool? Yes, he was worried. But a little needle of guilt had plagued him ever since she left the library. Indeed, he admitted, from the moment they'd met at the masquerade, thoughts of her never strayed far from his mind.

He rapped lightly on the door between their chambers. There was no answer, nor did he hear any movement. Opening the door, he glanced inside.

He strode back into his room. An hour. If he didn't see her within the hour, he'd check with the servants.

The thought had no sooner flitted through his mind than he did see her, alone in the courtyard. From the corner window of his room, he watched her. She wore no bonnet; indeed, she rarely did, whereas most women would dare not venture a single step outdoors without one. And most women probably wouldn't be out walking in the sunlight without a parasol.

A faint smile creased his lips. Maura was like his sister Anne in that regard. Vanity was not in Anne's nature. There was not a shred of vanity in Maura's either. Faith, but she was so achingly beautiful it nearly stole his breath.

His smile died. Maura's head was low, her gaze directed downward, her hands linked behind her back. He couldn't discern her expression, but it took no stretch of imagination to see that her mood was pensive at best. Perhaps a little dejected . . .

Some strange, twisting emotion unfolded in his chest. There was something achingly poignant about her pose. Was she so unhappy, then? Was it because of him? Because they had made love?

A knifelike stab pierced his gut. It almost seemed she was following some aimless path, occasionally kicking at the pebbled pathway that wove through the flowers. His mind swerved back. He would never forget how he'd dumped out her precious treasure of pebbles and dirt from her home . . . the way it hurt her. The way he had hurt her.

Guilt seared him. If time could stretch back, if he could reclaim that moment — he would give every thing he owned, all that he possessed.

But time was unforgiving.

Time was everlasting.

He could never take back what he'd done.

Just then, out the window, a child ran up to Maura and seized her hand. A second little boy ran out and latched onto the other hand. Then another and another, until they were like a flock surrounding her. A girl no higher than Maura's hip clutched a tiny fistful of her gown. And all at once they were tugging her away, out of the courtyard and down the slope of lawn.

Alec was reminded of the other time he'd watched as Maura held court with the children. Scant wonder they adored her, warming to her from the first. There was a magic, a charm, a beauty in her that could not be captured in words. He delighted in her freshness, their bantering, particularly when pitting anything Irish against the Scots. She was witty and quick, ever ready with a comeback.

She was unlike any other woman. He wanted her as he'd wanted no other woman.

Drawn by a force he felt powerless to

resist, Alec left the house and followed, but he kept his distance. He couldn't have stopped himself from following even if he'd wanted to.

Gathering flowers from nearby, she guided little fingers in making daisy chains as they sat on the ground. The girls beamed as she placed a coronet of flowers on their heads. Little Greta dropped one onto Maura's head.

Maura began to sing — off-key, which made it all the more disarming. On her feet now, she danced an Irish jig. Like leapfrogs, the children jumped up and joined in. Their laughter shrilled into squeals. Maura kicked off her shoes. Her hair had slipped from its knot on her nape. Raven locks streamed wildly behind her as she danced. Then she and the children joined hands and skipped in a wild circle. Shrieks of glee filled the air.

Alec moved closer. Shielded by the trunk of a giant oak, he watched them romp, conscious of an odd sensation growing deep in his chest. He couldn't take his eyes off Maura.

A smile tugged at his lips when her garland of daisies slipped off. She snatched it up and plopped it crookedly atop her head.

Then one of the children spotted him. "Can his grace dance?"

He'd been discovered.

"Come, your grace!" shouted Andrew, Mrs. Yates's youngest grandson. "Come dance with us!"

Alec arched a brow, then held out his hand as Maura twirled close. Her fingers caught his and she pulled him in. Then somehow she and Alec were in the middle, while the little ones danced all around. Alec spun her around and around until Maura was gasping and laughing and dizzy, her face turned up to the sky.

He caught her up against him. Locked fast in his arms, Maura gazed down into eyes of deep blue fire. And in those fiery depths glimmered a fierce yearning.

He wanted to kiss her.

He wanted to kiss her.

What happened next was a blur. Maura was hazily aware of Alec tugging her by the hand. Blindly, she followed until he pulled her around and into his arms, back against the trunk of a tree.

"Alec," she cried. "Alec, what are you doing?"

"What I wanted to do in front of the children."

His eyes were burning. His words thrilled her as nothing else could have. The raw hunger on his face made her mouth go dry.

Her pulse clamored madly. She inhaled sharply. A battle raged inside her. She couldn't — shouldn't! — be with him like this. "Alec," she said weakly, "we can't. We mustn't."

"I know."

The words were a hoarse, ragged mutter.

He didn't stop kissing her. Nor did she want him to. She saw on his face the same desperate desire that she felt.

With stormy heart and quavering limbs, her arms crept around his neck. Everything inside her went weak as he brought her against him. She felt the shape of him through his trousers, quickening in one breath, pulsing and erect against her belly even before the next.

His kiss sapped her strength and left her utterly boneless.

Maura had little recollection of entering the hall by the back entrance. Caught up in his arms, they kissed wildly as he closed the door of his room with the heel of his boot.

Their clothing left a trail to the bed. He deposited her on the bed and followed her down.

"Maura," he whispered. "I want you, sweet."

His tongue sparred with hers. Her breasts

swelled. He caught one ripe, swollen nipple in his mouth. One hand caught her buttocks. The other caught his shaft. He rubbed it between her thighs, parting her damp, dewy pocket to find the nub within. He was fever hot, and hard as stone.

His fingers spread her wide. They were both half mad when he thrust inside. Neither could look away. She moaned. He groaned. It was wild. Tempestuous. He pumped frantically and Maura clung to him blindly, arching her neck as she shuddered her release.

Then Alec collapsed beside her, wrapped an arm around her and pulled her tight against his side. Catching her hand, he kissed her knuckles and drew her hand to the center of his chest, covering it with his own.

Maura laid her head against his shoulder, nestling against his warmth, welcoming the peace that settled over them.

They must have dozed for a time. The next thing she knew, a kiss as light as a feather brushed across her lips.

She pursed her lips and kept her eyes screwed shut.

"Maura" — laughter laced that low male voice — "you're quite enchanting when you pout, sweet. But if it isn't too much bother,

329

might I have a moment of your time?"

By then it was all Maura could do to smother a laugh. But she managed to keep her eyes tightly closed.

"Why is it that I am always rousing you from sleep? Let me ponder a moment." He released a mock sigh. "Hmmm. I believe I may have the answer. I think perhaps the only way to stop rousing you from sleep is to never let you sleep." The next thing she knew, her hand was lifted from its perch on his chest and placed on a muscled, hairy thigh.

Maura's eyes popped open. There was no question that this was a part of him that no longer slept.

Alec gave a husky laugh at her expression of shock.

"What?" she said faintly. "Again?"

"I see that I have your full attention now," he teased.

He propped himself on an elbow and gazed the length of her. Maura blushed to the very roots of her hair, prompting another husky laugh.

Alec's eyes, so warm and tender and so very, very blue, made her breath catch and her heart turn over.

Leaning over, he kissed her. There was no hungry demand, just an achingly sweet kiss she felt in every corner of her being.

He drew back. "Raise your hand, love."

An expression of soft confusion on her face, she looked to him.

He lifted her right hand. "Pick a finger," he whispered.

Maura was still confused.

"Let me choose, then." He carried her finger to his mouth. Washed it with the warm, wet heat of his tongue . . .

. . . and dragged it slowly down the length of her belly.

But he didn't stop there. No, he pushed her warm, wet finger through the dark fleece that surrounded her womanhood — sliding between soft, plump folds to find that pearl of sensation crowned within.

Maura's entire body jerked. Her breath tumbled to a standstill.

No, she thought, stunned beyond reason. Oh, no.

Instinct governed. She tried to drag her hand away. But Alec's hand still trapped hers.

"Alec!" she cried softly. "I — I —"

"Shhh." His whisper was dark and intense. "It's all right. Don't think. Just feel."

Her fingers guided by his, she pressed. Plumbed. Circled. Caught the rhythm and the pressure —

"That's it, sweet. Oh, yes, just like that."

It was shockingly erotic.

Unbearably rousing.

And when another finger joined the play, her mind hazed with a dark, forbidden pleasure.

She began to pant. "Alec —"

"No shame," he whispered. "Only pleasure."

It was true. Alec stared down at her, deriving pleasure from her pleasure.

She moaned. "Alec . . . I want —"

"This?" He slipped his finger inside her.

Her eyes squeezed shut. Her hips were twisting. Writhing. Churning around his finger . . . around her own.

She cried out her protest when he left her. She opened her eyes just as Alec levered himself over her. His arms were bulging, his eyes glittering blue fire.

Drenched in arousal, drenched with heat, she moaned when he plunged hard and deep. This was desire unleashed. Desire unchecked.

One single thrust and she spasmed around his rod.

And then it began anew. With every searing plunge, every heartbeat, shivers raced inside her. Her whimper of need kindled the rise of his. His kiss was greedy, his body hungry. Sensing the rise of his climax, she clutched at his shoulders as he erupted inside her again and again.

Spent, he slid to his back and gathered her against him.

Maura buried her cheek against the hollow of his shoulder. She couldn't look at him. Right now she wasn't sure she could ever look anyone in the eye again. "Alec," she moaned, "I cannot believe that I —"

He gave a soft laugh and wrapped her closer still.

Maura woke, stretching slowly. In the haze of her mind she was aware that she'd spent the night in Alec's bed. A vague memory lingered. A memory of a kiss light as air pressed upon her lips, along with throaty, male laughter. She remembered screwing her mouth tightly closed, for she was in the midst of a wonderful, lovely dream from which she protested awakening.

Alec was there, in her dream. *Why, where else would he be?* chided a most preemptory voice in the dream. They were on the beach in Ireland; Castle McDonough crowned the cliff top above. Alec was laughing. Laughing at a small, wiry figure she tried to see but could not. In some wispy corner of her dreamworld, she wondered why Alec would be carrying a stick, wielding it as if it were a mighty sword. But she was happy. Oh, happy as never before.

That same husky male laughter echoed through her dream state. She felt herself rising through it, yet she hated to leave it, for it was so very, very perfect and she knew she would never tire of that husky male laugh. And when it was gone, with a wispy breath she lapsed back into her dream with a sigh of wonder anew.

When she appeared in the dining room where breakfast was laid out on the sideboard, Mrs. Yates informed her that Alec had gone out with his estate manager. She was both grateful and disappointed. In the wake of the eroticism they had shared, a part of her wondered how she might face him. Yet another part of her longed for him, to throw herself into his arms as if she hadn't a care in the world.

Which was rather silly, really. So it was that frustration gnawed at her. Her presence was not needed anywhere. Not knowing what else to do — she was at a loss as to where she might search for the Circle next — she pored over the family annals once more. Alas, a futile effort that only brought more frustration.

Closing the leather-bound book that

contained the family records, she left the library. Her path through the house carried Maura past the family portraits. She paused, turned back. Her gaze immediately swung to the portrait of James, seventh Duke of Gleneden. Even as she smothered an oath, she prayed that his portrait might provoke some great revelation.

As always before, shivers plied along her nerves. That strange sense that the Circle was here at Gleneden returned in full measure. Here was the Black Scotsman, the Black Scotsman that no one else knew, jeering at her.

Turning her back to him, she wandered outside. The day was warm. There was no need to tug a shawl about her shoulders. Almost without conscious awareness, her steps guided her to the loch.

She sat down and slid her arms around her upraised knees.

In the morning sun, the loch was a brilliant blue, with pale patterns that trembled on it in silvery paths. Across the shore were densely wooded hills.

With a sigh, she lay back on the grass. Palms up, her hands rested beside her head as she stared at a few cloudy wisps high above.

All around lay peace. Serenity.

But her soul, her very being, was anything but tranquil. Doubt crowded her. Everything inside her cried out. Locked in her breast was a world of torment.

She was weary and bleak. Her search for the Circle had proved fruitless. Was she on a mission of triumph or was Alec right? Was she on a fool's quest?

She'd promised her father she would find the Circle — promised him on his deathbed. But now, doubt crowded her. How could she possibly find the Circle? Something she had never seen . . . that no one in two hundred years had ever seen?

Despair wrenched at her. Hope was meager.

It wasn't just her family lands that were at stake.

Her heart was in jeopardy as well.

From the very beginning she'd felt he was far too dangerous for peace of mind. Far too dangerous to her heart. Oh, Lord, who did she fool?

She'd surrendered to Alec McBride from the very first time she'd laid eyes on him at the masquerade, garbed as a pirate.

He'd stolen her heart.

Captured her, body and soul.

She couldn't love him. She didn't dare. He'd scoffed at the existence of the Circle.

Aye, he had helped her search, but it wasn't because he believed . . . Yet if she didn't find it, he would die.

He would *die.*

She couldn't bear to lose him. She couldn't bear to think he might suffer a long, painful death as his father had.

And he would, if she didn't find the Circle of Light.

It was but one more curse — her own curse to bear.

Thus were her thoughts when Alec found her.

He stretched out beside her. "Spinning daydreams?" he murmured.

Maura gazed up into the sky. Gazed up at him.

He traced the crease between her brows.

"What troubles you, Irish?"

Her eyes filled with tears. She shook her head, her throat clogged with emotion.

"I think you need a sprinkling of fairy dust." He clapped his hands and waggled his fingers.

The sound Maura made was half laugh, half sob. His eyes were so pure and blue, filled with tiny silver lights, his expression so tender everything inside her knotted. Her fingers came up, grazing the hollow of his cheek, a wordless caress.

He gave a mock sigh. "I lack your finesse, don't I?"

With a cry, Maura clutched at him, burying her face against the column of his neck. "Alec," she choked out. "Oh, Alec."

All Alec could do was hold her. Her expression cut him to the quick. It was as if she was bruised inside. And in the sound of his name, he heard the anguish in her soul.

His arms tightened. He gathered her against him. She clung to him, as if her heart were breaking.

While his was cleaved in two. He couldn't keep her here. But her course was already set. How, he wondered, could he ever let her go?

CHAPTER TWENTY

They lay there for a long time, Alec watching the sun spill through the treetops, while Maura snuggled against his side, reluctant to release the shelter of his arms.

But it was impossible for either of them to ignore the way they lay together for long. Indeed, it seemed they both became aware of it at the same moment.

Maura's head was tucked beneath his chin. Her fist rested on his shirt, just above the buttons of his trousers. Holding her breath, she wondered what would happen if she extended her fingertips down just a wee bit —

She jumped as his rod leapt beneath her hand.

Alec's laugh was low and full. "What can I say, Irish? You stir me" — his smile was decidedly wicked — "to great length."

"Oh! You needn't boast, Scotsman."

He noticed that her hand had returned,

however, stirring him to even greater length.

"Irish?"

"Aye?"

"Do you wish to see that which you touch?"

Maura flushed crimson.

"Yes, I see that you do."

Her jaw dropped as he proceeded to strip naked before her.

"Your grace," she stated primly, "you display a dreadful lack of modesty."

"Perhaps you should join me, then." He tugged her upright. Nimble male fingers began to dispense the buttons on her bodice. Her gown was soon tugged from her shoulders and deposited on the ground. Petticoats, stockings, and shoes were tossed on the pile.

She was now as naked as he. And he had dropped to his knees before her. "Alec," she whispered. Faith, but it was difficult to talk with his tongue tracing slow, tantalizing circles around her nipples. She gulped. "We are here in the open —"

He tugged her down to her knees as well. They were face-to-face now. Her hands climbed to his naked shoulders.

His ran his tongue over the graceful arch of her throat. "So we are."

Maura could barely think. "Perhaps," she

said weakly, "the boathouse —"

"The next time, Irish." His mouth closed over hers.

Beneath the pleasure of his kiss, her breath began to fray. Her tongue dueled with his. Conscious thought was abandoned.

"Maura," he said raggedly. "Touch me, love."

He dragged her hands to his chest. Maura slid her fingers through the dark mat of hair there, then explored the binding contours of his shoulders, twining through the dark hair on his nape. Her fingertips glided over the tautness of his skin, relishing the texture. She didn't want to think. All she wanted was to lose herself to the moment. Lose herself to sensation. Lose herself in him.

She was hazily aware of Alec tugging them down. She lay on her side, as did he; the grass was warmed by the sunshine, while she was warmed by him.

His fingers tangled into dark fleece, stroked sleek, pink folds. He found her dewy, damp and ready.

He rolled to his back.

His hands caught her hips. She sucked in a breath, for now she straddled his thighs. His shaft was poised at the very heart of her, his crown embedded in sleek wet curls.

His features were taut with need, his eyes

341

blazing and brilliantly blue.

"Tempt me," he said thickly. "Tame me. Take me."

He brought her down upon his swollen shaft. Impaled, her lips parted in shock. Alec's hand closed around her hips. He lifted. Guiding. Harder, faster, until she caught the rhythm. And then she was panting. Churning.

It was heated. Blistering. Exquisite. Fever scalded her blood. She braced her hand on his chest and rose above him. Riveted by the sight, she couldn't look away from the place where they joined. Her hips tilted again and again. And again and again he pierced her, filling her with himself, driving deeper with every hungry, soul-shattering plunge. Her sheath clung tight around his swollen flesh.

Alec gritted his teeth. She was melting him. Into him. Around him. "Yes, Irish. Oh, yes, that's the way."

He caught her against him, clamping her tight. Her eyes squeezed shut as she shuddered spasms of release. His . . .

And hers.

Later in the day, Alec closed the door to his study. Maura had declared her intention to nap before tea. He briefly entertained the notion of joining her, then thought better of it.

The rules had changed. The game had changed. Making love to her had changed everything. He didn't want to push her. Somehow, he must convince her to stay.

He didn't want her to leave.

Ever.

He wanted a marriage.

A true marriage this time.

For all the right reasons.

He was cautiously optimistic. Maura's lips couldn't disguise her feelings. No, her response to him concealed nothing in her heart. She might deny it, but he knew better. There was every chance she might prove stubborn. Indeed, he expected it. She could be stubborn and fierce, his lovely lady.

But somehow he must find a way to convince her.

He understood her need, her duty to her clan and lands.

But she belonged to him.

She had to realize it sooner or later. And he would much prefer sooner than later. Indeed, he would prefer now.

He directed his steps toward the great hall. Afternoon sunshine splashed through the windows of the corridor, as if to light the way.

But all at once the sunlight vanished, with the suddenness of snuffing a candle flame. Alec stopped, looking up toward the sky.

A single, dark, threatening cloud obscured the sun. How curious. He could have sworn it hadn't been there a moment earlier.

The thought scarcely flitted through his mind than the hairs on the nape of his neck prickled.

If he were given to such stuff and nonsense, he might have considered it the frosty breath of a presence that lurked directly behind him.

A distinctly ominous presence.

If he were given to such stuff and nonsense.

Which he was not, he reminded himself sternly. He lent no credence to such things. It was simply all this talk with Maura, with her curses and ancient relics.

He turned from the window to resume his way.

Only then, he realized, did he notice that the sunlight ceased before the portrait of James McBride, seventh Duke of Gleneden.

Alec stared at the portrait. It was just as he'd told Maura. He had always thought of this particular forebear as a nasty-looking chap.

No wonder Maura disliked him.

But he'd never before fancied that James, seventh Duke of Gleneden, was somehow gloating. His eyes seemed to glint.

The feeling grew stronger. With every breath. Every beat of his heart.

Alec's gaze narrowed. He matched James McBride stare for stare.

Something gnawed at him. The feeling that something wasn't right.

He scoured the portrait. James McBride stood next to a wide, rustic fireplace on the outer wall, one booted foot planted arrogantly on the hearth.

He and Maura had searched that room just a few days earlier; it was like a miniature version of the great hall, the ceiling and walls timbered and whitewashed. It had served as the counting room after Robert the Bruce gave title over to the first Duke of Gleneden.

It struck Alec now that in all those years, it seemed nothing had changed — since the time of Robert the Bruce and certainly not since James McBride had stood there, that smile on his lips. There was an air about the duke. Daring. Bold. Reckless.

Almost before he knew it, Alec was climbing the stairs to the third story and moving down the hallway to the room at the end. He swung the door wide and strode to the fireplace. The room had fallen into disuse long before his grandfather was alive, when the fireplace was deemed unsafe to burn.

Plagued with some strange sensation, Alec stood where James, the seventh Duke of Gleneden, had posed for his portrait. He placed his boot where James had planted his. Stood where James had stood.

The brick beneath his heel moved. Alec dropped to one knee. His pulse quickened, drumming in his ears. The brick was loose; what mortar remained was pitted with age. He tried to grasp it, only to scrape his nails and fingertips. He didn't give up. Caught fast in the grip of some inexplicable, unseen force, he glanced around, looking for something he could use to dig away what remained of the mortar. Seizing a remnant of brick that had fallen away from the other side, he scraped at the mortar holding the brick in place.

There! It was free. He didn't know what possessed him. It was as if he'd been seized by some outside force. He pulled the brick away, then reached inside the hole.

There was something there.

His pulse leaped. Lord above, was Maura right? Could this possibly be her Circle of Light?

Fingers straining, he caught hold of it and

346

pulled it out.

It was a small book, the binding tattered, the pages yellowed. He opened it with painstaking care, then sucked in a breath.

His heart stumbled. It was a diary, he realized.

The diary of James McBride, seventh Duke of Gleneden.

Maura wandered down the path that led to the wishing well. She had tried to nap, but her mind would not quiet. Alec filled her mind, to the exclusion of all else. One kiss. One touch. One look from those heated blue eyes and she trembled with desire. She despaired over her weakness, despaired over what their lovemaking meant.

Her heart twisted. It meant the world to her. Where Alec was concerned, she had no resolve — no will to resist him!

She couldn't trust her feelings for him. They were too colored by want. By need.

By passion.

Oh, yes, her thoughts were filled with torment.

Her heart with love.

But she wouldn't admit it. No, not to him. Despite the fact that she yielded her body, her pride was still too strong.

But she couldn't stay here at Gleneden forever.

And she couldn't forsake her quest for the Circle.

Her promise to her father. She was needed back in Ireland.

Thinking to soothe her unsettled mood, to distract her mind, she had brought a book of poetry from the library room with her. At the well, she placed the book on the stone bench. She didn't understand why Alec didn't find it charming. Indeed, she would go a step further and call it charmingly enchanted. Aye, perhaps it was a trifle plain. But all it needed was a dash of color here and there. She could well imagine how pretty it would be with roses scenting the air.

A faint smile on her lips, Maura moved to the wall of the well. She had no coins with which to wish, but she closed her eyes, inhaled deeply . . . and made a most fervent wish nevertheless.

All at once there was an eerie sense of quiet. The sunlight faded. She glanced up, stunned to see a thick black cloud.

She sat down and too late realized that the stones were not secure. They shifted beneath her weight and she felt herself tumble, plummeting down . . . She cried out as she landed jarringly on her side.

Maura tried to push to her feet, then stumbled. Her head ached. She felt battered and bruised to the bone. Gritting her teeth, she managed to struggle upright.

She steadied her nerves. She was lucky. She wasn't hurt, not really. Scraped up and bruised, perhaps, but it could have been much worse. But she knew she could not climb out under her own power. It was perhaps twenty feet to the top, and the walls of the well were slick with moss.

She called out. Her voice echoed back at her.

She wouldn't be alarmed, she told herself. Not yet, anyway. Until someone realized she was missing, she could only wait. There was little point in screaming herself hoarse if there was no one near.

An hour later, the dark cloud had passed, yet it was difficult to see. She glanced down and it was then she felt it —

There was water seeping into her shoes. Within seconds it began to rush around her ankles. For the first time, fear took root.

The water was rising.

Fast.

Still stunned, Alec moved to a wooden chair near the window. No power on earth could have stopped him from reading the words of his ancestor. He handled it with care; many of the pages were loose. Thumbing through it, an entry caught his eye.

At first I hated my father for insisting I follow in his steps and serve in His Majesty's Navy. I was not meant to serve others. But once there, well, I learned the sea was in my blood. And I acknowledged what I have always known. I braved danger . . . and relished it. I craved power . . . and found it. I am, after all, a duke.

And a pirate. I am also a scoundrel.

It amuses me to no end when the ladies whisper and shudder when they speak of the Black Scotsman. How the bold blackguard plunders the seas between Scotland and Ireland. Little do they know the Black Scotsman may indeed sit across the table. That he may be at their elbow. Little do they know the Black Scotsman is a man with two faces. A man with two sides. Little do they know the Black Scotsman is a nobleman — a duke yet!

Alec sucked in a breath. There had truly been a pirate called the Black Scotsman.

And Maura was right — the Black Scotsman was his ancestor, James McBride. He read on.

No one knows. Not even my lovely Gertrude. Not my daughter, Willa. Nor my sons, Gerald and Robert.

His eyes moved down the page, then stopped at a passage that jumped out at him.

I covet power. I covet riches. I covet the thrill. My shipmates are loyal. They covet riches as I do. But I have heard of a far different treasure, a mystic Celtic circle. They say it whirls and spins of its own power, through day and night. They say it has brought the Clan McDonough fortune through the ages. I have vowed it will be mine, this mysterious Circle of Light. It will surely bring me riches aplenty, and a man can never have too many riches.

Dear Lord, Alec thought. His eyes scanned the text that followed, then came to rest once more as if drawn to a particular entry.

The Circle of Light is mine. But I have paid a terrible price. For when I first touched it, I screamed with pain. It burned, burned like fire. I will forever wear its scar upon my hand, a terrible sight to behold. I must forever hide it, the hand that brought me the Circle, that no one will know I am the Black Scotsman.

There was more.

The Circle is cursed. Gertrude is dead. I heard the snap of her neck as she tumbled down the stairs. And my son — my boy! — swept by a wave as he walked along the cove. My sweet Willa drowned in the wishing well, which now stands bone dry. It is the Circle, I know. The Circle come to wreak vengeance on those I love. I have sent young Robert to England. I cannot lose him, too.
    The Black Scotsman is my only pleasure. I know now that the Circle of Light holds a terrible beauty. Yet I cannot bear to part with it. Neither can I gaze upon it, for I hate what it has done. It holds a power over me that I cannot break.

And later:

It is done. I have buried the Circle of Light. It is both triumph and curse. I know it is here. It lies within sight of

Gleneden. I cannot see it or touch it. But I know it is there, forever mine.

Alec closed the diary and got to his feet. Maura had been right all along. There *was* a family curse. A curse that touched both their families.

Where had James buried the Circle?

In the great hall, Alec hailed Mrs. Yates. "I believe she's at the wishing well, your grace," she told him.

His heart stood still. A chill ran through him.

The wishing well.

Where James McBride's daughter had drowned.

CHAPTER TWENTY-ONE

Maura had long since abandoned the choice to wait until she was missed. She shouted. She screamed until her throat was raw.

Fright now verged on terror.

Water swirled around her waist, making a gurgling sound. It wasn't rising at such an alarming rate, but it was still rising. And it was frigid. She shuddered. From cold. From fear. She fought to keep her wits about her, but a tiny little moan escaped. She could barely feel her toes. Her legs were starting to go numb. Though she fought it, another moan escaped her lips. Was this how she would die? No. No.

In desperation, she summoned all her strength. "Alec!" she screamed.

"Maura!"

Her face turned up. Was she losing her senses?

Alec's face appeared over the top of the well. His expression was frantic.

She could have wept with joy. He was here!

"Maura! We'll have a ladder in just a moment." He turned away. "Hurry!" she heard him shout.

The ladder was lowered. Maura was shaking with cold so badly that she could scarcely grasp the rungs.

"Hold on, love! I'm coming down."

Moments later a strong arm warm and hard about her waist, she held on tight as Alec ascended the ladder. At the top, several men helped her out of the well.

Someone dragged a blanket over her shoulders. Maura gripped the edges as Alec wrapped her in his arms. Above her head he raged and swore. "I'll have this place bricked up again. Tomorrow, by God —"

"Alec! Alec!" She drew back so she could see him, her brow furrowed. "You knew, didn't you? You knew I'd fallen into the well." She shook her head in wonderment. "How? How did you know?"

"I will tell you, sweet, but first we must get you back to the hall and see you —"

"Alec, no. I am fine, truly. Just — tell me now!"

He pulled her to the bench. "You were right, Irish. You were right all along."

"About what?" Maura had a very good idea what he was about to say. Precisely how she knew, she couldn't say . . .

"The Black Scotsman," Alec told her. "The Black Scotsman is — was — James McBride. And the Circle of Light — he stole it. From McDonough lands. Your lands."

Her lips parted. "You believe me?" she whispered.

"Oh, aye. I believe you." His features grim, he told her how he had stood beneath the portrait of James McBride. How, compelled by some strange force, he'd studied it, and how that same force lured him to the room depicted in the portrait.

How he'd found the diary — and what revelations it held.

How James wrote that the Circle had burned him, scarred his hand.

"So that's why he wore the glove in the portrait," she murmured.

"So it would seem. Within days of stealing the Circle, his wife died in a fall down the stairs. One of his sons was swept away in the cove, which is probably where James sailed from. And his daughter . . . she fell into the well and drowned. That's how I knew where you were, Maura. I can't say why or how, but I knew." Alec's voice grew rough with emotion.

"James wrote that he buried the Circle

within sight of Gleneden, in a place where neither he nor anyone else could lay hands on it again. He believed it held such power over him that he could never truly part with it."

"So it's not inside the hall," she said slowly, "but within sight of it."

"Yes. But the landscape has surely changed in two hundred years. It could be anywhere." His eyes darkened. "And I will see that the wishing well is bricked up again. Why, this well is surely cursed! My mother always loved it, as did my grandmother — and you. But this place is damned. My mother planted roses here many times, but they always shriveled up and died. My father laughed at her. He told her his mother and grandmother had the very same notion — to plant roses here — but they always died. Nothing will grow here."

Maura bit back a smile. She wasn't about to admit that she, too, would have loved to plant roses here —

All at once her smile wavered.

Alec noticed the odd expression on her face. "What's wrong?" he asked quickly.

She shook her head. Her mind was churning.

"Maura? Why do you look like that?" Alec's expression changed. "You think the

Circle is buried here near the well?"

"Not near the well." She took a breath. "In the well." She threw off the blanket and looked over at the wishing well, where two stable lads were pulling up the ladder. Her voice rang out clearly. "Leave it, please! And will one of you fetch a shovel?"

"A shovel?" Alec was on his feet. "Sweet, that will have to wait. The water in the well —"

He broke off. Standing at the well, Maura glanced at him, her brows upraised, a finger pointing down.

He sighed, prepared to indulge her, given her ordeal. He moved to her side, glanced over the side of the well —

And froze.

The well was bone dry.

"It's there," Maura whispered. "James said he buried it. And he did. He buried it in the well. Don't you see? That's why nothing will grow here. That's why the well mysteriously fills with water, then disappears just mysteriously."

Alec was still shocked. Disbelieving. "How is it possible? The water . . . the Circle. It would surely be ruined."

"No." Maura was adamant. "No. It's the Circle of Light, Alec. It doesn't belong here. The Circle . . . it wants to be home. Home in Ireland. Back at the church of St. Patrick on McDonough lands. Home."

The lad was back with the shovel. Maura reached for it, but Alec's long arm stretched out before she could grip it. He dismissed the boys and turned to her.

Blue eyes flashed. "You are not going down there," he growled.

"Then be about it, man!" Maura was impatient. She was soaked to the skin, but she didn't care.

She watched him descend the ladder and begin to dig.

"Have you found it?" she called after a while. "Do you see it?"

Alec cursed. "No! There's too many bloody stones!" Indeed, he was about to give up when the shovel struck something hard.

He climbed the ladder with a small metal box tucked under his arm. Maura's body was almost pulsing.

On the bench, with the box between them, Maura opened it.

Inside was a small silver circlet. She started to reach for it.

"Maura, no! Don't touch it! Remember how it burned James's hand?"

"No, Alec, it's all right. Look," she breathed.

She'd already picked it up and now cradled it carefully in both hands. Warmth spread throughout her, a curious sort of energy.

The Circle began to glow then. Slowly, it rose, suspended above her palms. It seemed as if every color in the world shimmered in its depths, shifting and swirling, ever changing.

"My word," Alec whispered, "it's a miracle."

"Aye, Scotsman." She smiled up at him. "So it is."

Back at the hall, Alec saw his lovely Irish bathed and fed. She was exhausted, but glowing, almost as much as her Circle of Light, tucked snugly in its box near the window.

Maura finished the last of her tea, setting the dainty china cup in its saucer. Rising, she joined him at the window.

Her arms slid around his waist. Drawing back, he traced the shape of her mouth with the tips of his fingers. "You haven't stopped smiling since we left the wishing well."

His arms linked loosely around her form, he rested his chin on the top of her head. He didn't see the shadow that flitted across her features, the waver of that very smile he praised.

Catching his hand, she tugged him toward the bed. Slender fingers unknotted the sash of his robe, then pushed it from his shoulders.

Alec sucked in a breath. "Maura, no! You've been —"

Her finger against his lips, she stifled his protest. Then, with a finger to his chest, she pushed him so that he sat on the edge.

In one sinuous move she shrugged from her robe — and onto his lap. Alec's eyes went dark. "Irish —"

"Are you unwilling, Scotsman?" A finger already swirled an idle pattern through the dense mat of hair on his chest. His belly. Clear to —

Words eluded him. But from deep in his belly came a faint sound.

A small, feminine hand pushed him down upon the bed. "I shall take that to mean that you are not. Are you unable, then?"

Small hands came down on his shoulders. She straddled his form. The proof that he was indeed able — and aye, quite willing — was caught snug between her slender white thighs.

She squeezed them ever so slightly, shaped them around his breadth and length. An erotic caress, it stole his breath.

Strong hands molded her hips. "My lady pirate has returned, I see." A shift, and he slid deep inside. His eyes began to smolder. "This pirate has missed her."

Oh, aye, she had returned, his pirate seductress from Ireland. Her hair was all around them, a silken black curtain, teasing his chest, his belly.

It was indescribable. She tempted him, seduced him, possessed him body and soul, until he was on fire. Their lovemaking was wanton and wild, shatteringly intense. A ragged groan tore from Alec's chest. He erupted inside her again and again, while the night shimmered and the Circle glowed.

And when it was over, he dragged her against him and held her tight, his beloved lady pirate. He captured her, bringing her fast against his side, reluctant to release her. Long into the night he held her, until exhaustion claimed him and he slept.

And in the morning when he woke . . .

She was gone.

On the pillow was a note . . . and the family wedding ring he'd placed on her finger. Disbelieving, his jaw tight, Alec read:

Dear Scotsman,
I am forever in your debt. I hope that

you will forgive my intrusion into your life, just as I hope you will understand why it was of such importance. I wish you well in life's journey, Scotsman, and pray you will do the same of me.

Most sincerely,
Maura

He was steaming when he bolted into the carriage house. Maura, he discovered, had requested a coach and driver at dawn. He had a very good idea where the chit had gone — to Stranraer, to take a ship back to Ireland. And bloody hell, she was a good three hours ahead of him.

If he was lucky, he'd catch her before she boarded.

Unfortunately, it seemed luck was not on his side. On the way to Stranraer his horse lost a shoe and he was forced to stop at a ferrier. To make matters worse, the skies opened up and he was soaked to the bone by the time he arrived at the port.

Someone hailed him then. Turning, he saw Thomas Gates.

Alec ducked under the eaves of a building.

"What luck!" Thomas said. "I was just on my way to see you, your grace! I've just returned from Ireland with news of your wife." Before Alec could stop him, he continued, "She is certainly who she says she is. I visited her home and prowled about the McDonough lands, and spoke with a few of the tenants. I confess, I've never seen anything quite like it. The lands are quite —"

"Barren?" Alec supplied.

"Aye!" said Thomas. "And the tenants I spoke with said it was because of a curse, and an ancient relic —"

"The Circle of Light."

The older man eyed him. "You certainly don't seem to have needed my services."

Alec smiled grimly. "Let's just say my wife decided to enlighten me. And, if you don't mind, Thomas, may I settle your fee when I return? Odd as it may seem, I'm hoping to catch the next ship to Ireland to fetch my wife."

Thomas shook his head. "You may have a wee bit of a wait, then. I overheard someone say the last boat just departed, and it's expected none will be bound for Ireland for at least the next two days." He gestured heavenward. "It's a devil of a storm that's blown in."

Alec cursed, long and loud, so loud it might surely have been heard across the sea in Ireland.

Indeed, he hoped it was.

It was home.

Home, on the very tip of the peninsula, in this place where the wind met sea and sky, and the sky the earth, where the Circle of Light floated on an altar of stone — floated with a power of its own.

All who came out stared in wonder at the shimmering light that glowed in the church of St. Patrick, lighting the night. They exclaimed in joy and wonder, and called it a miracle.

Among those who came out were Toothless Nan. Patrick the Woolly. On the steps of Castle McDonough stood Maura, Murdoch, and Jen.

Jen beamed, her hands clasped before her. Murdoch shook his head in awe.

Jen turned and threw her arms around Maura. "Ye've done it, child. Ye've done it!"

Murdoch laid his hand on her shoulder. "Yer father would be so proud of ye, lass."

"Aye. He would." It was all she could manage. Maura was smiling, but her throat was tight.

She hadn't cried from the moment she arrived in the village near Gleneden. At the inn, she'd flung herself into Murdoch's arms.

She did not speak of Alec. Murdoch did not ask. When they boarded the ship that took them back to Ireland, Maura stood at the stern for long, long minutes. She stood until Scotland was no longer in view.

As she had once stood watching Ireland disappear from view. Oh, how things had changed since then!

Everything had changed.

Three days later, inside her room at Castle McDonough, Maura glanced out the window. She had to shield her eyes from the sun's glare.

A faint smile rimmed her lips. Three days, she thought. The Circle had been home but three days — and already there were miracles. The fields were green, brilliantly green in every direction.

She'd fulfilled her vow to her father. She'd brought home the Circle.

Oh, but her heart . . . she was very much afraid she'd left her heart in Scotland.

The door to her room flew open then. It was Jen, her eyes huge.

Maura cried out. "Oh, Jen, no! What is it? What's wrong?"

"It's him, Lady Maura. It's him."

"Who?"

"The Black Scotsman. He's downstairs.

Oh, and he's not at all what I expected, Lady Maura! Should you ask me, the Black Scotsman is not so very black-hearted at all! He's quite charming."

Maura's heart tripped, then began to thud.

"Hurry, love, and change your gown. Let me dress your hair." Jen was as excited as a schoolgirl.

Seconds later Maura stood at the top of the stairs. Jen squeezed her hand. "Go, child! Go!"

Maura swallowed. She was shaking so hard she could barely walk. Alec was here!

He stood with his back to her. With the sun shining through the window, gilding his form in gold, he was all power and strength.

Strength! Oh, but she had none. She held tight to the handrail as she descended. At the next to the last step she discovered she could go no farther.

He turned.

He did not smile. His gaze was solemnly intent.

The silence spun out. Everything inside her wound into a knot. She discovered she couldn't go back, yet neither could she take that last step forward.

And then he smiled.

"Hello, Irish."

Maura opened her mouth. There was a

huge lump in her throat. She couldn't say a word.

She had hoped, prayed, that he would come. She needed to know that he wanted her. That he needed her as she needed him. That he loved her as she loved him. And the fact that he was here could only mean one thing.

His head tilted ever so slightly. Softly he spoke. "You know why I'm here, don't you, Irish?"

Her eyes filled with tears.

"I came to fetch the woman who crawled into my bed . . . and never left my heart."

Maura gave a half sob. Strong hands caught her waist and swung her from the step. She clung to him.

A finger beneath her chin, he brought her eyes to his. "I love you, Irish. And I would very much like to know if you love this wicked Scotsman. You do, don't you?"

Emotion clogged her throat.

"A nod will suffice for now," he teased.

Her nod was quite vigorous. Drawing her close against his chest, Maura broke into sobs.

"Don't cry, Irish." He kissed away her tears. "I love you. I love you, sweet."

Her arms twined around his neck. "Alec?" she whispered.

"Yes, love?"

"Welcome —" With a lopsided smile, she drew back. "— to my soggy bog of an island."

EPILOGUE

They married in the church on the hill. The Circle shone bright from the altar above.

Some four years later their son Connor played on the beach below Castle McDonough. His two-year-old-sister Madeline — or Maddy — as they called her — was asleep on a blanket, her bottom high in the air.

Home was Gleneden, but they always spent part of the summer here in Ireland.

Connor wielded a stick like a sword. "I am a pirate," he declared, "so you'd best beware."

Alec gave a mock sigh and glanced at his wife, walking barefoot in the sand. "Have you been telling him about the pirating days of Grace O'Malley?"

Maura feigned reproach. "My love, have you been telling him tales of the Black Scotsman?"

A slow, wicked grin edged along Alec's

lips. "Well, it is in the blood." He got to his feet. "Connor!"

Connor ran up. With black hair and blue eyes, he was the image of his father.

"Let me tell you a tale, lad. Many years ago there was once a pirate ship that set anchor in the bay."

Connor pointed his stick. "There, Papa?"

"That very spot, lad. But the pirate, well, he found himself smitten with the lady who lived in the castle there." Alec pointed to Castle McDonough, perched atop the bluff. "And when he saw this lovely lady —" With an exaggerated move, Alec spun his wife around and into his arms. "— he kissed her like this."

Alec availed himself of his wife's sweet lips, a long, lingering kiss that was interrupted only when an insistent little voice said, "Papa! What happened then?"

"Well, when the pirate boarded his ship, he had jewels in his chest — and the lady he'd kissed."

"Jewels," breathed Connor. "Do you think it could truly happen, Papa?"

Alec gazed tenderly into his wife's laughing eyes. "My boy," he said huskily, "I think it already has."

ABOUT THE AUTHOR

It was **Samantha James**'s love of reading as a child that steered her toward a writing career. Among her favorites in those days were the Trixie Belden and Cherry Ames series of books. She still loves a blend of mystery and romance, and, of course, a happily-ever-after ending. The award-winning, *New York Times* and *USA Today* bestselling author of eighteen romances and one novella, her books have ranged from medieval to Regency.